Veiled By Darkness

By the author of “LAST OF A DYING BREED”

A Novel

By

Leon “Buckshot” Anderson

This book is a work of fiction. Places, events, and situations in this story are purely fictional. Any resemblance to actual persons, living or dead, is coincidental.

ISBN: 1-4107-7197-0 (e-book)
ISBN: 1-4107-7198-9 (Paperback)

Library of Congress Control Number: 2003094968

This book is printed on acid free paper.

Printed in the United States of America
Bloomington, IN

1stBooks - rev. 07/25/03

Dedication

To America's local police forces, conservation officers and law abiding citizens, who ever vigilant attempt to keep our precious natural resources safe from those who misuse or seek to destroy them, I hereby dedicate this work of fiction.

Special "Thanks"

To Wisconsin Conservation Officers, past and present, Ben Bendrick, Chuck Wranowski, Duane Harpster, Mike Sealander, and John Walker of the Michigan Department of Natural Resources, plus thousands of others like them. These dedicated professionals, who enforce conservation laws, often face danger and death in their day to day and night to night patrols. Collectively, you are the inspiration for this story.

And finally; To Peggy, my "bride" of 45 years who has acted as a constructive critic and proofreader.

Table of Contents

Prolog

The black Ford pickup truck turned west off Michigan Highway 77 unto a narrow two rut dirt road and extinguished it's lights, despite the fact dusk had already settled in. A quarter mile further the vehicle slowed to a crawl and finally stopped behind a screen of low bushes at the edge of a large clearing. The two men inside each popped open their third can of beer and tossed the empty containers out the open windows. The individual on the passenger side slipped a loaded clip into a scope mounted .223 semi-automatic rifle and aimed it at the rapidly darkening field to test it's light gathering capabilities. The two brothers were on another mission.

The field that lay before them was bursting with fresh green grass. The two local individuals knew this field was frequently used by the local deer herd as a spring feeding area after a tough Upper Peninsula winter. It was only a matter of time until the four legged visitors they sought would begin arriving.

Several hundred yards beyond the field a mature doe, with her pair of four-day-old fawns, rested in a thick grove of balsam trees. The doe rose from her daytime bed, stretched and nuzzled her offspring to also rise. For the next fifteen minutes the tiny babies nursed from their mother's milk sack to satisfy their perpetual hunger. The doe then left her new born family in the safety of the thicket and headed for the lush, grass covered field.

Ten minutes later the doe reached the field's western edge. She hesitated, testing the gentle wind currents for any sign of danger. Satisfied the area was free of natural predators, such as coyotes, wolves or cougars; she entered the field and began grazing to satisfy her own hunger. Minutes later a young buck joined her.

Within a half-hour the field contained nearly two dozen deer, all enjoying the tender, young grass they had craved throughout the long, severe winter. A nearly full moon was just cresting the eastern horizon, illuminating the field as though dawn was breaking. Off to the south a wolf howled. The deer froze for several moments, then satisfied their second worst predator was not close enough to present immediate danger they resumed feeding. Their worst predators were preparing for an attack.

The brothers in the black pickup truck were well into their second six pack by the time the moonlight provided enough light to clearly see their victims in the riflescope. The entire herd of deer froze as an intensely bright spotlight blazed across the field. The beam settled on the doe that had been the first to enter the field. The sound of the rifle blast never reached her ears, as the bullet had already passed through her brain before the sound of the shot reached her falling body.

Many of the older deer bolted from the field, but several young animals remained frozen in place. The gunner successfully dropped three additional animals before the field had emptied. It had been a good harvest.

Within minutes the four carcasses were quickly loaded into the box of the pickup truck and the two violators were headed towards an old vacant farm to begin butchering their illegally taken prizes. As their vehicle reached Highway 77, the driver turned on the truck's headlights while his partner popped the tabs on their last two beers. After draining down several gulps the pair gleefully grinned and gave each other "high fives". Their nighttime crime would yield them a nifty price in the illegal venison market.

The fate of the two motherless fawns was sealed. They would stay in the protection of the thicket until starvation ended their suffering. Or possibly wandering natural predators would complete the gruesome task.

The scourge of the outdoor world had struck again. They constitute a small, but formidable army of societies misfits, who nationwide, illegally kill tens of thousands of big game animals yearly. They are uncaring, cold blooded killers, stealing game for profit rather than sport. They steal a resource that is managed by government agencies for the welfare of the resource and the citizenry. They are criminals in the true sense of the word. They are "Poachers"!

****

Conservation officer Brian Matson was worried. For the past several weeks his phone had been ringing off the wall with calls from various citizens who lived throughout the vast district he patrolled. The calls where basically the same. People had been hearing numerous large caliber rifle shots well after dark. And during the season of spring that could mean but one thing. Deer poachers were on the loose.

Fairly new to the force, Brian was beginning his second year as a game warden. His primary jurisdiction included an area nearly five hundred square miles. Policing an area of that immense size without assistance was an impossibility. Fortunately, lots of help came from the citizens living in this vast area in the form of "tips", called in on the Department of Natural Resources "Poacher Hotline". It was common knowledge that nearly eighty per-cent of all arrests involving major fishing and hunting violations were a result of citizen involvement. Attitudes had changed considerably since the time his grandfather had served as a game warden. Back then, poaching was often necessary for survival in depressed rural areas, and few citizens bothered to inform the authorities of poaching activities.

Officer Matson was investigating a series of calls he had received from persons who lived along Michigan Highway 77 between the communities of Seney and Blaney Park. A half dozen citizens claimed they had heard rifle shots well after dark for the past several nights.

Slowing his unmarked truck at every unpaved side road, Brian scanned the dirt for signs of fresh tire tracks. Most of the primitive roads looked as though they had been driven on recently. For most of the morning he drove up and down a dozen or more dirt "two tracks" searching for any evidence of poaching. It was nearing eleven o'clock when he hit pay dirt.

At the end of one side road that meandered west off highway 77, and ended at a large field at the southeastern edge of the Seney National Wildlife Refuge, he spied tire tracks that had crushed the tall grass in the field. He parked his vehicle and followed the course of the tracks on foot. Fifty yards into the field he found a substantial stain of dried blood. A few yards further was another. And beyond that were two more. Someone or someone's had recently shot four deer within the boundaries of a Federal Wildlife Sanctuary!

Officer Matson returned to his truck and phoned the Seney National Wildlife Office to report his findings. The time was eleven forty seven a.m.

Returning to highway 77 he turned his vehicle north and continued to examine additional side roads for evidence of recent travel. Several miles later he passed what looked like an abandoned farm. Over a forested area beyond the dilapidated barn he observed a large flock of crows, some of which were sitting in the treetops and others were swooping down into the woods. Brian made a u-turn and headed his truck down the driveway leading to the old farm. He noticed the road looked well worn from vehicle traffic. "Odd", he thought.

Two men and a black pickup truck were in the old barn. The men were almost finished skinning and quartering the seven deer they had poached the previous evening and night. They stopped their work to peer through the cracks in the barn wall at the sound of an approaching vehicle. The large radio antenna on the roof of the truck gave away the identity of the driver. It was a game warden!

Officer Matson continued past the barn following the seemingly well used road leading to the edge of the wooded area where all the crows were congregating. At his approach the noisy scavengers rapidly vacated the area. Brian stopped his truck, turned off the ignition, and got out. He followed what looked like a well used path for about a hundred feet to where it entered a dense grove of pine trees. The officer suddenly stopped and gazed at a grisly spectacle. A large area under the protective cover of the mature trees was littered with the remains of dozens and dozens of deer. Some of the bones looked to be as much as several years old, but many were fresh. Piles of meat scraps and internal organs were definitely fresh! Brian was stunned by his discovery!

The two poachers quickly and quietly left their butcher shop and hurried on foot to the officer's truck. From their vantage point they easily saw the warden had discovered their secluded dumping ground. Without hesitation the older of the two brothers centered the cross hairs of a scope mounted semi-automatic .223 on the back of the young warden's head and pulled the trigger.

Mrs. Brian Matson became a widow, and her two young children were fatherless.

Chapter One: "Home Again"

Part One: "Reborn"

It was as though he had been reborn. At least that's how Hap Larson put it. Since returning to his boyhood home near Newberry, Michigan and settling in with a completely new life style, possibly it did feel like being reborn. Hap's new wife, Edna, agreed with Hap's feeling.

The previous year had been hectic, to say the least. It was difficult to believe so much had transpired in Hap Larson and Edna Sullivan's lives in less than a year's time. Who could have imagined a couple of senior citizens would be thrust into so many challenging situations in such a short time. Especially two people who had lived such quiet, sheltered, unobtrusive lives! But all in all they had handled the challenges like they had been used to dealing with adversity all their lives. They were indeed a unique couple.

It was only last May when the whirlwind of change struck Hap and Edna. Upon arriving in Nitchequon, Quebec with his stash of winter furs, Hap had been assaulted and robbed. A few days later he saved the life of an officer and friend, who was a Royal Canadian Mountie, by killing one of the men who was holding the officer prisoner and subduing the second criminal.

Both were the same men who had assaulted and robbed Hap less than a week earlier.

Next, Hap began to fall in love with a widowed Irish lass who owned the one and only boarding house in Nitchequon. Then, following the press sensationalizing Hap's heroics in saving the life of Sergeant Osborne and ending a crime spree that had plagued the Province of Quebec for nearly a dozen years, Mr. Larson became somewhat of a National Hero. An hour long televised special about his life as a wilderness trapper and doer of good deeds resulted in him being dubbed "The Hero of the Wilderness".

News of Hap's expertise in surviving in the out of doors, plus his trapping skills, aroused the interest of a group who were developing a "Historical and Cultural Theme Park" depicting major elements of Quebec's history and culture. Hap was hired as a consultant in coordinating the building of "The Trapper's Exhibit". During the five months he worked for The Society on that project he inadvertently caused the downfall of a major drug dealer and his henchmen.

And then to top it all off, Hap and Edna left Quebec, returned to his boyhood home near Newberry, and were married Christmas Eve!

The newlyweds were sure their time had come to just sit back, relax, and enjoy their newfound freedom.

Part Two: "Honeymooning, The Planning"

The days following Hap and Edna's wedding continued to be rather hectic. The small entourage that had assembled for the wedding stuck around for the Holidays and despite the fact most of their friends and relatives rented motel rooms in Newberry, the Larson homestead continued to be a prime location for yuletide celebrations.

Much to the newlywed's relief, by the third of January all the well wishers had departed and scattered to their respective home locations. Edna informed her loving husband it was time for the Honeymoon.

True to the simple lifestyles they had long been accustomed, the couple opted for a simple honeymoon. Hap suggested they simply spend a week or so, as Hap put it, "Touring the U.P. and showin' ya all the neat stuff we got up here in God's Country". Edna, having been born, raised and lived in eastern Canada up to now, gleefully agreed, "That would be a splendid idea! Let's go!"

Hap contacted Joe Hilgala, a local handyman who worked several part times jobs for several area businesses. Joe had been ever so helpful in assisting Hap and Edna during their brief visit to Newberry the previous June. The couple had made a quick visit to Hap's boyhood hometown to take care of some loose ends after the death of Hap's parents, and Joe had been their "chauffeur".

Hap and Edna needed someone to tend to their five sled dogs during their honeymoon, and Joe eagerly accepted the job. Sadie, the Larson's Black Lab, would accompany them on their exploration of the Upper Peninsula. Sadie was spoiled. Sadie generally went everywhere Hap went. And she rode in style! Inside the topper covering the back of Hap's truck was a large, soft dog bed, water bucket and dog food bowl. And Sadie loved to travel.

A well planned itinerary was being pre-planned over a road map of Michigan's Upper Peninsula, as well as Edna doing some searching the web with her new computer. Hap, acting as the travel agent, dictated the sequence of travel and Edna recorded the route in a small spiral notebook.

"O.K. Edna, here's our route. Boy, it's bin a long time since I traveled these highways with my folks. I bet I ain't gonna recognize lots of places. It's hard ta believe I've bin gone from here fer forty years! This is gonna be fun!"

Edna smiled at her excited husband and agreed. It was going to be fun! And if it turned out not to be fun all the time, well, they'd MAKE it be fun! Sadie wagged her tail and agreed too.

Hap began his dictation. "We'll make our first day on the road a short one. We're gonna follow Highway 28 to Marquette. Along the way I'll let ya stop in Christmas, seein' it's the Holiday Season. They got lotta nice shops women folks like ta snoop around in. While yer doin' yer snoopin', I might jist hit that casino in town and put a few nickels in one ah those one armed bandits. Or, ya can come with me and make yer fortune too."

Edna giggled and Sadie continued wagging her tail.

"We're gonna spend our first night on the road in Marquette. There's a nifty old hotel in the downtown area that's been all remodeled and spiffied up to make you think you jist stepped back into the 30's or 40's. It's called The Landmark Inn. And the food's almost as good as yer cookin', Edna. It's kinda like that cuisine stuff we had at Del Monico's in Quebec."

"Sounds like something I'm really going to enjoy, sweetheart, just so we don't get into the same mess we got into at Del Monico's.", replied Edna, with another giggle.

"I kin guarantee we won't meet any assholes, like Blair Blakey, in Marquette. Ya gotta remember Edna, yer in Yooperland now, where everybody is friendly. Well, almost everybody."

"You're right Hap, everyone I've met so far are down to earth, friendly, wonderful people. This sure is a beautiful part of the world in which to live. Where are we headed after we leave Marquette?"

'Well, we'll be on highway 41 then and head north and west past Ispeming. But first we're gonna stop there at a place called Da Yooper's Tourist Trap. They sell all kinds of typical gift store stuff, plus lots of silly, funny things. We kin also buy some of those tapes full of Yooper type songs sung by a group of entertainers called, Da Yoopers. Then we kin listen ta some good music while we're travelin'."

"Oh, I've heard some of their songs on the radio. I heard several, including "Grandma Got Run Over By a Reindeer", "The Rusty Chevrolet", and I remember another one, "The Second Week of Deer Camp". I'll have to admit their music is silly, but funny. Hap, I've been meaning to ask you,......what exactly is a Yooper?"

"Well Edna,......that's a tough question ta answer. A Yooper is a term applied ta someone who lives in Michigan's Upper Peninsula,......da U.P. It's bin said we got a little different what ya'd call culture in the U.P. It's kinda hard ta explain, but as ya live here longer and longer, yer gonna figure it out." Hap had a questioning look on his face, as though he wasn't sure where to go with his explanation from here.

"Life has always bin tough in the U.P. Still is. The economy never was great, even when the loggin', iron and copper mines were goin' full throttle. So the folks up here developed into a very proud and independent lot. We don't think we're any better than other folks in other parts of the country, but we do think we're tougher. Not in the sense of more muscles, but stronger fiber."

"Now I'm beginning to get the drift of this Yooper thing.", smiled Edna.

"As long as we're on the subject I might as well tell ya the rest. We refer ta the southern section of Michigan as The Mitten." Edna looked puzzled. "Take a good look at this road map here on the table. Look at the part of Michigan south of the Mackinaw Bridge."

Edna looked. "Oh my God! It is shaped like a mitten! Here's the thumb,……and……it is a mitten!" Edna's education continued.

"We Yoopers call the folks living in Lower Michigan,…Trolls", grinned Hap.

Edna looked even more puzzled. "Trolls?, Why on earth do you call them Trolls?"

"Heh, heh, heh, because they live south of or, beneath, the Mackinaw Bridge! Har de har, har."

"That's terrible Hap. How would you like to be known by some negative sounding label?"

"Well, heh, heh, heh, I've bin called a Dumb Swede a few times. Don't bother me none. Edna, that Troll thing is jist an example of how strongly the natives feel about our independent style of livin' up here. We really don't hold any animosity towards our fellow man. We're jist plain proud ta be Yoopers."

"Tell me then oh honorable Yooper man,……how can I tell a true Yooper from all us common folks?" Edna had a smirk on her face.

"Easy. Yoopers drive pick up trucks. There'll be a gun hanging on the gun rack in the rear window of their truck, maybe two or three. And there's at least one dog riding in back. And the dog will be either a retriever or a hound. Haw, haw, haw. Our deer season in November is considered a sixteen-day holiday, jist about every male over the age of eighteen spends most of the season in a Deer Camp. She ranks right up there with Christmas, Easter and the 4th of July. Hap was delighted by Edna's last question.

But she thought she had caught Hap short handed. O.K. Mr. Smart Ass, I've got two more questions. One. How come you don't have a gun hanging on a gun rack in the rear window of our pick up truck? And, two,…just where does the U.P.'s female population fit in during your male chauvinistic sixteen day Holiday during deer season?

"Well, as to the gun question,...I've got my .44 under the front seat, and for your question about what the ladies do during deer season,......they all get together and take a vacation by shopping in Green Bay. Thought ya had me, hey Edna?" Hap had won this round.

"Now that ya know all the history about us Yoopers, let's git back to plannin' our trip." Edna shook her head and nodded in agreement.

After we leave Ishpeming, we'll stay on U.S. 41 to L'Anse and Baraga. Them's two nice towns nestled at the end of a big bay of Lake Superior called Keweenaw Bay. The French had a big fur tradin' business goin' on there back in the sixteen and seventeen hundreds. Baraga was named after a famous priest, Father Baraga, who spent much of his life administering to the Indians and attempting ta pound a little Christianity inta their heads. We'll pass a gigantic statue of the good father, which is right by the side of Highway 41.

We'll eat lunch at the Best Western in Baraga. It's right on the lakeshore and their dining room overlooks the lake. The bay will be all iced in at this time of the year but it's still a right nice spot. And if you've had enough drivin' for one day, we'll rent a room and spend the night. Maybe even drive up the hill in Baraga and spend some time in their casino. We're not on any schedule ya know."

"That's for sure darling, we're both retired seniors and there are no deadlines to meet. We both agreed we were going to spend our Golden Years just enjoying life. And so far this honeymoon trip sounds totally relaxing." Hap squeezed Edna's hand and gave her a little peck on the cheek.

From Baraga we'll keep going on 41, pass through a little village called Chassell, which is filled with antique shops and stores for women folk. If ya treat me real nice in the motel, I'll stop the truck and let ya shop a bit."

Edna smirked again. "Don't worry old man, I'll give you more in the motel than you can handle."

"Ya got me there Edna. I ain't gonna argue that point!"

After the Chassell experience, we'll pass through Houghton and Hancock; big college town full of yoop it up college kids, and continue on ta Copper Harbor, which is where U.S. 41 ends. It's not much of a town for size, but it's in one of the most beautiful spots in the world. See here on the map Edna, it's almost at the tip of the Keweenaw Peninsula. Maybe we'll take some real warm clothes with us, rent a couple of snowmobiles, and ride out ta the very tip of the peninsula. My pa took me out there one spring ta fish for trout off the big rocks that hang out over the water at the point. It's awesome!"

"If the weather isn't terribly cold, I'd love to do that.", replied an eager Edna.

"There ain't a lot of places ta stay, and sometimes at this time of the year the town is packed with snowmobilers. If we can find a room, we'll spend the night there. The town is famous for a couple of good eating-places and there's one up on the hill overlooking the town I'd love ta show you." Hap was bubbling over with enthusiasm.

"After leaving Copper Harbor I'll drive ya over the scenic road that follows a high ridge where the view is breathtaking. That's if it's plowed. Edna, ya think we git snow here in Newberry,...jist wait till ya see the banks and drifts in the Keweenaw! Yer gonna see it and still ain't gonna believe it!" Edna looked at Hap and didn't believe it.

"Hey Edna. Are ya still writin' all this down? If ya don't, we're both goin' ta fergit where we're goin' and git lost fer sure!" Edna frowned, nodded, and pointed to several pages of notes. Hap continued the verbal tour.

"We'll hafta backtrack to Houghton,...then take highway 26 south ta U.S. 45. Take a right and head north ta a town called Ontonagon. Old town, but real nice. Right on Lake Superior. Maybe it'll be iced over and maybe not. I useta have some relatives living in Ontonagon. My pa had a brother and a sister in law who lived there. They had a whole flock of kids, but I've no idea where they all wound up. We'll see if any of 'um still live around Ontonagon when we git there." Edna completed her notes. Hap droned on.

"From Ontonagon we'll head west on highway 107 ta Silver City. There's a couple of nice motels right on the lakeshore. We'll hole up there for night number four. Once we're up and had breakfast, I'll show you one of the most beautiful and spectacular sights in the U.P. Nestled in an old fault line at the top of the Porcupine Mountains is a vista that overlooks Lake of the Clouds. It's one of the most photographed places in

Michigan, or the entire mid-west for that matter. We gotta make sure we bring our new camera and lots of film."

"It's already packed, sugarplum." replied Edna with a sigh and a smile.

Now, the next leg of our journey is iffy. We'll make it if the road is plowed and take the long way around if it ain't. After leavin' the Lake of the Clouds, hopefully South Boundary Road will be open ta vehicle travel. Sometimes the road crews don't open it during the winter and let snowmobiles run on it. The road goes from Silver City at the east end of Porcupine Mountain State Park ta the west end where the mighty Presque Isle River enters Lake Superior. It's nearly thirty miles of pure natural beauty."

"Well, if it's not plowed, we'll just go back and visit the area next spring or summer. Remember Hap darling,......we're retired and not on any schedule."

Anyway, one way or another, I'll get ta the park at the mouth of the Presque Isle and we'll walk the trail ta the shore of Old Gitche Gumee" You'll love the suspension bridge ya gotta cross ta git ta the other side of the river. She swings a bit when ya cross. You won't be scared, will ya dearie?"

Edna punched Hap in the arm and gave him an obscene jester while replying; "Maybe I'll throw you off the bridge and collect your life insurance."

Hap laughed and added, "How ya gonna live on a hundred bucks?"

Hap continued with his tour on the map. "After that we'll pick up U.S. 2 at Wakefield and head ta the westernmost town in the U.P., Ironwood. There's an old theater in the downtown area that was built before I was born. It's been given a major facelift and features live plays that rival that stuff you'd see on Broadway. Probably a lot better! We'll check on what's playin' and take in a real show. How'd ya like that Edna?"

"I didn't think anything was older than you, honeybun, but as long as you're buying the tickets, I'll love it!"

"Me buy the tickets? Hell's Bells sugarplum, yer the gal with all the moola! My monthly allowance of ten bucks will be spent by the time we git there!"

"Oh just admit the truth Mr. Scrooge. Deep down inside you're a tightwad, penny pinching old geezer."

"What da ya mean a tightwad? Didn't I buy you a chain saw and a snow blower for Christmas?"

"Very funny. Where do we go when we leave Ironwood?"

"Jist follow my finger on the map and you'll see. We head back east on U.S. 2 ta Watersmeet. Then we'll swing north on U.S. 45 and I'll take you ta see one of the U.P's premier waterfalls, Bond Falls. But I'm gonna blind fold ya till we git past Watersmeet so ya don't see the casino."

"Oh goodie, another casino! You can drop me off there and pick me up after you get done looking at Bond Falls." giggled Edna. Hap knew he'd probably be stopping at Lac Vieux Desert Casino for at least a couple of hours.

"Well Edna, maybe ya kin put yerself out long enough ta come and see the falls with me, then if yer behavin'

real good we'll head back ta Watersmeet and spend the night at the casino and hotel. You kin play yer slot machines and I'll take a nice swim in the pool. How's that sound?"

"You're reading my mind, sweetheart!"

"That ain't sayin' much. There ain't much left ta read. Heh, heh, heh."

"And then, after it gits dark, I'll drive ya north of the casino a few miles and show you what is known as The Paulding Light."

"And what may I ask, is The Paulding Light?"

"Well, actually, nobody knows fer sure. It's a strange light that dances around near the bottom of a big valley most every night after it gits dark. It's bin there since before the white man arrived. The Indians were scared to go there and considered it an unholy place. Thousands of visitors visit the site annually to look at the light and be awed. Numerous scientific groups have studied the light but have come up with nothing to explain it's existence. You'll love it Edna!"

"If you say so darling."

"Now if I'm keeping track of the days correctly, when we leave Watersmeet we should be in day seven of our honeymoon tour. Is that right, oh faithful guide?"

"Yep, that's right. And by the afternoon of day seven, after following U.S. 2 east for another hundred and twenty miles or so, we'll come ta overnight stop number eight."

"And where pray tell will that be?"

"Jist another casino and hotel in a little crossroads place called Harris. This is a pretty big casino and hotel too. They got a swimin' pool area that looks like yer in a tropical paradise. She's called The Island. Useta be called The Chip Inn. Right fancy joint. And ya better like this one cause it's our last overnight. We'll be back here in our home sweet home on the afternoon of day nine."

"And I'm sure we'll be glad to get back. Trips and vacations are always nice, but it seems like coming home is as much fun as the trip."

Edna placed her pad full of notes in her purse. The honeymoon was planned. Tomorrow they would be beginning the tour!

Part Three: "Honeymooning, The Trip"

A few soft snowflakes were drifting earthward as Hap and Edna finished packing their truck for the greatly anticipated, as Hap put it, "Our Honeymoon Tour Of Da U.P." Hap's final chore prior to departure was letting his five sled dogs out of their kennel for a romp in the snow, plus he took time to pay special attention to each dog. Edna always marveled at how much Hap loved dogs and how much the dogs returned the feeling. But she understood that during her husband's thirty plus years living and trapping in the wilderness of Quebec required the trust in a good team of dogs to guarantee survival. And Hap had survived, despite many harrowing experiences.

"Come here Wolf! Good Boy! Yer old master is gonna be gone a few days but Joe'll be here every day ta let ya out fer a run and feed the bunch of ya. He'll probably even hook ya all up ta my sled and take a run along the river ta keep you guys in shape." Hap gave Wolf, his lead dog, a dozen or so friendly pats and strokes and then repeated the process with Meathead, Star, Rusty and Bubba. In turn each dog gave their master a few loving licks and sad looks as if they knew exactly what Hap had told them. Edna was sure the dogs had understood their master would be gone for a few days. There was a time when she didn't think much of animal intelligence, but all that had changed since she had fallen in love with Hap,……and his dogs. After all, their loyalty and bravery had once saved her life, or at least saved her from a severe beating from two thugs.

The trio of vacationers left Newberry shortly after eight a.m. on January sixth, turned west on highway 28, and began their nine day "Honeymoon Vacation". Hap was excited to revisit places he hadn't seen for forty or more years, and he was equally excited to be showing his new bride his beloved U.P. Nearly every few minutes Hap would point out some landmark or relate a story pertaining to some event that had occurred on or near their present location.

"We're comin' inta Seney. It ain't much of a town today, but back in the hay day of the lumberin' boom it was a bustlin' community. Later, after the lumber jacks cut all the big pine and left, the town burned down. What you see now is what was rebuilt. And just ahead we'll be crossin' the Fox River. It's one of our best trout streams. Even Ernest Hemmingway fished here back in the 20's and 30's. Told everybody he caught all his trout in The Two Hearted River north of where we live, but the old Fox was his favorite." Edna was getting an education.

Later, as the vacationers began the long downgrade into the coastal community of Munising, Hap pointed out a highway sign at the intersection of highways 28 and 94. "See that sign that says Chatham, 18 miles?" Edna looked and nodded. "That's where that tabloid you get such a kick outta is published."

"You mean the U.P. Magazine, The Porcupine Press?", asked a smiling Edna. Hap grinned and nodded. "That's the funniest newspaper I've ever read. And besides the funny stuff, it contains lots of U.P. history and stories about famous U.P. people,...and,...and,......it's a delightful paper. I'm going to subscribe to it when we get back from our trip!" Edna liked to read.

The well-planned trip continued to be an extremely relaxing and entertaining experience. Hap mentioned several times that their trip was "goin' like a well oiled machine". Plus Edna was getting more and more information about becoming, as Hap put it, "Yooperized". Edna was a good student.

Several of the motels they encountered had rooms that contained two of the couple's favorite added attractions. A hot tub and vibrating mattresses. And they made good use of both tools.

Relaxing in bed watching the ten o'clock news after one of their rousing, intimate love making sessions, Hap had a question. "Say Edna darling,...what da ya think some of that new Viagra stuff might do fer me?"

Edna giggled and pulled on Hap's whiskers, "I really don't think you need any sexual stimulants, honey,......at least not yet!"

"Ya, yer the only stimulant I need Edna, and you do a dandy job of stimulatin'. Besides, I heard a story one mornin' down at the coffee shop in Newberry that made me think twice about usin' that Viagra stuff."

Edna cast a suspicious eye at her husband and waited for the rest of the story.

"Herb Whitney said his wife bought him some of that stuff ta make him more horny. But he wouldn't take it. So his wife poured the whole bottle of pills down their well, thinkin' every time old Herb took a drink of water he'd be rarin' ta go ta bed." Hap hesitated and looked at Edna.

"All right, I'll be your straight man,......What happened Hap?"

"Well, his wife's plan backfired. The stuff worked so good that she couldn't push the pump handle down! Har de har har!"

Edna moaned, rolled over and went to sleep.

The days and miles rolled by,...all too quickly. Only two of Hap's pre-planned routes had to be changed. The scenic road running along the high ridge near Copper Harbor was not plowed, nor was the South Boundary Road in the Porcupine Mountains. They were minor interruptions in an otherwise well-planned trip.

Edna hit a jackpot on a quarter machine in Baraga, then lost most of her winnings in the gift shops of Chassell.

The theater in Ironwood presented the touring couple with a wonderful performance of "South Pacific". When Edna asked Hap what part of the play he liked the best, he answered, "The nice pair of coconuts on the leading lady". His remark and the smirk on his face cost him another punch in the arm. The newlyweds were thoroughly enjoying their honeymoon and each other!

Edna slipped on an icy rock at Bond Falls and nearly fell in the river. Hap suggested he should have given her a harder push, because, as Hap put it, "You could use a cold bath ta cool off". Hap's arm was getting black and blue.

Hap won almost a hundred dollars playing Blackjack at the casino in Watersmeet, but Edna lost thirty-five in the slots. Still, they had enough profit to pay for a wonderful prime rib dinner and an expensive bottle of wine,……
which they consumed in their room while, as Hap put it, "Foolin' around a little bit."

Both enjoyed the warm sand beach and the pool area during their last night's stay in Harris at the Island Resort and Casino. And after a yummy dinner of chicken and ribs they retired to their room for the last night of their honeymoon. Both expressed an eagerness to, as Hap put it, "Git back ta livin' a normal life in the peace and quiet of our home on the banks of the Tahquamenon River."

The couple's final day on the road took them along the north shore of Lake Michigan, which was dressed in a virgin white mantle of winter. And yet another breathtaking view. As they neared the community of Manistique, Hap's memory kicked in to recall something he hadn't thought of for many, many years. And of course he excitedly told Edna.

"Hey Edna, I jist remembered something! I might have some relatives livin' here in Manistique."

"Oh", questioned Edna, "is it someone you've told me about?"

"Heck no! It's bin so long since I visited old Uncle Dewey and Aunt Betty, I dang near forgot where we usta go ta visit them. Aunt Betty was my mother's younger sister and once in a while we'd visit them here in Manistique and then they'd come up and see us in Newberry. There was two kids in the family, just a bit older than me, a boy named Tom and a girl named,……oh what the hell was her name,………oh ya, Sarah. Wonder if any of 'um are still around?"

"Well darling, it's nearly lunchtime. Let's stop at a cafe, have some lunch, and ask. Maybe somebody knows the answer to your question."

"Ya, my gut's growling a bit. Good idea Edna. We're makin' good time so we kin take a break, grab a bite ta eat and see if anybody knows if any of my shirt tail relations still live around these parts."

A short distance from Manistique's city limits Edna spotted a sign advertising an establishment that served food and beverages that appealed to her woman's intuition. As usual, her choice was a good one.

"Teddy's Pub and Bristro", grumbled Hap, "sounds kinda fancy ta me. But when it comes ta pickin' places ta eat, you ain't done too bad a job, Edna. Teddy's it is."

The cheeseburgers and fries were done to perfection, and the iced schooners of tap beer topped off a perfect lunch. When their waitress returned to check on her two customers, Hap gave her the name of his aunt and uncle and asked if any of the family was still living in or near Manistique. Hap was amazed to discover both his relatives were still alive and living in an assisted living complex for seniors. Directions to the location were received and ten minutes after leaving Teddy's, Hap and Edna were knocking on the door of Hap's relatives, which he hadn't seen for over forty years!

A little over an hour and a half later Hap turned his truck north at Blaney Park on Highway 77 and he, Edna and Sadie began the last leg of their journey home. Midway between Blaney Park and Seney Hap pointed out a large flock of crows and ravens that were congregating in a wooded area behind an old barn and farmhouse. "Look at that bunch of crows and ravens Edna. They must have found a dead deer or are harassing an owl, which is one of their arch enemies." Edna looked, but seemed unimpressed.

"Hap, I've been thinking about your aunt and uncle, Betty and Dewey,…they sure were a spry old couple for being well up into their eighties. Your uncle sure seemed proud that one of his grandchildren was following in his footsteps and became a game warden. What did he say his grandson's name is?

Hap looked at Edna and replied, "Brian Matson".

Chapter Two: "Conspirators"

Part One: "Just Relaxing"

The months of winter and early spring that remained after Hap and Edna returned from their honeymoon consisted of the much-anticipated relaxation the couple had been seeking. Hap joined the local sportsmen's club and Edna became involved with a local book club and reading group. Edna had always been an avid reader.

In order to keep himself in shape and prevent boredom, Hap set out a modest trap line along the banks of the Tahquamenon River, which flowed through his property. This in turn allowed him to run his dog team nearly every day to keep them in shape. As Hap put it, "This retirement stuff ain't bad, Edna".

The couple also took their team of dogs to several dog sled races. Hap took first place in the "Beginners" five-dog event at Land O' Lakes, Wisconsin, collected a second in Ironwood, and Edna drove the team to another first in Sault Ste. Marie. As Hap put it, "Ain't too shabby fer a team of young dogs!" Edna wasn't surprised by their victories, as her husband worked hard keeping his dogs healthy and fit, plus he had molded the young dogs into, as Edna put it, "a well-oiled machine."

Several times Hap took Edna and Sadie ice fishing. He purchased a portable ice fishing shanty and a small propane heater to keep the enclosure warm. Hap caught northern pike and walleye, which made superb eating, but Edna usually brought along a good book to read and sat close to the propane heater.

During the March meeting of the Newberry Sportsmen's Club, a local conservation officer, Brian Matson, presented a short talk to the members about the Department of Natural Resources deer management plan. It was with a great deal of pleasure Hap got to meet one of his distant relatives. And he took an immediate liking to the young officer. As Hap put it when he told Edna, "That kid's got some of the Larson bloodlines all right!"

Edna was quick to point out that the "bloodlines" came from his mother's side of the family, the Baldwin's. Hap's reply was, "Close enough!"

April arrived, offering some occasional hints of real spring weather, although snow still blanketed the U.P.'s landscape, in places over a foot deep. The early trout-fishing season opened in late April, and Hap, Edna and Sadie spent several days fishing for salmon. They rented a cabin at Rainbow Lodge, a well known fisherman's destination at the mouth of the Big Two Hearted River, and despite the cool, misty weather the trio did manage to land a half dozen Coho and spring run steelheads. Returning to their home in Newberry, Hap built a "smoker", using a fifty five gallon steel barrel, and soon supplied some of his neighbors and friends with smoked fish.

By mid May, spring finally wedged its way between winter and summer. Arbutus and marsh marigolds blossomed, followed by Juneberry, Black Cherry, Pin Cherry and Choke Cherry, as well as a host of other wild flowers and flowering shrubs. The U.P.'s atmosphere was drenched with the sweetness of spring.

Flocks of wild ducks, geese, robins and numerous songbirds began their spring ritual of mating and nesting. Daily, the amount of green on the deciduous trees increased. Newborn fawns began to appear, waddling along behind their mothers and frolicking in fields of fresh spring grass. Yes sir, Old Ma Nature was putting on one of her finest shows!

Next, the couple took time to complete another chore they had anxiously been waiting to tackle. Hap's parents had owned a vintage '57 Chevy Nomad Wagon, in nearly mint condition. Hap inherited the vehicle after his folks died. Besides needing to replace all four tires, the engine and drive train needed to be carefully checked, and all the fluids needed to be replaced before the car could once again be driven. It had been sitting in the garage at the Larson homestead for nearly four years.

Hap and Edna jacked up one wheel at a time, blocked the axle with pieces of six by six timbers, removed the rims, and had new tires installed at the Jiffy Lube in Newberry. Once the new tires were back on the old Chevy, a tow truck from the local General Motors dealer towed the classic car to their repair headquarters and put the Nomad back in perfect running condition. Edna now had a vehicle of her very own! As Hap put it, "A classy dame drivin' a classy car."

A few days before the Memorial Day Weekend Hap and Edna received a phone call from Hap's cousin, Charles Baldwin, who with his wife Shirley, lived in Sept lies, Quebec. The Baldwin's had some exciting news.

"Well, well, well, cousin, good ta hear yer voice. How's everything out east?", responded Hap to his cousin's greeting.

"Everything's just fine, Hap. All of us are well and the boys are busy expanding their chain of hardware stores that Shirley and I turned over to them when we retired a year ago.", Charles answered. "How are the two newly weds adjusting to married life? It was wonderful to be a part of your wedding party and we had a great time visiting you and getting to see your hometown. The U.P is every bit as nice and beautiful as you claimed it to be. You recall I only got to visit there one other time and that was when you and I were about fourteen years old. I really didn't remember much about the area."

"So, what's new cousin. I know ya ain't callin' just ta pass the time of day. Somethin's brewin', ain't it?" Hap had a knack of keeping ahead of most conversations.

"You know me too well Hap. Shirley and I have been talking all winter about what we want to do in our retirement years. We're lucky, at this point at least, money is not a problem. As I told you last spring when my oldest son, Jason, and I visited you in Nitchequon, our chain of hardware stores made Shirley and I a lot of money. So,......we've decided to spend some of it."

"I'm diein' ta find out on what, Charles. Quit talkin' in riddles and come out with it. What's up yer sleeve?"

"Shirley and I are flying to Sault Ste. Marie sometime around the Memorial Day weekend. We're going to rent a car, drive to Newberry, where we'll reserve a room at the Sportsmen's Bar, Supper Club and Motel,......we have some business to attend to."

There was an awkward pause as Hap's mind whirled trying to think of what to say or ask next. "Yer still beatin' around the bush, cousin. And if yer comin' ta Newberry, we'd want ya ta stay at our place. Why'd ya go and rent a motel room?"

"Well, Shirley and I didn't want to impose on your hospitality, and we've not sure how long we may have to stay in the area until we find what we're looking for."

"Gull dang it cousin, would ya jist tell me what yer comin' here for? Yer drivin' me nuts!"

"We are going to buy a summer residence somewhere near Newberry, hopefully on a lake or stream, and spend the summer and early fall seasons in the U.P. Do you think we'd make good Yoopers?" Charles ended his confession with a laugh.

Hap was once again speechless.

Part Two: "Complications"

For the Welchek Brothers, Cory and Todd, the days before the upcoming Memorial Day Weekend began as a gigantic nightmare. As deer poachers, they had been very successful. But adding murder to their list of criminal acts was something much more serious, and was going to complicate their lives beyond their wildest dreams. The murder of Conservation Officer Brian Matson opened a whole new can of worms.

Immediately following the murder, the two had gotten into a terrible argument. Todd, the younger of the two and somewhat brighter than his brother Cory, was livid with rage. The unexpected arrival of Officer Matson to the location of their illegal butchering and dumping ground had caught the pair completely off guard, which contributed to Cory's ill advised decision to kill the officer.

However, the argument was short lived and a plan of action was quickly developed. The brothers drove the officer's truck into the barn where it would not be seen by anyone passing by on Highway 77. Next, they wrapped the young officer's body in a plastic tarp and carried it into an area of dense, bushy balsam trees almost a quarter mile further into the forest and buried it in a shallow grave.

After dark, Todd drove the officer's truck, with Cory following in their black Ford pickup, to a secluded location deep within an uninhabited area between the east and west branches of the Manistique River. They doused the truck with gasoline, set it on fire, and later covered it with mounds of tree branches and shrubs. At the moment their plan sounded like a winner.

Early the following morning the phone rang at the residence of Randolph Redman. The nightmare was spreading.

"Hello", inquired a sleepy sounding Mr. Redman.

"Randy? This is Todd. We've created a real problem here and feel you should know about it before the shit hits the fan. Cory and I think we've got our problem solved,……but there's going to be some fallout before the dust settles."

Randolph's mind began to clear as he recognized who was calling. "Christ sakes, what the hell could be so pressing as to call me at six in the morning?" Mr. Redman wasn't happy with the early call and was soon to become much less happy.

"Cory did something really stupid and has created what might become a real mess. I gotta tell you what we did in trying to solve our problem, but there may be additional things we should do before all hell breaks loose. We don't know who else to turn to. We both know you're a real smart man,……seeing as you were the one we have to thank for figuring out how to create our plan of distribution."

"O.K. spit it out. Now what have you two gotten yourselves into? It better not be another drunk driving ticket, or one of your barroom brawls. I'm getting damn sick and tired of bailing you two idiots out of trouble. I hope this is something simple and not as bad as you're indicating."

"Naw, Mr. Redman, this ain't simple,………Cory killed a game warden."

By seven a.m. Mr. Redman had completed two additional phone calls pertinent to the serious situation of which the Welchek Brothers had informed him. One was to a Mr. Corbet O'Keefe in Lansing, Michigan and the second to Mr. Kenneth Bradford in Washington D.C. The entire chain of command had been notified of Brian Matson's murder.

Obeying Mr. Redman's directive, Todd and Cory parked their pickup truck behind a run down bar on the east shore of

Manistique Lake. "The Howling Beagle Bar and Grille" was presently owned by a two time divorcee of questionable character. The bar was a frequent hang out for many of the local "good old boys" who liked to whoop it up on week ends or stop in for a couple shots and beers after work. Those who didn't have jobs often spent much of the day in the Howling Beagle. For those who were not patrons of the establishment, The Howling Beagle was usually referred to as "That Dive at Manistique Lake".

Being a Wednesday, and nearly eleven p.m., the small parking lot was empty, and but one neon sign shone inside a small, dirty window. It blinked, "It's Miller Time", over and over. Two additional cars were parked behind the bar when Todd and Cory arrived. The owner's well used red Jeep Cherokee and Mr. Redman's new blue Ford Explorer. Todd and Cory entered through the back door, said a quick hello to the owner, April Ravovich, and retreated into the bar's living quarters. Randy Redman was seated at a small table in the kitchen area inhaling a homemade cigarette and consuming his second glass of Jack Daniels on the rocks. And Mr. Redman didn't look happy.

The late night meeting lasted for nearly an hour. Todd and Cory related the events leading up to the murder of Officer Matson and gave the gruesome details of the aftermath. Randy Redman, the brother's immediate "supervisor" of their illegal poaching business, listened intently as his mind raced to comprehend the scope of the consequences the events being described to him might create. But what had happened couldn't be reversed. For the moment, Mr. Redman could only hope the steps Cory and Todd had taken to hide the evidence of their untimely crime would shield everyone involved in the illegal poaching conspiracy. But the sick feeling in the pit of his stomach suggested otherwise. But at the moment, nothing more could be done.

It was after midnight when the meeting broke up. Todd and Cory, their faces looking like something you'd see in a wax museum, left the bar and disappeared into the night. Randy Redman, who had told his wife he was headed for an important meeting in Iron Mountain and would not return to his home in Escanaba until the following day, entered the bar and had a double shot of Jack Daniels.

For the next hour and a half, between the sheets of her bed, April attempted to sooth Mr. Redman's soul. Usually April's skill worked miracles to sooth any number of troubled souls. In fact, April derived a considerable amount of her income from "soothing men's souls", after the bar closed. But on this night, after a rousing round of lovemaking, Randy Redman spent the next four hours tossing and turning in fitful sleep. And his macabre nightmares included finding a rotting corpse in a shallow grave.

Part Three: "Search Plans"

Hap and Edna, as well as many others in the western upper peninsula, were first made aware a conservation officer had disappeared, when on Wednesday the evening news broadcast from WSSM-TV in Sault Ste Marie broke the story. No particulars were mentioned, nor was the name of the missing officer released. The brief story only mentioned a conservation officer was missing and presumed lost, or stuck, or perhaps some other simple explanation might be forthcoming to explain why the officer had not returned from his patrol shift on Tuesday. The commentary ended with assurances the young officer would be located safe and sound.

The story was hardly earth shaking news, as game wardens often got stuck in some out of the way, God forsaken place. Often their radios often didn't work, or phone batteries went dead, or they might be in a "dead spot" when cell phones didn't work, or,……sometimes they were simply just too bullheaded to call for help. Officers who did call for help, when poor judgment or carelessness got themselves into trouble, such as getting stuck in the mud on some wilderness cow path, were usually the object of severe kidding or practical jokes delivered by their peers or superiors.

The morning news broadcast contained a much more serious tone.

"A full-fledged search is underway for Conservation Officer Brian Matson of Schoolcraft County. He was last heard from about noon on Tuesday after he had radioed a report to the office of the Seney National Wildlife Refuge indicating he had found evidence that a number of deer had been shot within the boundary of the sanctuary. The refuge is located just southwest of Seney along Highway 77. At the moment foul play is not suspected, but search planes are presently in the air attempting to locate his vehicle or any distress signals that may be originating from the ground. Officer Matson was driving a dark blue Dodge Ram truck with Michigan Municipality license plates number, SH-414-62. If anyone has any information as to the whereabouts of Officer Matson, please call the Michigan DNR hotline, DNR-HOT-TIPS."

Hap turned off the television set, filled his corn cob pipe with Bond Street, put a match to the bowl, and began pacing the floor. "Somethin's wrong Edna. Real wrong. That young Matson fella jist struck me a bein' too savvy an officer ta git lost or be stuck somewhere fer this long. Good God,……today's Thursday already. If the last they heard from him was Tuesday noon,……somethin's damn wrong!"

Edna agreed, and sensed her husband's deep concern over his missing relative. Edna knew her husband had experienced numerous "close calls" during his nearly four decades of living in the wilderness of Quebec's sub-arctic. There were so many circumstances, which could challenge or take the life of someone alone in the wilderness and in trouble. So far neither Hap nor Edna factored in the possibility of foul play.

Brian Matson's father and mother, Tom and Beverly were sitting on their screened in porch at their retirement home in Naples, Florida having coffee and reading the morning paper when the phone rang. It was a call from Tom's dad, Brian's grandfather, who lived in Manistique. The news was not good.

As soon as Tom hung up he placed a hurried call to a travel agent, which resulted in successfully booking a flight out of Naples to Atlanta. Their departure time would be 9:45 the following morning. The remainder of their flight schedule included a two-hour layover in Atlanta, then after boarding a second plane, they would continue on to Detroit. Here, after another hour and a half lay over the couple would switch to a commuter service and fly them from Detroit to Sault Ste. Marie. Arrival time at their destination was expected to be 6:45 p.m. From Sault Ste. Marie the couple would rent a car and drive sixty miles to Newberry. Two new players would be entering the search.

By Thursday morning, the DNR office in Escanaba was abuzz with frenzied activity. Every available conservation officer in the area, all their trainees, plus representatives from the county sheriff's office, the state police and the local search and rescue squad were assembled in the largest meeting room. Also in attendance were two Federal Wildlife Officers. A serious faced Chief Warden, Paul Vandenburg, filled the assembled multitude in on the sketchy details.

"You are all aware of why we are here. We've got a missing warden who hasn't been heard from since just before noon on Tuesday. His last confirmed location was at a field at the southeast corner of the Seney National Wildlife Refuge. At eleven forty seven a.m. he made a phone call to the refuge office. He informed the ranger on duty that he had found bloodstains in a field, indicating at least four deer had been recently killed there. He added he was going to continue searching for more evidence. Why he didn't call that information into this office is unknown."

A deputy sheriff raised his hand and was recognized by Officer Vandenburg. "Go ahead Doug."

"I was up and down Highway 77 from Seney to Blaney Park twice that day and did see Brian in his truck shortly after noon. I was south bound and he was north bound. We waved at each other. I know that's not much information, but at least we know which direction he was heading after he made his call to the refuge office."

"Thanks Doug. Yes, you're right, every little scrap of information helps. It may help narrow the search area. As most of you also know, we've had several planes up combing areas on both sides of 77 and both north and south of 28 and U.S. 2. Today the search areas are going to be expanded west all the way to 94 and east to 117. Hard telling where Brian went later Tuesday afternoon. He could have wound up anywhere in that vast area, and as most of you know it's some damn wild country. At this point all we can do is keep our eyes and ears open, hope perhaps some citizen might know something,……or Brian may walk though that door on his own power."

Warden Maki had a question. "Paul, has there been any effort to bring additional manpower into the search? I mean, have any citizen groups been asked or volunteered to assist in helping to attempt to locate Brian"?

"Yes! The Newberry Sportsmen's Club and the committee members from Duck's Unlimited Chapters in Escanaba and Munising have called to offer assistance. I'll be meeting with them later this morning and will set up some sort of zone for each group to cover. Maybe we'll get lucky and find some clue as to what happened to Brian or where he is. If he's laying out there somewhere hurt,………well, God damn it,……time may be running out." Being no further questions or comments, the members of the audience quickly filed out of the room, picked up maps of their individual search areas, and began the task of looking for a needle in a haystack.

Chief Warden Vandenburg was about to return to his office when the door to the meeting room bust open. Another concerned person, who had been invited to the meeting, rushed through the door apologizing for being late.

The senior warden smiled at the late arrival and replied, "Have a seat, I'll fill you in on what you missed, Senator Redman".

Part Four: "Searching"

The volunteers who met with Officer Vandenburg left the DNR Office in Escanaba shortly before eleven a.m. There had been over fifty individuals in attendance, twenty-two from the Newberry Sportsmen's Club, seventeen from the Duck's Unlimited Chapter in Escanaba, and thirteen from the D.U. Chapter in Munising.

After receiving the same briefing as had been given to the earlier group of law enforcement personnel and the search and rescue squad from Escanaba, the volunteers from each organization were given specific areas to assist in the coordinated search for Brian Matson.

Seeing that the last known sighting of Officer Matson had been made as he was heading north on Highway 77, the major part of the search would be concentrated in that general area.

The two groups representing the Duck's Unlimited Chapters were assigned an area from Blaney Park, north, along both sides of 77 to Germfask. An additional area of about forty square miles to the south and east of Germfask, and bordered by paved highways, was also the responsibility of the D. U. group.

The volunteers from Newberry would begin their search pattern on 77 at Germfask, checking all the side roads on both sides of 77, north to Seney. In addition, the Newberry Sportsmen's club volunteers were assigned an area north and east of Germfask. It too was bordered by paved highways and contained in excess of forty square miles, which included Manistique Lake.

After receiving their maps of the area to be searched, the volunteers created "teams" of two or three individuals and each team selected areas they would search along their assigned routes and within their assigned area.

The entire body of searchers spent the remainder of Thursday afternoon combing every side road and any other seemingly possible place that Officer Matson may have ventured into. Individuals and families who resided in the search area were questioned. The search netted exactly nothing! Zero! Zip! Hope of finding the young warden alive was rapidly waning.

On Friday morning Hap Larson arose before sunrise and drove to Germfask, where the continuing search would begin. He was the first volunteer to arrive. Hap suspected most, if not all the volunteers would call it a day by mid afternoon and return to their respective homes in anticipation of enjoying the Memorial Day weekend. But bullheaded Hap Larson had decided he wouldn't quit looking for Brian Matson until dark, and at this time of the year it didn't get dark till nearly nine o'clock. After all, how much longer could Brian hold out if he was badly hurt? Hap continued to suppress the notion that the young officer may already be beyond help.

The D.N.R. had set up a temporary "nerve center" to coordinate the search efforts. The senior ranger in charge of the Seney National Wildlife Refuge had arranged to provide a room in one of their administration buildings to house the nerve center. One member of each search team was assigned the task of reporting the team's findings at the completion of their day's search.

By mid-afternoon on Friday the team leaders began arriving to file their reports. Once again, there was nothing new to report. By five p.m. all but one team leader had filed their report and left. Hap Larson was still searching!

Before leaving Germfask, Hap carefully studied the quadrangle map that had been supplied to the searchers by the D.N.R. He thoughtfully stared at the marked location where

Brian had phoned the Seney National Wildlife Refuge Office after he found evidence deer had been illegally poached. Even though Hap knew the area had already been searched for clues by several different teams of searchers,……well, he just had to take a look for himself.

It was shortly after five p.m. when Hap reached the boundary of the wildlife refuge. Large yellow signs with bold, black letters were affixed to posts on either side of the narrow, two-rut road, which proclaimed;

Seney National Wildlife Refuge

NO SNOWMOBILES, ATV'S OR ANY WHEELED VEHICLES BEYOND THIS POINT

Hap parked his truck short of the signs and noted that the searchers who had preceded him had done likewise. Walking out in the field, he found four blaze orange strips of surveyor's tape attached to stakes marking the location of the bloodstains Brian Matson had discovered on Tuesday. At least the earlier investigators had looked hard enough to find what the young officer had reported.

Hap looked back towards the edge of the field where his truck was parked. Slowly and carefully he studied the foliage and brush which bordered the field. Mumbling to himself he said, "Now if I was a dang poacher, where would I set up an ambush?" Rubbing his chin thoughtfully, suddenly his eyes zeroed in on an area a hundred or so feet from where the old road entered the field. A thick, low screen of pussy willow and hazel brush caught his attention. "Guess I better have a look at that spot over there.", Hap ordered himself.

Pushing his way through the thick screen of bushes, he stopped and allowed his eyes to scan the ankle high grass. Something shinny about twenty feet to his left drew his gaze. Walking slowly to the location of the mystery object, his eyes continued to scan the grass-covered ground. The shinny object was an empty beer can. He sniffed the hole in the top of the can and easily caught the odor of stale beer. The can had been left there fairly recently.

Continuing to scan the area, he discovered nine additional cans, all the same brand with all the same code numbers. And then another small, shiny object caught his attention. He leaned over and picked up an empty .223 cartridge! Smelling the open end of the cartridge produced a fairly noticeable odor of burnt gunpowder. This cartridge had been fired recently. "Probably the same night the beer was guzzled.", Hap informed himself.

Looking more closely now, Hap soon found three more empty .223's. "Damn, the guy who's doin' the shootin' is a pretty decent shot." Being careful not to put too many of his fingerprints on the empty casings, he dropped each cartridge into separate fingers of one of his brown cotton work gloves he kept in the glove compartment of his truck. A plastic bag from Pamida, which was located under the seat of his truck, became the depository for the ten empty beer cans.

Returning to the location where he found the beer cans and empty cartridges, Hap continued to look for whatever else the poachers might have left behind. His efforts produced six cigarette butts, all in a comparatively small area, and about fifteen feet from where the shell casings were found. These were stored in the second cotton work glove.

Hap returned to stroking his chin whiskers as he started putting all the pieces of the puzzle together. Five empty beer cans had been found fairly close together and five more had been found fifteen to twenty feet from the first five. All the empty cartridges had been found close to the second batch of empty cans, while the cigarette butts were interspersed where the first five cans were lying. "HHHUUUUUMMMMM?" thought Hap.

Further Investigation of the area between his discoveries Hap found four small areas where the grass had been flattened. "Yep", mumbled Hap, "here's where the bastards parked their truck,...or car,...or whatever they were drivin'. The driver was the smoker and the passenger was the shooter. An' both of 'um was drinkers. It all fits,......plain as day!"

Detective Larson had at last produced some "hard evidence"!

Tom and Beverly Matson landed in Atlanta on schedule and spent nearly two hours impatiently pacing the terminal waiting for their next plane to depart. Within fifteen minutes of departure time the Security Office received a phone call indicating a bomb had been planted somewhere in the airport terminal. The entire complex was evacuated. No bomb was uncovered. This delay added an additional four hours to Tom and Beverly's wait.

Upon finally arriving in Sault Ste. Marie at ten fifty five p.m., they discovered all the car rental agency booths were closed. And with the Memorial Day Weekend loomed ahead in just a few hours, phone calls to all the "emergency numbers" of all four car rental companies were only successful in obtaining a recorded message that the rental offices would open at nine the next morning.

Reluctantly, the frustrated couple called a cab and were ushered to the local Super 8 Motel.

Chapter Three: "The Farm"

Part One: "Discoveries"

It was a few minutes after six p.m. when Hap turned his truck north on highway 77 and headed for the D.N.R. nerve center to file his report and present the authorities with his newly discovered "evidence". The nerve center was locked up, as was the refuge office. It looked to Hap as though the staff of both offices had finished their "nine to five" jobs and scattered to their homes, or wherever, to enjoy the Memorial Day Weekend.

Returning to highway 77, he turned south to intersect County Highway H-44, which was a shortcut back to Newberry. He reluctantly resigned himself to give up the search, at least for the present, and return home. Edna would be expecting him to return in time for dinner, and he was already late. And being late for any appointment was something Hap Larson was rarely guilty of.

A few minutes later he passed what appeared to be an abandoned farm. Behind the barn, over the wooded area behind it, swarmed a large flock of crows and a few ravens. A light bulb flicked on in Hap's head. This was the same place he and Edna had spotted a large flock of crows when they were returning from their honeymoon tour in January!

Hap took his foot off the gas, braked slowly and parked his truck on the shoulder of the road. As he watched the pesky birds diving and swooping into the thick stand of evergreens, curiosity got the better of him. What could be in the woods that caused such a large group of scavengers to continue to congregate in the same place for such an extended period of time? It was a puzzling question that needed an answer. Hap checked the road in both directions, found it vacant, did a U-turn, and turned his truck down the farm's driveway towards the crow-infested trees to investigate.

The outcome of the meeting at the "Howling Beagle" between Senator Randolph Redman and his two poacher pals, Cory and Todd Welchek, resulted in outlining a course of action which would hopefully shield the poaching organization from the investigation that would follow the ultimate realization that Officer Matson was dead.

At a direct and firm order from Senator Redman, the two brothers wasted no time returning to the old farm on Highway 77 and removed a considerable amount of damaging evidence that was contained in both the house and the barn.

But in their haste, they failed to consider the amount of illegal material that was present at the old farm. They neglected to bring along their large covered trailer, and therefore did not have enough space in the bed of their truck to haul all the illegal venison plus what was in the basement of the old farm house in one load. And due to the lateness of the hour, the brothers opted to call it a night, get a few hours sleep, and return to the farm for the remainder of the damning evidence on Thursday morning.

Then they made their next mistake. Before retiring for the night, Cory and Todd consumed a half bottle of cheap whiskey and the better part of a twelve pack. It was nearly noon on Thursday before they crawled out of bed.

On Thursday afternoon the brothers made several attempts to return to the old farm and collect what they had forgotten to remove Wednesday night, after their meeting with Senator Redman. But by Thursday afternoon Highway 77 was literally crawling with vehicles. They encountered numerous D.N.R. trucks, sheriff's cruisers, state troopers, and even a few pale green National Forest Service vehicles. Besides all the official traffic, trucks and cars of all descriptions were parked along the roadway and others were often viewed entering or leaving a number of secondary side roads. Many of the individuals they saw along the highway were carrying hand held walky talkies.

Cory and Todd encountered the same problem Friday. And they hesitated to continue driving up and down past the old farm for fear of arousing suspicion as to why the occupants of a black Ford pickup had such an interest in such a short stretch of Highway 77. The Welchek Brothers were suffering from a bad case of the jitters, and it didn't take a rocket scientist to tell the search of Brian Matson was in full swing!

As Hap slowly drove his truck past the seemingly deserted farmhouse, his ever vigilant eyes recorded several unusual items. Although the yard and shrubs, as well as the surrounding small fields, suggested the farm had not been active for many years, the driveway and the dirt road that ran past the barn, and continued on towards the trees full of crows, seemed awfully well used to simply be part of an abandoned farm. As his truck slowly passed the backside of the badly weathered barn, Hap saw two large double doors. Likewise, the dirt wheel tracks leading to the doors were not overgrown with grass and weeds, suggesting wheeled vehicles of some type had frequently entered and left the barn. Also, a large padlock was visible. "Odd.", he thought. But then again possibly the farm was owned by a neighboring farmer or a logger, and the barn was being used as a storage shed for some type of mechanical equipment.

Reaching the edge of the wooded area the dirt road ended. A turn around area showed more evidence of heavy use. A well-used pathway entered the wooded area and disappeared into the shadows beyond. Hap shut off his truck's engine, got out, and followed the path into the thick evergreens. The time was six thirty p.m.

The Welchek Brothers returned to their secluded home, which was located just east of the little community of Curtis, four and a half miles southeast of "The Howling Beagle". Frustrated and worried about not being able to remove the material from the basement of the old farm house, Todd once again called Senator

Redman at his home in Escanaba. "Hello, Mr. Redman,......this is Todd."

Todd's conversation with his boss lasted less than two minutes. Irritated at the realization his two venison suppliers had screwed up once again, Senator Redman blew his stack! His instructions, heavily accented with vile language, told the twosome to return to the farm house after dark and get, as he put it, "That God Damn stuff out of there before someone thinks to search the place!" And Randolph ended with, "And don't call me again at this number!"

Hap cautiously followed the well-worn path into the now quiet grove of evergreens. And like Officer Brian Matson's reaction four days earlier, Hap was stunned by what he discovered. For another ten minutes the veteran woodsman slowly meandered through the piles of leg bones, back bones, decaying deer hides, heads, scraps of discarded meat, rotting internal organs, and tallow. The place reeked!

As Hap was returning to his truck his gaze settled on an area just to the side of the path that was infested with buzzing flies. He leaned over and looked to see what had attracted so many of the filthy creatures. The forest floor was covered with brown pine needles, and with the waning light at first Hap could not detect anything out of the ordinary. He kneeled down for a closer look.

He removed his hat and swished it at the congregation of flies to make them fly. A dark, discolored mass of something about a foot in diameter covered the brown needles. Hap poked a finger at the mass, found it to be somewhat solid, and then picked up the entire glob. Taking a sniff of the unknown material made Hap's eyes widen. It was dried blood!

Returning to his feet, Hap strained his eyes to detect any other un-natural objects or clues that might give him an idea as to the origin of the bloodstain. Faintly, he detected two strips of disturbed pine needles with minor depressions in the sandy soil, which rested beneath the dead vegetation. It looked at though something had been dragged a short distance from the location of the bloodstain to the base of a very bushy white pine tree.

Suddenly, Hap jolted upright. His entire body became rigid. A horrible picture began to take place in his mind. The drag marks looked very much like the heels of two boots had been dragged across the pine needle covered ground. Yes, he was sure! Some one had dragged a body from the bloodstain to a point under a very bushy white pine tree! Something very evil had taken place here besides dumping the remains of dozens of illegally taken deer! And then, Hap's mind put a face on whom he thought had probably been the victim. It was the face of Officer Brian Matson!

At seven p.m., about the same time Hap Larson was beginning to piece together the clues of what he considered to be the scene of a murder, State Senator Randolph Redman was busy making phone calls. He updated Corbet O'Keefe in Lansing, MI. and Kenneth Bradford in Washington D. C. as to what was transpiring in, as Mr. Redman put it, "the situation created by those two dumb assholes, the Welchek brothers." As expected, the top two men in the poaching enterprise were greatly disturbed."

Upon returning to his truck, Hap drove to the back of the barn and began searching for a way into the building. Understandably nervous about breaking into locked, private property, he left his vehicle close to the barn making it impossible for someone to see it from the highway. Even if someone drove as far as the farmhouse, Hap's truck would still be shielded from view.

The early evening sun was now nearly below the tree line to the west, and twilight would soon engulf the landscape. Hap took his flashlight from the truck's center console and began phase two of his investigation at the old farm.

He tried shinning his flashlight through the cracks in the barn wall. He could make out nothing inside. Next, he walked all around the building, looking for any possible point of entry. He noted the electrical wires leading to the barn seemed to be of a much larger gauge that would normally be required to service a few lights in a barn. And the electrical wire looked to be fairly new. At one point in his investigation of the barn's exterior, he could hear some sort of electric motor or compressor running. His curiosity deepened.

Completing his circuit around the barn, Hap looked above the locked double doors and saw another large door that probably led to the hayloft. He turned his truck around, and backed up until it was but a few inches from the old barn. Next he climbed up on the roof of his truck's topper, and using the handle of his jack he attempted to pry the door to the loft open. It was unlocked!

Forcing the door open enough to allow his entry, he was able to pull himself up and into the second story of the barn. The loft area still contained a number of musty smelling bales of hay, and hundreds of dust particles danced in the beam of his flashlight. A ladder led him down to the ground floor.

Even in the rapidly dimming light of day, Hap easily saw what the barn had recently been used for. Several large wooden tables were encrusted with dried blood, plus deposits of reasonably fresh blood. A dozen or more knives of various sizes and shapes lay on one table. Two cleavers and a meat saw rested on another. Boxes of large plastic bags, wrapping paper and freezer tape were stacked on shelves. Without a doubt, this was the poacher's butchering room.

An open doorway invited Hap to search the rest of the ground floor of the barn. It was here he discovered the source of the sound he had heard when he was making his circuit of the barn's exterior. A walk in cooler had been installed in one corner of the barn, and it was nearly twenty feet square. The interior of the cooler was empty, except for more dried and fresh blood on the floor, plus several dozen meat hooks that were suspended from metal railings attached to the ceiling. It was easy to determine the operators of this poaching operation were well equipped for doing a lot of business.

By the time Hap lowered himself to the roof of his topper, and then returned to earth, the sun had set. Twilight was beginning to fade into the darkness of night. Hap still had one more building to investigate.

Leaving his truck parked behind the barn, Hap made his way to the old farmhouse and once again searched for a way to enter the locked building. As he circled the old house he noted all the windows were covered from the inside by what appeared to be thick material resembling quilts or blankets. In the rear of the house he found the solution to his need. A large coal shoot angled downward into the basement of the house. And it was just large enough to allow Hap Larson to slide down. The time was eight forty-five p.m.

Part Two: "Missing"

It was nearing seven p.m. when Edna began looking out the living room windows for any sign of her husband's return. By eight o'clock her apprehension began to grow, and by nine she was growing frantic.

Between nine and nine thirty Edna made phone calls to a half dozen members of the Newberry Sportsmen's Club inquiring if any of hem had seen Hap or knew were he might be. One informant remembered as he was leaving Germfask a little before five p.m., he had seen Hap standing by his truck looking at a map which was spread out on the truck's hood.

Edna's seventh phone call was to 911.

Shortly after nine p.m., the Welchek Brothers left their residence and once again headed for the old farm on Highway 77. They were pulling a large covered trailer behind their black Ford pickup. They were positive all the searchers would by this time have vacated the area. But their assumption was incorrect.

Edna's call to "911" aroused the interest of the dispatcher at the sheriff's office when she informed him that her husband, Eric Larson, better known as Hap, was way overdue returning from a day of helping the authorities search for the missing Conservation Officer, Brian Matson. She added that her husband was always punctual, and ALWAYS returned home at the time he said he would. Edna's sketchy details of where Hap had last been seen wasn't much to go on, but the dispatcher put out a call to all available law enforcement officers anywhere in the area of Germfask.

Edna was put on hold for several minutes and then the dispatcher came back on the line. "Mrs. Larson, the nearest officer is a deputy sheriff from Luce County, Officer Douglas Nordahl. He is presently at the scene of a one-car accident on U.S. Highway 2 between Gulliver and Blaney Park. He is waiting for an ambulance to transport an injured victim to a hospital and will respond to your call as soon as the ambulance arrives at the accident scene. Being a holiday weekend, many of our law enforcement personnel are on vacation leave. It's the best I can do."

With trembling voice Edna thanked the dispatcher for his assistance.

Before breaking the phone connection the dispatcher added, "If your husband arrives home, please call and inform us he is safe and sound. Perhaps he just stopped off at some bar for a couple of beers with his friends."

By the tone of the dispatcher's voice, he sounded as though Edna was simply overly worried about a common occurrence. A husband coming home late on a Friday night. Edna's apprehension became mixed with anger! Her Irish temper was rising rapidly!

Five minutes later, Edna was heading towards Germfask in her '57 Nomad. Huddled together in the cargo area were two of her companions. Sadie and Wolf.

Hap's rapid head first descent down the dirty, cob web and spider web infested coal shoot landed him in a heap on a hard cement floor. Had he been able to see himself, he would have seen someone who resembled a coal miner who had been working in coal dust for too long a time. The old coal bin was dark and musty smelling, but strangely the temperature in the basement was very warm and very humid.

Before turning on his flashlight Hap remained motionless, listening for any sounds that might indicate someone was in the building. The house was as quiet as a tomb. As his eyes began adjusting to the near total blackness, he saw a narrow band of very bright light glowing beneath what appeared to be a doorway a few feet in front of where he stood. He snapped on his flashlight and discovered it was a door. Cautiously he moved forward, slowly turned the doorknob, opened it a crack, and squinted as a ray of extremely bright light spewed into his eyes.

It took several more seconds for his pupils to re-adjust to the sudden change in light conditions. Hap blinked several times and stared into the room before him. "Holly Shit, would ya look at this!", was Hap's first exclamation to himself. The entire room before him was filled with heat lamps and pots filled with marijuana plants! Besides being poachers, the persons who were using this property were also dope growers!

Next the inquisitive woodsman climbed the stairs and searched the main floor of the old farmhouse. Most of the rooms were empty except for a few ancient wooden chairs and a table in the kitchen. Satisfied there was nothing more of interest upstairs, Hap returned to the marijuana garden in the basement with the intention of taking one of the illegal plants and adding it to the other items of evidence he had stored in his truck. The time was nearing nine thirty.

As the Welchek Brothers turned off Highway 77 into the driveway leading to the old farm house they switched off their lights and carefully parked their truck and trailer in front of the farm house door. Todd unlocked the entrance, flicked on his flashlight, and with Cory following the pair crossed the hardwood floor to the doorway at the top of the stairs which lead to the basement.

Hap heard the sound of the truck as it pulled up in front of the house. Likewise he heard the upstairs door squeak open and footsteps on the floor above him. He quickly returned to the coal bin, ducked down behind it's retaining wall, and waited, wondering if the person or persons who had arrived were the same ones who murdered Brian Matson. A final thought passed through Hap's mind before he heard the voices. "Damn, I left my .44 in the truck!"

"Cory, let's get this over with as quickly as possible. I think all these pot plants will fit in the trailer. We'll pack 'um together as close as possible so they don't tip over. This stuff represents a lot of dough fer us."

"Ya, we'd git a lot more dough if that damned Senator didn't take such a big cut of the profits. We do all the work and take all the risks and he takes most of the cash." Cory was making a point.

"But you forget brother dear; it's that damned Senator who makes all the connections so we got someplace to send all the meat and the weed. We'd be shit outta luck without his help. I mean,.........who the hell are we? We ain't got no ideas of how to distribute and sell venison and pot." Todd was making a point.

For the next half-hour the Welchek Brothers hauled load after load of their illegal plants up the stairs and carefully stored them in their covered trailer. Hap simply sat crouched down in the next room, listening to their muffled conversations and hoping his hiding place in the coal bin would continue to conceal his presence. His major discomfort was the nauseating smell of coal dust.

By ten o'clock Edna was nearing the intersection of H-44 and MI. 77, where the tiny community of Germfask was located. She had no plan of action, but just simply felt she needed to be looking for her missing husband. The sheriff's dispatcher had pissed her off. The only decision she had made was to drive to Germfask, turn north on 77 and drive to Seney. Maybe she would see Hap's truck parked along the road somewhere. It was slim chance, but Edna reasoned, it was a chance. Fear for the safety of her husband was beginning to consume her. Damn, she loved that man!

Deputy Doug Nordahl sat in his police cruiser and finished writing up a brief report at the scene of the accident, which he had investigated. The ambulance crew, being a volunteer organization, had taken longer than normal to assemble and respond to the site of the accident, due to the upcoming holiday weekend.

It was nearing ten o'clock when he swung his squad car north on Highway 77, intending to drive to Seney and back, looking for a dark green Dodge Ram with a matching topper, license number LU-7747. The dispatcher indicated it would probably be a wild goose chase, as he suspected the caller, an Edna Larson, was probably simply overly concerned because her husband had not returned home "on time". Doug smiled to himself as he engaged the cruise control and recalled numerous similar calls from wife's who sent officers searching for a spouse who was probably sitting at a bar someplace or playing around with another woman.

"Oh well," thought the deputy, "I've got another four hours on my shift. Might as well take a leisurely joy ride."

Cory and Todd finished loading their contraband and returned to the basement of the old house to turn off the lights and heat lamps before taking their cargo to their residence for safe keeping. Cory was about to switch off the lights when a strange sound emanated from the next room where the old coal bin was located. It sounded like a muffled sneeze. It was a muffled sneeze. The coal dust had worked it's evil.

"What the hell was that?", Both brothers uttered the same question almost in unison. "Sounded like a sneeze! Some son of a bitch is back there!", suggested Cory.

Todd extracted a pistol from his belt and Cory readied his flashlight as he jerked open the door separating the pot room from the coal bin. The flashlights beam cut through the dust and gloom to rest upon a bearded man, encrusted with soot. Spider and cobwebs were draped over his cap, and in his crouched position Hap resembled some yet to be discovered nighttime creature.

Momentarily, the Welchek Brothers gasped, and took a step backwards, not really believing what the beam of the flashlight had revealed. Hap shielded his eyes from the bright light and stood up. But as he did so, he quickly slipped his wallet out of his rear pocket, and flipped it into the darkened corner of the coal bin. His mind was racing, asking a question, "How the hell am I gonna git outta this pickle?"

Part Three: "Captured"

Cory stepped forward and grabbed Hap by one arm, then jerked him through the doorway into the brightly-lit room that had recently housed the crop of marijuana. Hap briefly considered resisting, but being outnumbered and looking down the barrel of Todd's revolver, he opted to take a different course of action.

"WHO THE HELL ARE YOU, AND WHAT IN THE HELL ARE YOU DOING ON OUR PROPERTY?", asked Cory, in a tone that quivered with rage.

Hap blinked several times as he sought to organize his line of defense. "I,...I,...I'm a homeless bum. I was hitchhiking on the road out there, didn't have any luck hitchin' a ride,......saw this place,......she looked abandoned,...so I figgered I'd sleep here out of the night's chill. I tried yer barn first,......but she was locked." Hap tried to look dumb and innocent. His physical appearance had already convinced the Welchek Brothers that he quite possibly could be a bum!

The brothers looked at each other as if to silently ask, "Do you believe his story?" Todd took over the questioning. "How'd the hell did you git in here? This place was locked up tight?"

Hap took on the look of a kid who had just been caught with his hand in a cookie jar. Lowering his eyes and shuffling his feet, he answered, "I,…I,…slid down the coal shoot."

"Well that would explain why ya look like some black faced vaudeville comic from the '20's. But ya saw what was in this room,……didn't ya?" Todd's question was the brother's main concern, and Hap continued to play dumb.

"Yea, right nice crop of tomatas you had growin' in them pots. Ya should be able to sell them buggers after they blossom and start producin'." For a few seconds Hap thought the two dope growers had bought his story.

Again Cory and Todd looked at each other, silently asking, "Do you believe this guy?" Todd was the first to respond.

"BULLSHIT! I don't buy your BULLSHIT! You ain't that stupid, old man! If you are who you say you are, just some old homeless bum,……well then you've come across pot before. And by yer looks, ya probably smoked a few joints yerself!"

Cory agreed. He moved around behind Hap, padded him down looking for a weapon or a billfold, found neither, but did remove a handful of coins and a jack knife from Hap's pants pockets. Then he poked the barrel of his revolver in Hap's ear and continued with, "Ya ain't even carrying a billfold. No I.D. either. NOW WHO THE HELL ARE YOU MISTER?"

Hap went into a submissive mode. "Please,…please, don't shoot me! I'm jist a wandering old homeless bum. I ain't never bothered nobody. Ya,……I knowed the stuff was pot. Planned ta take some with me when I went on my way in the mornin'. I wouldn't a took much. Jist a little ta give me a buzz. If ya let me go,…I promise I won't come back,…nor tell anybody. Honest!" Hap even put a little fear in his eyes, although inside he was fuming with anger.

It was Todd's turn again. "So what's yer name old timer, and where ya from?

During the few minutes that had elapsed since his capture, Hap continued formulating a plan. He knew sooner or later the two bozo's questioning him would come around to asking the questions which the younger brother had just asked. "My name is Carl Winters. I was born in Iron River." Hap figured the less information he volunteered, the better off he would be.

Cory took over. "So how come yer homeless,……wanderin' around the countryside like ya claim. Under all that soot and coal dust ya look pretty dang healthy fer bein' a bum. I think somethin's fishy about this character, Todd."

Todd kept staring at Hap, searching his facial expression for any sign of nervousness that might suggest the stranger in their basement was lying. To Todd, their prisoner looked scared. "Ya, I don't know what to make of this guy. His clothes look a little too good, other than the filthy coal dist on 'um, fer what a bum would be wearin'. I think we better take him along with us and keep him locked up until we get a chance to check up on his story. It's awful funny he ain't got a wallet or some kind of I.D. on him someplace. Christ sakes, he's only had a few cents and a little jack knife on 'um."

Cory had a different suggestion. "Maybe we should put him where we put that other guy who was snoopin' around our private property. I can't stand snoopy trespassers."

Every fiber in Hap's body froze at hearing Cory's statement. Hap was sure Cory was referring to Brian Matson. The patch of dried blood mixed with the pine needles near the remains of the poached deer hurtled into Hap's mind. Now he was sure he had been correct in has analysis of what had taken place in the pine thicket! And the murderers were the ones presently holding him captive!

Todd raised his voice slightly in responding to his brother's suggestion. "NO, that won't be necessary. I don't think this guy who claims he's just a bum poses any danger to us. At least that's what I think at the moment. We're gonna take him with us to our place and lock him up in you know where. Then we'll do a little checkin' around and see if anybody else knows this guy. After that we can make up our minds what to do with him."

Hap emotionally relaxed a bit. At least he had bought some additional time. Time to think, Time to figure a way out of, as Hap had put it, "this pickle I've got myself into".

Part Four: "Imprisoned"

At gunpoint, Hap was forced into the front seat of the Welchek Brother's truck, where they placed a paper shopping bag over his head. Cory pushed the revolver into Hap's ribs and told him to sit still, shut up, and don't make any sudden moves. Hap said a silent thank you that the two kidnappers hadn't bothered to check the area around the house and barn, or Hap's truck would have been discovered and his cover story would have been destroyed. At the moment that fact was a gigantic plus.

The truck with the trailer full of pot plants eased towards the highway with it's lights still off. Nearing the end of the driveway Todd noted the glow of headlights approaching from the south. He decided to delay tuning unto the paved road, which would have required him to turn on the truck's lights. A lingering fear of the ongoing search for Officer Matson still played deeply on his mind. The oncoming vehicle just might be the authorities or one of those damn game wardens. Todd expected the darkness would shield their presence. It was not to be.

Edna had entered Highway 77 at Germfask a few minutes before Todd and Cory had forced her husband into their truck. Her slow speed north towards Seney had been planned in order for her to scan both sides of the highway for any sign of her missing husband or his truck. About two miles north of Germfask a glimmer of reflected light from reflectors on the side of a truck caught her eye. She slowed even more, hoping against the odds that it might be the truck she sought.

As the Nomad glided past the driveway to the old farm Edna saw the truck was not Hap's. But, faintly, she did see what looked like three people in the front seat. And the person in the middle looked like they had something over their face! "Odd", thought Edna as she continued north.

After the vintage Chevy had passed, Cory remarked, "Boy that car was sure an antique. Probably some old lady coming back from bingo." Todd laughed, turned on the headlights and turned the truck south on Highway 77.

Twenty minutes later Hap was locked inside an old chicken coop,…chained to an iron post.

Chapter Four: "Win Some,...Loose Some"

Part One: "Lucky Break"

Edna continued north at a modest pace, still scanning the roadsides for any sign of her missing husband, or his truck. A glance at her watch indicated the time to be five minutes after ten. However, her mind kept replaying the scene of three individuals sitting in the front seat of a black Ford pickup truck. A truck parked just off the highway, on what looked to be a driveway or unimproved secondary road, with its lights off! But what really puzzled and bothered her most was the image of the person seated between the other two occupants in the truck. The one who appeared to have their face covered.

An inner voice began telling her to return to the location where she had seen the black Ford, and look around. But for what? But then Edna recalled one of her husband's basic rules of survival. "Always believe in your first hunch. Most of the time it'll steer ya in the right direction. Whatever yer gut tells ya is instinct, an' instinct don't tell no lies!" Edna looked in the rear view mirror, noted the road behind her was vacant, made a u-turn and headed south.

Deputy Nordahl touched his brake peddle to cancel the cruise control and slowed his squad car to the legal speed limit as he entered the village limits of Germfask. As he passed the intersection of Highway 77 and H-44 he met a black Ford pickup truck pulling a large covered trailer. It had its left turn signal blinking; indicating the driver was going to turn east on H-44. As the two vehicles passed each other, the officer instinctively looked in his rear view mirror and noted the trailer's taillights were not working. He touched his brake and considered following the vehicle to pull it over and inform the driver of the violation. But he vetoed the impulse and continued north towards Seney.

Edna reached the location where she had earlier viewed the suspicious black Ford pickup truck and it's three occupants. She slowed nearly to a stop, and then swung her vehicle left into the dirt road. Almost at once her headlights outlined an old farmhouse. She rolled her window down for a better view, but saw nothing out of the ordinary. Continuing down the well-used two-rut dirt road she spotted the outline of another building. As she got closer she could see it was a barn, and there was a vehicle parked in back. Swinging her car to the right, the headlights illuminated a sight that made her heart leap to her throat. It was her husband's truck!

Doug Nordahl's mind was wandering as he continued his joy ride north towards Seney. His thoughts were of the upcoming holiday weekend. He and his girlfriend were planning to head north to Muskallunge Lake where they had reserved a rustic cabin, and just spend the weekend relaxing and doing a little fishing. He had slightly more than three more hours left on his shift and was anxious to finish it, file his reports, and get in at least a few hours sleep before beginning his mini-vacation.

As he was passing the location of an old abandoned farm, he detected a glow of headlights shining behind a building of some sort. His first thoughts were someone was shining deer. After all, recent events had caused every officer to be on the lookout for just that sort of illegal activity. He swung his squad car around in a squealing turn, flipped on his overhead flashers, and thundered down the dusty driveway.

Hap's kidnappers had treated him fairly well, at least up to this point. If you could call being chained to an iron post in a stinking old chicken coop being treated well. Todd provided some straw for him to lie down on and gave him a threadbare wool blanket to cover up with. Hap also received a canteen of water, a sandwich, which Hap was sure was made with fried venison, and an empty milk jug to use as a toilet. Cory checked the chain which secured Hap to the iron post, grinned evilly, and then the two brothers turned out the light and shut the door, leaving Hap all alone in his chicken coop jail cell.

Through the cracks in the wall of his prison he could see stars, and streaks of color from the Northern Lights. His thoughts drifted back and forth between what Edna must be thinking and what eventual fate awaited him. Tonight was the first time he and Edna had not been together since she came to live with him in his old trapper's cabin in Quebec, after she had put her boarding house up for sale. That had been almost a year ago. God, he loved that woman!

Part Two: "The Chicken Coop!"

Deputy Nordahl's first impression of what his spotlight and headlights revealed could best be described as "mixed emotions". A vintage '57 Chevy Nomad was parked with its lights on, which were illuminating a fairly recent green Dodge Ram pickup. The passenger side door of the truck was open and a red haired woman was apparently vandalizing the vehicle or searching for something. Two dogs, a black Lab and a monstrous breed of unknown origin were racing around the barn with their noses to the ground as though they were trailing something.

As the squad car came to a halt in a cloud of dust, the woman turned and began running towards it, shouting, "Thank God you've found us!" Deputy Nordahl's shift was about to be extended.

After making sure their captive was securely restrained for the night, Cory and Todd unloaded their trailer full of pot plants and stored them in a garage. When the chore was completed they walked to their house and started enjoying one of their favorite pastimes. Getting drunk. While finishing a bottle of whiskey, washed down with numerous cans of beer, the two began enjoying one of their other favorite pastimes. Getting into a fight. With each other.

It started out as a discussion about what to do with the bum in the chicken coop. The discussion degenerated into a quarrel. The quarrel intensified into a shouting match. And then Cory threw the first punch.

After the drunken brawl finally ended in a draw, Cory sprawled out on a couch and fell asleep in a drunken stupor. Todd, still angry about Cory's insistence that their prisoner should be killed to keep him quiet, left the house, got in the truck, and drove to "The Howling Beagle". And even though the hour was nearing eleven o'clock, the Friday night crowd was having a rip-roaring time.

It took Edna nearly ten minutes to explain to Officer Nordahl why she was parked by an old barn at night, searching another person's truck, allowing two dogs to run wild, and was so happy to see a police officer. Next she displayed the mystery items she had found in Hap's truck prior to Officer Nordahl's arrival. First there was a plastic bag containing ten empty beer cans. Edna explained to the officer that her husband rarely ever drank canned beer, but preferred tap beer. And even then, he never consumed more than a glass or two.

A second mystery centered on the items contained in the fingers of Hap's brown cotton work gloves. Four empty .223 cartridges in one glove and a half dozen cigarette butts in the other. Edna informed the officer her husband didn't own a .223 nor did he smoke cigarettes. A pipe, yes, but cigarettes, never. And why would he, or someone, put such objects in the fingers of gloves? Officer Nordahl scratched his head and shrugged.

However, Edna decided to skip telling the deputy about Hap's .44, which she had found under the driver's side of the seat. This she had tucked into the waistband of her slacks and covered the exposed handle by buttoning up her windbreaker. At the time, she had no idea what she was going to do with a gigantic Ruger Super Blackhawk revolver, but she felt better knowing it was in her possession. After all, Hap had taught her how to use it.

For the next ten minutes Edna and Doug followed the two dogs as they sniffed all around the barn, then did the same all around the old house. Sadie and Wolf finally stopped and sniffed the door covering a coal shoot. Edna told Officer Nordahl she was certain they had followed the scent of their master, her missing husband. It appeared to Edna that Hap's trail ended at the coal shoot. Both she and Officer Nordahl were mystified as to why anyone would want to enter an old abandoned farm house by sliding down a coal shoot.

The dogs also spent an unusual amount of time sniffing the area in front of the house, leading Edna to believe Hap had recently been there. It was at this moment the pieces of the puzzle fell into place in her mind! Edna quickly related what she had witnessed when she passed the driveway to the old farm earlier in the evening.

"When I drove past here earlier, I saw a black Ford pickup truck parked in the driveway next to the highway with its lights off. There were three persons in the front seat. The individual in the middle appeared to have their face covered with some object. Oh my God,……I bet that person was my husband! Those other two people were taking him somewhere! But why?" Edna looked into Officer Nordahl's face, searching for an answer she knew she would not get. A knot of fear and uncertainty began forming in her stomach.

At the mention of a black Ford pickup truck, Officer Nordahl's eyebrows lifted. "Mrs. Larson, tell me again about that black Ford pickup truck you saw parked in the driveway next to the highway. Was it by any chance pulling a large covered trailer?"

Edna replied in the affirmative.

"Shit", exclaimed the officer, "I think I let the persons we are looking for slip right through my fingers!"

After convincing Edna to return home and allow the authorities to track down her missing husband, and attempt to find the people who might be responsible for his sudden disappearance, Officer Nordahl called the sheriff's office. He explained the situation in which he had become involved, then pinpointed the area where he would begin searching for a black Ford pickup, asked for assistance as soon as possible, and ended his report by saying he'd keep in touch with the dispatcher at regular intervals.

Before returning home, Edna removed the keys from the ignition of Hap's truck, and locked the doors. It was nearing midnight when she entered her empty house. She lay down on the couch and tried to convince herself that Hap was going to be found, and that he'd be unharmed. But doubt and a deep feeling of foreboding had crept into her soul, dampening her earlier optimism. A short period of fitful sleep followed, but by one a.m. she and her two loyal companions were once again heading for,.........Edna wasn't sure where.

Hap's spirits lifted a tad when he heard his captor's truck leave the premises. Expecting that both of his jailors had departed,......to who knows where, he could begin trying to formulate some sort of plan which might allow his escape from his makeshift jail. The possibilities looked bleak, at least at the moment. The chain that held him was tightly wrapped around his waist, and securely fastened with a padlock. Hap had already tried unsuccessfully to slip the chain over his hips, and even though he was slight of build, there was no chance of success.

On hands and knees he explored the darkened prison searching for anything that might be used as a weapon, should the opportunity present itself when his captives returned. The chain that secured him only had enough slack to allow movement but a few feet from the iron post to which it was fastened. The four-inch diameter post was set in concrete and supported the row of boxes the chickens once used when nesting. It was a very substantial restraining device!

Besides finding a considerable amount of dried chicken scat and an old three-pound coffee can, Hap's search was uneventful. However, he did avoid being cut by the jagged lip on the coffee can, so he was thankful for that.

Returning to the iron post, he leaned back against it and began to think, and ever so slowly his inventive mind began to formulate a plan.

Part Three: "The Great Escape"

Deputy Douglas Nordahl returned to Germfask where his earlier indecision had allowed two unknown individuals, and possibly the missing husband of one Edna Larson, to slip through his fingers. He swung his squad car east on H-44 and slowly began to search for a black Ford pickup pulling a large covered trailer. Although the area was sparsely settled, a few homes were scattered along the route. Using his squad's spotlight, the officer scanned every driveway for the vehicle he was seeking. It was a long shot, but he had to take it.

Reaching the intersection of H-44 and H-33, he turned south towards Curtis and continued his search pattern. As he was passing the east shore of Manistique Lake, the neon lights of The Howling Beagle Bar and Grille loomed ahead. The parking lot contained over a dozen vehicles, all pickup trucks. The deputy slowed his cruiser and carefully looked at each truck. There were two Toyotas, four Chevy's, three Dodges and four Fords, but only one was black!

Officer Nordahl continued past the bar, shut off his headlights, and parked his cruiser well out of the dimly lit parking area. Seeing no one outside the bar, he walked to the black Ford, and with his small penlight examined the ball on the truck's trailer hitch. The ball was shinny and free of rust, which suggested it had recently been used to pull a trailer. Next he recorded the vehicle's license number and returned to his squad.

"Hello Walt. This is Doug. I'm at The Howling Beagle out on H-33. I think I may have found the truck I've been looking for. Run a check on this number."

Inside the bar, the joint was jumping. Nearly two dozen persons were wildly celebrating the coming of a three day weekend. However, on most Friday nights, the same individuals were celebrating upcoming two-day weekends. Sweet smelling cigarette smoke filled the room and Todd Welchek was doing a land office business selling his homemade joints. In fact, he did so well he had enough money to coax April from behind the bar and into her bedroom for, as Todd put it, "a quickie". In less than fifteen minutes April was twenty-five dollars richer, and Todd was sound asleep in April's bed.

It took but a few seconds for the police dispatcher to bring license number LU-9601 up on his computer screen. He whistled softly as he digested the information highlighted on his monitor. "I'd say you found a real dandy, Doug. It's registered to the Welchek Brothers, Cory and Todd."

Officer Nordahl shifted slightly in his seat and responded. "Oh Shit! Not those two assholes again!"

Walt chuckled. "I'm glad it's you out there and me in here. Do you need an update on the darling Welchek Brothers?"

"Not really, but go ahead anyway. Maybe there's something new I haven't heard about.", grumbled Doug.

"Well, each one has two DWI's. One more and it's bye bye driver's license. They've been hauled to the cooler four times for starting a brawl in two different bars, but three of the times it's been in The Howling Beagle." Another chuckle came from Walt. "Two of the brawls were Cory and Todd fighting each other. Har de har har!"

"Very funny Walt. Keep reading."

"They were arrested two years ago for attempting to deliver a controlled substance, but the case never got to court. Reading between the lines, it looks like somebody with some clout got the charges dropped. Four years ago they were pinched for shinning deer. And last but not least they both did six months in the county lockup for resisting arrest and beating the hell out of a state trooper. Looks like a couple of model citizens to me, Doug."

"Walt, is there anybody close to me that's available for assistance or at least some back up support. What I've got going here is a possible kidnapping,……or maybe worse. I need to put the arm on these two as soon as possible and ask a few questions. I told you about what's going on out here when I called in from that old farmhouse about an hour ago."

"Geeze Doug,…the nearest help I've got is a state trooper just west of St. Ignace. I'll give him a holler and directions to the Beagle. But he won't be there for at least an hour and a half."

"Thanks Walt. Keep the lines open. I'm going to have to go it alone. I can't wait that long. There just might be too much at stake if I delay. I'll keep you posted."

It was nearing one thirty a.m. when Cory awakened from his drunken slumber. His jaw hurt where Todd had smacked him with a frying pan, his nose was swollen from being elbowed in the face, plus he had a rip roaring head ache and a stomach that felt like it was about to turn inside out. He just made it to the door when he heaved up the contents of a six pack and a half-quart of whiskey all over the front porch. He nearly fell down the steps, grabbed the nearest tree and retched with dry heaves for nearly a minute.

As his eyes cleared, he glanced beneath the yard light and noticed the truck was missing from it's parking spot. "God damn that son of a bitchin' brother of mine", snarled Cory under his breath. His next thoughts went unspoken. "He better damn well not have let that noisy bum go lose. Wouldn't put it past him though. Todd's got no backbone. I'll hafta take care of that snoopin' trespasser jist like I did that damn game warden!"

Cory stumbled around to the back of the garage to where the old chicken coop was located. He kicked open the door, pulled his revolver from his coat pocket, and flipped on the light switch. The feeble glow of the dirt encrusted sixty-watt light bulb dimly outlined the shape of their captive, who appeared to be curled up under his thin blanket and sound asleep. Cory took two long strides to where Hap was stretched out on the straw and gave him a kick in the back.

"Wake up ya snoopy son of a bitch. You and me is goin' fer a little walk in the woods,......and only one of us is comin' back!"

Edna decided she might as well be driving around looking for her missing husband and the black Ford pickup that she was positive had taken him away, rather than pacing the floors of their house waiting for a call from the police that might never come. As she was heading west on Highway 28, planning to return to the area around Germfask, she saw the highway sigh for County Highway H-33. She remembered looking at a road map and noticing H-33 and H-44 were a "shortcut" to Highway 77, the very area she intended to search. She made a left turn onto H-33 and headed south.

Deputy Nordahl reached the door of the Howling Beagle, stopped, and listened to the noise inside. The jukebox blared as Willie Nelson related being "On The Road Again", while what sounded like a drunken woman sang backup. A muffled argument was in progress as to who was the best trout fisherman. Somebody was bragging about how drunk they were going to get during the weekend and everything was mixed with the clunk of pool balls banging together. The officer unhooked the strap on his holster, swallowed hard, and opened the door of The Howling Beagle.

Hap rolled over at being kicked in the back and feigned confusion by rubbing his eyes with one hand. "Huh," he grunted.

Again, grinning evilly, Cory kneeled down and stuck his revolver in Hap's face, while handing him a key. "Take this key and unlock that padlock,...you and me is goin' fer a little walk in the woods. I'll be comin' back, but yer only goin' one way, Mr. Snoop."

As Hap reached for the key with one hand, his other hand quickly materialized from under the blanket holding a coffee can. With a flick of his wrist Hap threw a yellow liquid mixed with dissolved chicken scat into the face and eyes of his jailor. Cory's reaction was instantaneous!

He let out a howl as the horrible smelling and tasting mixture entered his nose, mouth and eyes. The urine stung like fire and Cory clutched at his eyes with both hands as his pistol clattered to the floor of the chicken coop. Hap quickly looped the slack in his restraining chain around the back of Cory's neck and jerked him forward,......head first into the iron post.

There was a sound like a watermelon being dropped on a hardwood floor,...followed by silence. Cory Welchek was in la-la land! Hap located the key to his freedom, unlocked the padlock and wrapped the chain fairly tightly around Cory's neck. He re-locked the padlock; put the key in his pocket, picked up the revolver, then extracted his pocketknife from Cory's pants pocket. Looking at his unconscious captor, Hap whispered, "Thanks fer keepin' my knife for me, scumbag." Then grinning slightly he added, "Turn out the lights, the party's over asshole." Hap then turned out the light, closed the door of the chicken coop, and vanished into the night.

Chapter Five: "Almost, But No Cigar"

Part One: "One Down, One To Go"

As the door clicked shut behind Deputy Nordahl, all eyes in The Howling Beagle turned to see who was so late coming to the Friday night bash. Within seconds the only sound in the bar was Willie Nelson, still "On the Road Again". The atmosphere in the bar was hazy and liberally laced with the sweet smell of pot. Officer Nordahl cleared his throat, tried to look cool, calm and collected, although his stomach was as tight as a drum, and quietly asked, "Are Cory and Todd Welchek in here?"

No one answered at first, but there was noticeable activity as a half dozen individuals hastily got rid of their joints. April finally answered the officer's question. "No, neither of them has been here for several days now."

"Then who is driving their truck?", Doug questioned back.

Again there was an awkward pause. And the deputy was unable to see one of the customer's slip through the back door into April's living quarters.

Again April came to the defense of the Welchek Brothers. "Oh ya, their truck broke down a few days ago. They haven't been back to pick it up and take it somewhere to be fixed." April's cheeks blushed pink between her strands of long, straight blond hair.

"That's damned funny, when I walked past their truck in your parking lot I felt the hood. It's still warm. Sure must take an engine a long time to cool off in these parts. NOW WHERE THE HELL ARE THEY?" Deputy Nordahl was tiring of the lies.

Within a few seconds after Todd was shaken awake and informed a cop was in the bar looking for him, he pulled on his shorts and pants, then quickly fled out the back door of April's living quarters. Veiled by darkness, he began running north along H-33, away from the now quiet party in The Howling Beagle. His mind was racing, trying to clear the cobwebs, which the alcohol had draped over his brain, trying to decide what to do next.

Within a few minutes he reached the intersection of H-33 and H-44. He paused to catch his breath and make a decision as to which way to continue fleeing. And then just ahead, the lights of a vehicle came around a corner in the highway.

Hap shoved Cory Welchek's pistol in his belt and carefully made his way along the narrow dirt driveway. He had no idea where it ended, as his head had been covered by a grocery sack during the drive from the old farm house to what he assumed was the Welchek's residence. The moon was already sinking below the western horizon, and the deep darkness made travel on an unknown surface difficult. After covering nearly a quarter mile, Hap emerged onto a blacktop road. Looking in both directions he noted a faint distant glow of light off to his right. He turned north and headed towards what he hoped would be a friendly residence. Hap needed to find a phone and call the authorities as quickly as possible.

Edna easily noticed the road sign informing her that the intersection she was looking for, H-44, was just ahead. She slowed her Nomad, flipped on the right turn signal, even though no other vehicles were present nor had she seen any since leaving Highway 28. As she turned the wheel to enter H-44, the headlights illuminated a man standing in the middle of the road wildly waving his arms! "My God" thought Edna, "Someone's in trouble or had an accident!" She was correct about being in trouble.

Edna stopped just short of the frantic individual and rolled down her window, expecting the stranger would ask for a ride to somewhere, as his face expressed deep concern and a trace of fear. She was totally unprepared for what happened next!

The stranger in distress jerked open the car door, grabbed Edna by the arm and dragged her from her vehicle. Edna started to protest, but her assailant gave her a hard push that sent her sprawling on the blacktop. Edna screamed, "You dirty bastard!" Todd Welchek was totally unprepared for what was about to happen next!

Deputy Nordahl, hand on the butt of his service pistol, slowly walked through the small, but crowded barroom. He looked at each male customer, but somehow he knew the two individuals he was seeking were not going to be among those present. His act of crashing the party was met by hateful scowls as he made a circuit of the bar. But seeing as Deputy Nordahl was six foot three, and a muscular two hundred and thirty five pounds, the assembled partygoers were content with just the hateful scowls.

Satisfied the objects of his search were not in the barroom, and he was legally unable to search the private residence without a warrant, he retraced his steps to the door and quickly exited The Howling Beagle. Not sure of what to do next, he returned to his squad car and radioed a report to the police dispatcher as to his lack of success in locating either of the Welcheck Brothers. He also asked once again if any additional officers had been located who might come to his aid in continuing to look for the two suspects.

Walt's reply was that no additional help could be located near Doug's present location. The young deputy was still on his own.

Edna's scream brought her two companions in the rear of the station wagon to full alert. After all, they had heard Edna scream once before when Bruno and Bruce had attempted to attack her, mistaking Edna for her husband. Bruno and Bruce had paid a fearsome price. Todd Welchek was about to see history repeat itself!

Just at Todd was attempting to enter Edna's car and flee, one hundred and thirty pounds of pent up fury, armed with tooth and nail, hit Todd like a middle linebacker. Now it was Todd's turn to be slammed sprawling on the blacktop!

Wolf pounced on top of the younger Welchek Brother, pinning him on his back, and began to rearrange Todd's face and neck. As the terrified carjacker attempted to fend off the beast that had surprised him, Sadie leaped from the car through the open door and clamped onto Todd's thigh, removing pieces of his pants, skin and flesh.

Edna quickly regained her feet, rushed to her car and removed an object from beneath the driver's side front seat. She gripped the .44 in both hands and began yelling at Wolf and Sadie to abort the savage attack. Edna was not the only person yelling!

Sadie responded quickly, but Wolf, being part what his name implied, was having too much fun. Edna was finally forced to give her savior a kick in the posterior, which caused Wolf to finally back off.

Todd, clutching his torn and bleeding face, rolled over, got to one knee and was attempting to regain his feet, when Edna's Irish temper reached the boiling point. Still using both hands, she stood over her attacker, raised Hap's massive .44 high above her head, and brought it down with full force on Todd's skull. There was a dull "thud" sound, as if a coconut fell from a tree. For the second time in one night, a second Welchek Brother was in la-la land.

Part Two: "Joining Forces"

For several seconds Edna stood over her unconscious attacker. Her rapid breathing began to return to normal and her Irish temper began to subside somewhat. She thought about what her next move should be for nearly a minute, then ordered Sadie and Wolf back into her car and got in herself. Not sure of what to do next, or which way she should go seeking assistance, Edna saw a small arrow sign nailed to a tree. It was pointing south, down H-33, and proclaimed, "The Howling Beagle Bar and Grille, 1 mile". Edna sped south, leaving the still form of Todd Welchek lying motionless in the center of the intersection.

Deputy Nordahl sat in his squad car and pondered his next move. He knew where the Welcheks lived, and it was only a short distance from where he was now located. But he wasn't sure if he should enter their private domain without backup. After all, the two did have a nasty history of not being too receptive of visits from the police. But still, it was highly probable that Mrs. Larson had been correct in her assumption that Cory and Todd were the ones responsible for her husband's disappearance. However, he had no earthly clue as to why the Welchek's might have kidnapped Edna's husband. But he knew he must investigate, due to the possibility that Mrs. Larson was correct. She certainly seemed to be a level headed, intelligent individual.

What bothered the deputy most of all was the obvious fact that the Welcheck Brothers had recently been to The Howling Beagle. If they had kidnapped someone it was doubtful they would have brought their captive along to the Friday night bash. What if Mr. Larson had already been............He didn't want to think of that possibility. A sudden feeling of urgency swept through his body. He was going to the Welchek residence and see what he could find.

Just as the officer was about to pull out onto H-33, a car came screeching to a halt behind him. Looking in his rear view mirror, Deputy Nordahl saw the familiar grill and hood ornaments of a '57 Chevy.

The glow of lights became brighter and brighter as Hap neared the final bend in the highway that would allow him to see the dwelling from which the light emanated. Much to his surprise he recognized where he was. "I'll be damned", he muttered to himself; "I'm over on H-33 by Manistique Lake."

Looking at his watch he noted the legal closing time was near, and there were still over a dozen vehicles parked at The Howling Beagle. "Must be some party.", he told himself. As he neared the parking lot, Hap's eyes saw four things that made his heart sing with joy. One was a police cruiser,...two was a '57 Chevy Nomad Wagon, and three and four were a deputy sheriff and Edna! He began jogging the final fifty yards.

Cory Welcheck slowly began to regain consciousness a few minutes after Hap rendered him unconscious. His head throbbed and his stomach felt like it was on fire. He rolled over and wiped a gob of dried chicken scat from his face, spit out a few additional small chunks, and then suddenly remembered what had happened. Sitting up and leaning against the iron post, he then felt something cold pressing against his neck. He quickly rubbed the area with his fingers and discovered a chain was securely fastened around his neck. Next he rubbed the top of his throbbing head to discover a lump the size of a chicken egg. His fury returned, but in his present situation there was no one on which to vent his anger.

Deputy Nordahl whirred around at the sound of crunching gravel. Instinctively, he put his hand on the butt of his pistol, but did not draw the weapon. With his other hand the officer withdrew a flashlight from his duty belt and flipped it on, aiming it's beam at the sound of oncoming footsteps. What his light revealed did little to relieve his apprehension.

A man was jogging towards he and Mrs. Larson. The stranger's face was covered with some sort of black substance. His clothing was filthy, and strands of straw clung to his shirt, pants and cap. Doug and Edna had similar first impressions. Whoever this person was, he certainly had to be the dirtiest bum in Michigan! As he drew nearer, the jogger waved and sent out a greeting. "Boy am I glad to see you two!"

Edna's eyes opened wide as she recognized the voice that reached her ears. "Oh my God,...IT'S MY MISSING HUSBAND!" And despite Hap's filthy condition, Edna rushed to meet him and gave him a hug,......and a kiss on his coal dust encrusted lips.

"Hap darling,...I was so afraid something dreadful had happened to you. When you didn't come home in time for supper,...and,......and, then two more hours passed, I took Sadie and Wolf and went looking for you. I just happened to be passing by that old farm on Highway 77 and saw what I later knew had to be you sitting between two other persons with your face covered. Hap, this is Deputy Sheriff Douglas Nordahl. He's been helping me search for you, and the men who took you, for the past several hours." Edna was excited and relieved.

Edna rambled on. "After I passed that truck you were in,......I didn't suspect it was you until much later,......well, I got this feeling inside to turn around and go back where I saw that truck." Edna paused to catch her breath and then resumed her high-speed story. "What I thought was weird, was the fact the truck was parked in the driveway,......right at the edge of the road you understand,.........with it's headlights off. That's how I was able to see what looked like three people sitting in the front seat. I mean,......my lights allowed me to see inside the truck. Well, when I got there and drove down the driveway I found your truck behind the barn,.........and,......and, that's when all the pieces of the puzzle started falling into place." Edna gave Hap another hug and another kiss on his cheek and continued.

"About then this wonderful officer happened to find me, and,......and, we looked all around to try and find you,......and,......and, Sadie and Wolf seemed to be following a trail of your scent all around the barn and then they sniffed all around the old house. They finally stopped at the door of a coal..........." Edna's voice trailed off as she suddenly realized what all the black material was on her husband's face and clothing. "You slid down the coal shoot to get into that old farmhouse,......didn't you?"

Hap grinned. "Yer gonna make a detective yet sweetheart. Now let ME tell YOU about all the missing parts of the story."

For the next ten minutes Deputy Nordahl listened to two unbelievable tales. First came a short version of how Hap had gotten into this mixed up mess. He explained how he found the beer cans, empty .223 cartridges, and the cigarette butts in the field where Warden Matson was last heard from. Next, he filled his listeners in on his abduction, imprisonment and escape, plus a brief summary of what he had discovered in the old barn, the farmhouse and the wooded area beyond.

Next Edna gave her account of the brief encounter with a would be carjacker. When Edna described the physical appearance of the man who had attempted to steal her car, Doug was sure it had been Todd Welchek. There was little doubt the one whom Hap had left chained to an iron post was Cory.

By the time the Larson' completed their unbelievable tales, Officer Nordahl had decided on a course of action. "Let's take a run north to the intersection of this highway and H-44 and see if Todd Welchek is still lying in the road. I'll lead and you two can follow my squad. We could all go together, but those two dogs would make a slight overload. Besides, if Todd is still there, he'll be handcuffed and riding in my back seat."

Todd Welchek slowly returned to the world of the living a few minutes after Edna bashed his head with a two-pound pistol. Upon standing, he staggered uncontrollably for several seconds, partly due to the amount of alcohol he had consumed and partly because of the lump on his head. As his brain cleared sufficiently to think somewhat rationally, he decided that to continue following a highway might not be a good idea. Within seconds the forest had veiled him in darkness.

The longer Cory remained a prisoner in his own chicken coop, the angrier he became. The fact that his own brother had left for who knows where, without telling him where he was going or taking him along, fueled his anger.
Then of course was the botched attempt to permanently silence the wandering bum that had discovered their illegal pot factory and possibly their illegal poaching activity. He silently made a vow that somehow, somewhere, sometime, that bum was going to pay dearly for what Cory Welchek was presently enduring.

As the time of his imprisonment increased, Cory rehearsed what he was going to tell his brother when he returned. He planned a speech, which basically consisted of every foul swear word known to man. And a number of his favorite four-lettered curse words were to be included several times. Cory was steamed!

After finding that Todd Welchek was no longer laying at the intersection where Edna had foiled the attempted carjacking, Deputy Nordahl radioed the police dispatcher with an update. Again Walt was the bearer of more bad news. The State Trooper who had been summoned to assist Doug had been forced to stop and take charge of another accident on U.S. 2. A motor home had struck a deer, causing the vehicle to leave the road and topple over into a swampy area. Deer/vehicle collisions were the most common highway accident in the Upper Peninsula. No one had been seriously injured, but the trooper had to stay at the scene and wait for a wrecker to remove the motor home from the swamp. And who could tell how long that might take.

From the vacant intersection the threesome headed for the Welchek property to see if Cory was still chained to an iron post in the old chicken coop. It was nearing three a.m. when the squad car and Edna's Nomad parked in front of the Welchek's house.

At the sound of a vehicle returning to the Welcheck's home, Cory assumed his brother had finally returned. At the sound of a car door closing he began his verbal attack. Hap jerked his thumb in the direction of the vile shouting and grinned. "Yep, he's still chained up".

Cory was well into his pre-planned verbal attack on his brother when Deputy Nordahl pushed the chicken coop door open and directed his flashlight beam on the prisoner inside. Hap flipped on the electric light. Cory's oration died like a fire that had been doused with a bucket of cold water. Upon seeing an officer of the law, plus the dirty bum who had outsmarted him, and an attractive red haired lady, Cory's lips continued to move, but no sound emanated from his mouth. I guess it could be said that Cory Welchek had received an unexpected surprise.

Deputy Nordahl took control of the situation. He informed the chained man he was under arrest for the kidnapping and illegal imprisonment of one Eric Sever Larson. The officer then read him his rights, and commanded his prisoner to extend both hands so he could be handcuffed. Cory did not resist, but sat in stunned silence with his mouth hanging open.

Hap extracted a key from his pocket and unlocked the padlock that had kept Cory securely attached to chain around his neck. It was at this point Cory's voice returned and he began verbally assaulting Hap. Doug Nordahl grabbed the front of Cory's shirt and jerked him to his feet. Staring down at the smaller man, the officer uttered one short sentence. "Shut your foul mouth or I'll shut it for you!" Cory shut up.

Edna, who had been standing just outside the door of the chicken coop couldn't resist getting her two cents worth in. "My my! Such a dirty mouth you have! What you need Mr. Welchek is a good old-fashioned mouth washing with hot water and soap!" Cory glared at Edna but kept his mouth shut and his thoughts to himself.

The deputy placed his prisoner in the rear seat of his police cruiser and then conversed with his two helpers.
"Well Mr. & Mrs. Larson,..."

Hap interrupted. "Jist call us Hap and Edna."

"O.K.,...Hap,...Edna. I can't thank you both enough for all the help you have contributed in bringing at least one of the Welchek Brothers to justice. I'm sure the other one will be rounded up soon. Before I leave here I'll call the dispatcher and bring him up to date on what we've accomplished so far. Then he'll get the ball rolling to start a major investigation into all the seemingly illegal activity you seem to have uncovered."

Hap interjected his thoughts. "Ya better git a couple of search warrants and check out that farm and this here Welcheck place. And don't forget to have someone look over those beer cans and empty .223's fer fingerprints.

. I got an awful feelin' in my gut that these two Welchek's is behind the disappearance of Warden Watson."

"Yes, I've got all that on my mind's list of things that need to be done, and done quickly. But thanks for reminding me, Hap. The way you operate, I think you'd make a hell of a good cop.", replied Doug sincerely.

"Thanks! And if there's anything else that Edna and me kin do ta help, jist let us know. We've got a special interest in the missing warden, Brian Matson. He's my nephew, twice removed.", added Hap.

"Oh, I didn't know that. No wonder you have become so involved. It's a high probability that we'll be getting in touch with both of you,...and soon. I know the sheriff, as well as the wildlife officers, will probably want to talk to you about your discoveries."

"Our phone number is in the directory. Give us a call when yer ready."

"Why don't you two head on home and get some sleep. I know I'm tried and you Mr. Larson,...ah,...Hap, must be exhausted. You too Edna."

"Ya, I'm a mite dirty too. I jist hope all this dirt don't plug up the drain in our shower." Hap chuckled at his own remark. We're both ready to catch some shuteye, ain't we Edna?" Edna smiled and nodded in agreement. "But first we're gonna drive back ta the old farm so I kin git my truck. Then we're goin' straight home. Ain't we sweetheart?" Edna was already in the car motioning Hap to join her.

Deputy Nordahl left the Welchek property, turned right on H-33 and drove to The Howling Beagle, where he removed the keys from Cory and Todd's truck. One additional vehicle was parked in back, nearly out of sight. It was a new blue Ford Explorer. Unknown to the officer, April Ravovich was earning a little overtime money.

The squad car, with Cory safely behind the security screen in the rear seat, headed for the county jail in Newberry. From time to time Deputy Nordahl glanced in his rear view mirror to make sure Cory was behaving himself. As his gaze returned to the road ahead, suddenly a large deer bust from the shoulder of the road and dashed directly in the path of the oncoming cruiser.

The officer reacted to instinct, jerked the steering wheel to the left and careened off the road. The vehicle struck a large rock, became airborne, and rolled over several times down a steep embankment, finally coming to rest by smashing into a large red oak tree.

The deputy's head struck the roof of the car, rendering him unconscious. The impact sprung both rear doors open, and Cory Welchek was hurled out of the vehicle into a bushy spruce tree, which cushioned his fall. Upon untangling himself from the tree's branches, Cory approached the upside down squad car. The officer was hanging motionless upside down also, supported by his seat belts. Cory chuckled at his good fortune.

He kneeled down, located the officer's flashlight, and with the aid of its beam, retrieved the keys to the handcuffs and the deputy's pistol. In less than a minute Cory Welchek disappeared into the forest, just as the eastern sky was beginning to blush dawn's pink.

Chapter Six: "The Plot Thickens"

Part One: "Unraveling The Clues"

Saturday morning dawned bright and clear, a perfect beginning to the Memorial Day Weekend. Tom and Beverly Matson arranged for a rental car from their motel room in Sault Ste. Marie, which was delivered at nine thirty a.m. The couple arrived in Manistique a little over two hours later and checked in at The Bayview Motel, where they had reserved a room for a week. From there they drove to the senior's assisted living complex to meet with Tom's parents, Dewey and Betty, to learn if any progress had been made in locating their missing son, Brian Matson. The update was very upsetting.

Deputy Douglas Nordahl regained consciousness just as dawn had broken on a lovely Saturday morning. He was able to free himself from the seat belts that had prevented a more serious injury than a lump on his head. He immediately radioed the dispatcher's office to report his accident, and the escape of Cory Welchek. Now both of the Welchek Brothers were at large and hiding,......who knows where.

Walt, the dispatcher, awakened Sheriff Bill Ostermeir, who in turn gave on order to call all off duty officers and inform them to report to his office ASAP!

Next, Chief Warden Paul Vandenburg was notified, and he likewise gave orders for all available Conservation Officers, including any Federal Fish and Game Wardens, to report to the nerve center at the Seney Wildlife Refuge.

By mid morning the information and evidence that Hap Larson discovered in the field where Brian Matson made his last phone call prior to disappearing, plus what he found in and around the old farm on Highway 77, was disclosed to those in attendance at the two separate meetings. Search warrants had been secured to search the old farm and the Welchek residence. By eleven a.m. both locations were swarming with law enforcement officials.

Back at the Sheriff's Office, the empty beer cans, the .223 cartridge casings, and the cigarette butts were carefully dusted for fingerprints. There were lots of them. The evidence was then carefully packaged to be shipped to the State Crime Lab in Lansing, Michigan for further analysis and confirmation as to the identity of the individuals who made the fingerprints. The package was addressed to "Chief of Criminal Investigation", Corbet O'Keefe.

The search parties confirmed what Hap claimed to have discovered was accurate. The search also turned up additional hard evidence that needed to be investigated. From the Welchek property, foremost was a scope mounted Ruger Mini-carbine in .223 caliber. Four other firearms were also found in the house and likewise confiscated. In addition, the stash of marijuana plants in the Welchek's garage were confiscated, as well as the remains of seven deer, which were found jammed into a chest type freezer in the brother's basement. An officer was sent to the phone company with orders to impound the Welchek's phone records.

A wrecker was dispatched to The Howling Beagle and the Welchek's truck was impounded and hauled to the Sheriff's Office in Newberry to be gone over with a fine toothed comb.

A complete search of the old farmhouse, the barn and the wooded area beyond simply validated the information Hap Larson had already supplied to the authorities. One item, which would be of interest to Hap Larson, was his wallet, which the officers found in the corner of an old coal bin in the basement of the farmhouse, exactly where he said it would be.

Investigators were also able to find the area of dried blood in the pine needles that covered the forest floor near the discarded deer remains. It would be examined to determine if indeed it was human blood, as Mr. Larson had suspected, or the blood of some other type of animal. The authorities that located the bloodstain were of the opinion it was simply blood from one of the many deer that had been butchered nearby.

The evidence that bothered the investigators most, was the tremendous amount of rotting deer bones, hides, entrails, heads, tallow, meat scrapes, etc. that Hap discovered in the thick wooded area east of the barn. The amount of material strongly suggested a major poaching operation had been uncovered! It was apparent that the Welchek Brothers lacked the ability to deliver and distribute such quantities of venison as the dumping ground suggested was being "harvested". So, the next question was,......who else was involved and how did the distribution system function?

Hap and Edna slept as though drugged, after what had been over twenty-four hours without sleep. It was nearly noon the day following their ordeals before they were once again, as Hap put it, "among the land of the living". Just as the couple was finishing what might be described as "brunch", they received two phone calls. One was from Sheriff Ostermeir. He invited Hap to come to his office in Newberry and pick up his wallet. That was the good news. Next, the sheriff informed Hap of Deputy Nordahl's accident and the escape of Cory Welchek. The second news item caused Hap to frown deeply. The sheriff also suggested Hap should come to his office "at his convenience, but the sooner the better". And Bill Ostermeir ended the conversation by saying, "We need to have a little talk".

The second call was from Hap's cousin, Tom Matson, who with his wife Beverly, were getting ready to leave Manistique on their way to the sheriff's office in Newberry.

Hap and Edna arrived at Sheriff Ostermeir's office a half-hour later. The chief law enforcement officer invited the couple into his office and offered them comfortable chairs in front of his desk.

"Well, Mr. Larson, first of all, here's your wallet. My secretary cleaned the coal dust off of it as best she could. I think she got most of it. Now, could you tell me how your wallet ended up in the corner of a coal bin in a deserted farmhouse?" The sheriff's voice was mixed with curiosity and a bit of mirth.

For the next ten minutes Hap once again gave a first hand account of his activities after all the volunteers and law enforcement officers had ended their day of searching for clues as to the whereabouts of Officer Matson. The sheriff listened intently, stopping Hap several times to ask a specific question. The information Hap related concerning his hunch that the dried blood and the two drag marks in the pine needle covered forest floor, where the remains of all the deer were located, were indeed the marks left by the heels of someone's boots. And Hap made his feelings known that he suspected the heels of Brian Matson's boots made the drag marks,......after he was killed!

"I certainly respect your opinion, Mr. Larson,..."

"Hey sheriff, cut out that Mr. Larson stuff. Jist call me Hap."

"O.K. Hap it is. What I was saying,......I know enough about you to realize that nearly your entire life has been spent in the out of doors. Your very existence and survival have been dependent on your ability to read signs and follow your instincts. The information that was faxed from the headquarters of the Royal Canadian Mounted Police seemed to indicate you must be one of the top guru's of the outdoor world."

Hap squirmed in his seat upon hearing the sheriff's words of praise and admiration. Edna smiled, reached over and took her husband's hand, and replied, "My husband isn't ONE of the top guru's, he IS the top guru!"

Sheriff Ostermeir smiled and remarked, "If you say so Mrs. Larson, I'm not one to question your opinion. But seriously,.........so far there is no REAL evidence Officer Matson is dead,......let alone murdered, as you suggest Mr.........ah, Hap."

Hap slowly stroked his beard and appeared to be deep in thought. Then grinning slightly he answered. "Then I guess I better jist git busy and prove to you folks what I'm positive happened."

The intercom on the sheriff's desk interrupted the conversation. The voice of his secretary crackled with urgency. "Sheriff, I know you told me not to interrupt your meeting with the Larson's, but you have a call from Paul Vandenburg that is quite urgent."

Part Two: "A Break!"

Chief Warden Paul Vandenburg did indeed have some earthshaking information. Sheriff Ostermeir's eyes opened wide as he digested the words that flowed into his ears during the brief phone call.

"Bill, this is Paul. I think we've just got a break in the Brian Matson disappearance. Two high school kids were riding their ATV's out in the boonies between the east and west branches of the Manistique River and found a burned up Dodge pickup truck hidden under a big pile of brush and branches. The boys said there was no sign that anyone had been inside the vehicle when it burned. As we speak, the boys are leading several of my wardens to the truck's location. I suspect you or your deputies might want to swing over this way,...I'm at the nerve center at the Seney Refuge,...and take a look at what's left of the truck. At this point we can't be sure it's Brian's vehicle,......but I've got a hunch it is. If I'm correct, this changes the entire nature of our search and investigation."

"Oh my God!" The sheriff looked at Hap. "Unfortunately, if your hunch is right,...then so is Hap Larson's. I'll grab one of my deputies and be there in a half-hour."

The sheriff quickly filled Hap and Edna on the substance of the phone conversation, bid them a hasty good-bye, grabbed his hat and rapidly departed. Hap and Edna stared at each other for several seconds, and then Edna whispered, "You told them so. Now maybe they'll believe the rest of your theory."

For the Welcheck Brothers, life had definitely taken a turn for the worse! Todd, regaining consciousness after Edna smacked his head with her husband's .44, had stumbled through the darkened forest, not knowing nor caring where he was heading. Tree branches frequently brushed against his already painful face and thigh. Blackberry briars tore at his arms and hands. Several times he stumbled on the uneven floor of the forest or stubbed his toes on exposed tree roots, causing some nasty falls. Todd was definitely not having a good time.

His meanderings eventually led him to the northeast shore of Manistique Lake, which was actually only a few hundred yards from the intersection where two dogs had attempted to kill him, and then some red headed woman driving an antique '57 Chevy Nomad Wagon had clobbered him.

Todd washed the bleeding and torn parts of his anatomy in the lake, and then rested under the overhanging branches of a cedar tree until morning. When daylight dawned several hours later, he spied a cottage nestled on the shore of the bay that lay before him. He cautiously approached the building and found it to be apparently uninhabited. Removing a screen and forcing open a bedroom window, he entered the dwelling and searched it's interior. It appeared to be a seasonal cottage that hadn't been occupied for some time, although the electricity and water were both operational.

In the bathroom's medicine chest he located a bottle of hydrogen peroxide, which he applied liberally to his wounds. He grimaced as the liquid seeped deep into his flesh and began to fizz. Next he applied band-aids and taped gauze over the worst of his injuries. In the kitchen he found cupboards filled with canned goods, crackers, dried cereal, coffee, potatoes, onions, and bags of cookies. He ate liberally. The refrigerator contained very little, some ketchup, mustard, a jar of pickles, and a few apples and oranges that were nearing the end of being eatable. The freezing compartment was filled with a treasure trove of goodies! Steaks, chops, fish, hamburger, chicken and shrimp.

In a hallway closet he discovered a well-stocked supply of various kinds of liquor and beer. The dressers and closets in the bedrooms were filled with men and women's clothing of all types.

To Todd, this looked like a perfect place to lay low for a few days and attempt to figure a way out of the mess into which he had been thrust.

Cory Welchek, on the other hand, began his unexpected escape from the clutches of the law with a plan. Upon removing the handcuffs, and stealing Doug Nordahl's pistol, he too had plunged into the forest. With the aid of dawn's first light, he was able to navigate a course using the rising sun as a compass of sorts. Cory decided he would strike out to the south and attempt to reach The Howling Beagle, where April would afford him security, and perhaps some womanly pleasures, while he decided his next move.

His flight took him across highway H-44 and to the shore of Manistique Lake. Now all he had to do was follow the shoreline south to The Howling Beagle. As he carefully made his way along the tree lined shore; he suddenly came to a small cottage nestled in the remote corner of the lake's northeast bay. It looked deserted. Cory cautiously approached it.

Hap and Edna were about to leave the sheriff's office when Tom and Beverly Matson arrived. Not having seen each other for so many years, a half hour evaporated before they had become reacquainted and brought each other up to date on where their lives had taken them. Then the conversation turned to a much more serious subject.

"Hap, I've had phone conversations with my son's supervisor, Paul Vandenburg, and Sheriff Ostermeir, concerning the investigation into Brian's disappearance. Both of them told me that you were the individual who accomplished the most towards uncovering information that might be helpful in locating our son."

Hap and Edna could tell by the tone of Tom's voice that he was still hoping his son would be found alive, but suspected the odds were tipped in the opposite direction. "Ya, I jist got lucky I guess. I stumbled onto a few things that might help in findin' him." Hap always seemed to underestimate his own skills and determination.

"Level with me cousin,......what do you think happened to Brian,......and do you have any idea where he might be?"

Hap looked at Tom and Beverly. Tom looked highly distraught, and his face was pale. Beverly was wiping two tears from her cheeks with a paper tissue. Hap shuffled his feet nervously, cleared his throat and answered his cousin's pressing question. "I'll be honest, Tom. For a couple of days after he disappeared I had hope we'd find him stuck or lost or hurt or something like that,...but it's bin jist too long now. I don't think we'll find him alive." Beverly broke down in uncontrollable sobs, as Tom hugged her tightly attempting to lessen the impact of realizing what they both already suspected.

With a pleading look, Tom asked another question. "I know you've already been through a bit of hell during your attempts to find our son,......but will you help us,......help us find him? I know it's a lot to ask,......but we need to find our son,......we need to know what happened to him!" And Tom finally let loose all his suppressed emotions.

Edna hugged both grieving parents and held them tightly until their sobs subsided. Hap grabbed his cousin by the shoulders and gave him a supportive squeeze. "I made up my mind before I met you folks,...I ain't givin' up the search. And in my mind I know who's responsible for Brian's,............" Hap stumbled as he attempted to select the proper words to complete his sentence. "accident." It was a kind suggestion.

"Do you really believe our son had an accident?", asked Tom.

Hap hesitated, then looked his cousin in the eye and answered. "No,...no I don't. I'm sure he was murdered. I came to that conclusion based on several things I found. And something else you two don't know yet, 'cause the sheriff jist found out from the wardens." Hap hesitated again, not sure if what he was going to tell Tom and Beverly was factual. "They think some kids found Brian's truck. It's way out in the boonies and had been burned and covered with brush. But there was no indication that Brian, or anyone, was in the truck."

Beverly looked like she might faint, but managed a weak voiced suggestion. "Maybe we should go out to where the truck is. Maybe we can help find him. Maybe........" Her voice trailed off as more sobbing began. Tom put his arm around his distraught wife and gave her a hug.

Hap took command. "No use goin' there. They ain't gonna find Brian anywhere near that truck,......and it may even turn out ta NOT be his truck. Come on, let's all go ta our place and we'll talk. I think I know where Brian,......Brian's remains are hidden. If ya want ta go lookin' with me,...well, I could use some help."

Part Three: "Secrets In The Forest"

Cory Welchek scanned the cottage from the security of a bushy spruce tree, as his eyes searched the building for signs of life. After ten minutes of seeing or hearing no activity he decided it was safe to walk on by the dwelling and continue his trek towards The Howling Beagle. As he was passing the front of the house he suddenly heard a door open. Whirling around and withdrawing the stolen pistol from his belt, he saw an individual step out on the porch.

"Hey Cory, it's me,...Todd. What the hell are you doing here?" The Welchek Brothers were once again reunited.

After arriving at the Larson residence, the two couples settled into the living room. Edna made a fresh pot of coffee and materialized from the kitchen with a heaping plate of homemade cookies. When everyone was comfortable, Hap poured out his story of what had transpired from the time he decided to continue the search late Friday afternoon, through Deputy Nordahl's accident and Cory Welchek's escape. He left no detail to anyone's imagination. Hap emphasized certain points, which were critical in explaining, how, why and where he thought Brian had been murdered. He ended his account by admitting his theories were simply his opinion, basically based on circumstantial evidence. But he added, "I ain't braggin',...but usually my instincts take me in the right direction."

Tom and Beverly thought about what they had heard for nearly a minute. Tom had questions. "Why don't the police share your opinion,...I mean,...why aren't they looking for Brian in the area where you think the murder took place? If indeed there was a murder. The evidence I've heard so far lacks for substance".

"Probably 'cause there ain't any real HARD evidence,......yet! And now that they've located what might be Brian's truck, if it turns out to be Brian's truck, it's a good bet they'll be looking in that area for a body. And I'm dang sure they ain't gonna find one there. Brian probably stumbled onto that pile of deer remains the same way I did. I only met your son once, but he sure impressed me as being a highly observant young man and sharp as a tack. I'll bet my last dollar the Welchek's found him at their dumpin' grounds and realized their poachin' operation had been uncovered. And they killed him! Right there in the woods next to all those bones and such. I know I'm right and as soon as that sample of dried blood is tested,......it's gonna be human and it's gonna be the same type as yer son's!" Hap was very convincing.

"All right cousin, let's assume for sake of argument that you're right. And the police are barking up the wrong tree. What's our next move?"

Hap looked at his cousin with a slight smirk on his face and packed his corn cob pipe with a load of Bond Street. "What'd mean, "our" next move?" Are ya tellin' me ya want in on what I'm gonna do next?"

"YES! I can't just sit around and wait for something to happen. It seems to me the more eyes we have doing the looking the better the chances SOMETHING will be discovered. Hap, you're the general,...I'm the private. What's your plan?"

"Well, it's only a quarter ta three. We still got at least six more hours of good daylight left, and where I'm goin' and what I'm gonna do when we git there ain't gonna take all that long.", replied the general with an air of confidence.

Edna had a comment. "That's what you thought yesterday afternoon when you went snooping around all by yourself! And look at the mess you got yourself into! Why don't you just keep your nose out of this situation and let the authorities handle it" Edna really didn't agree with Hap's investigative plans.

"Ya, that was yesterday. Today's today. And I got myself an army to back me up now." Hap grinned at Edna and gave her his best wink.

"Well at least tell me where you're going and what you plan to do, you old bullhead! That way if you don't show up for supper again, I can come to your rescue,......darling!" Edna didn't smile nor did she wink. It was obvious she really didn't approve of her husband trying to act like Sherlock Holmes.

"I'm goin' back ta that old farm, look around a bit more, and maybe find what we're lookin' fer. I got an idea in my head that jist might work." Hap narrowed his eyes into slits and tried to look investigative, then added, "And look who's callin' who BULLHEADED!"

Tom interjected. "There's two problems. Bev and I have a motel room rented for a week in Manistique. If we don't get back until after dark,...well, I don't like driving these country roads at night with all the wildlife running around trying to make money for the collision repair shops. Plus mom and dad will worry if we're late in returning."

Hap immediately had the answer to Tom's problems. "Heck, Edna'll call yer motel and yer folks and tell 'um yer gonna stay with us tonight. Edna and Beverly can git better acquainted while you and me is out playin' detective. The gals kin whip up something for dinner,......Edna's a fair ta middlin' cook. Then you two kin drive back ta Manistique in the morning." Hap was flirting with getting more than a punch in the arm, but Edna sighed, shrugged her shoulders and resigned herself to the inevitable.

Ten minutes later Hap, Tom, Sadie and Wolf were heading towards an old farm on Highway 77.

Charles and Shirley Baldwin were busy packing suitcases in anticipation of their flight from Sept-lies, Quebec to Sault Ste. Marie, Michigan. Their excitement, concerning the planned purchase of a summer vacation cottage near where Charles' cousin, Hap Larson, lived was running high. The earliest flight they were able to schedule was on Tuesday, the day after Memorial Day.

A phone call interrupted their packing. It was a call from the reservations desk. The attendant informed the Baldwin's there had been two cancellations on a commuter flight from Sept-lies to Montreal. From Montreal there was room available on an Air Canada flight, which stopped in Sault Ste. Marie on it's route west to Vancouver, British Columbia. If they were at the terminal by four p.m., they would be able to purchase tickets and be on their way three days earlier than anticipated. A half-hour later the couple arrived at the airport.

The driveway to the old farm was closed off with strips of yellow plastic crime scene tape that warned; "Crime Scene, Investigation in Process, DO NOT CROSS". Hap directed Tom to lift up the strip of tape so he might drive under it and into the farm's driveway. Tom obeyed, but looked nervous in doing so. A flock of crows cawed noisily in the trees beyond the barn.

Hap drove slowly down the dirt road, passing the old farmhouse and the barn. As he did so he explained how he had entered the buildings, despite the fact they had been locked. Tom couldn't help noticing a small smirk on Hap's face as he enjoyed telling the story. As they approached the wooded area beyond the barn, in which the remains of the poached deer were located, more yellow crime scene tape criss crossed the path leading from the turn around to the rotting mess beyond. Hap parked his truck, removed his .44 from under the seat, stuck it in his belt, and then opened the tailgate and leashed Sadie and Wolf.

Tom, who had also exited the vehicle, began walking around the truck through a patch of tall grass. Something shinny caught his eye. He bent down and picked up an empty cartridge casing. "Hey Hap! I found something that might be of interest."

Hap ordered his two dogs to "sit", and walked toward Tom to view the object he had discovered. "Ya, this is real interesting! She's a .223! The same caliber and make as the ones I found Friday in the field where your son discovered four deer had recently been poached. And I bet a ballistics test will confirm it was fired from the same gun."

Hap peered down the path and squinted. Then he pointed. "Look jist to the left of the opening where this path enters the woods. See that little balsam tree besides that bigger red pine?" His cousin nodded in the affirmative.

"That's right where I found that patch of dried blood I figured came from Brian when he got killed. Now it looks like you jist helped me figure out how. Those bastards shot him!"

Tom blinked several times and swallowed hard, trying to repress the emotions that were surging through his body. Then he looked at Hap, as though waiting for more of an explanation as to what had brought his cousin to that conclusion.

"Now it makes sense that if Brian drove down here,...jist as I did,...wonderin' why all them crows was hangin' around these pines,......he probably parked in about the same place I did. Does that make sense to you?" Again Tom nodded, "yes". "Then let's say those two Welchek bastards saw him, or his truck, and walked down here to investigate. They probably saw Brian looking at that mess in that stand of pine jist ahead. I'll show ya that in a minute or two,......hope ya got a strong stomach. Now those two son of a bitches decided to shoot the warden who jist discovered their dumpin' ground,......well, here's about where they'd shot from. And the empty would have bin kicked out and landed about there." Hap pointed to where Tom had discovered the empty casing to emphasize his theory.

Tom remained speechless.

Hap placed the empty cartridge case in his truck's glove compartment, and then he, Brian and the two dogs followed the path into the stand of pines. Tom's reaction was one of repulsion and disbelief. "OH MY GOD! Even though you told me there was a huge amount of deer remains,.........wow,......I sure wasn't prepared for this much! And UK, what a stench!"

"Ya, and as the weather continues to warm as we git deeper into spring and summer, It's gonna git real ripe!
Follow me, we'll walk to the upwind side of this mess so we won't have to gag on every breath."

Hap led his cousin to the base of a large white pine, ordered Sadie and Wolf to "sit" and sat down himself with his back against the tree trunk. He pulled out his corncob pipe, filled the bowl with tobacco and struck a match to it. Looking up at Tom, he grinned and said, "Pull up a tree trunk yerself and have a seat cousin. We're gonna sit and rest a spell. I gotta see if my plan is gonna work."

Tom slowly settled himself onto the cushion of pine needles next to his cousin and leaned back as Hap had. But

Tom's face reflected an extremely puzzled look. "I thought we came here to look for my son's remains. Now we're sitting next to a pile of rotting deer parts and you said you have a plan? Could you let me in on your little secret?"

Hap chuckled softly. "Guess I better explain. I've bin studyin' a quadrangle map of this region. This stand of pine is on the edge of a fairly large, low, swampy area. What that means is the water table is probably only a couple of feet beneath the surface. Now I'm sure Brian, or somebody, was killed right over there." Hap pointed with the stem of his pipe for effect. That's where I found a large amount of dried blood. There was also two drag marks in the pine needles that even disturbed the soft sand underneath. In other words, whatever got dragged was fairly heavy. The twin marks were only a few inches apart and jist the right size to be the heels of somebody's boots."

Tom shook his head and responded. "Hap, I've only been around you for a few hours and I've noticed from what you've said and already showed me,……your power of observation is unbelievable!"

"If ya lived in the boonies as long as I did, ya'd have the same ability, or ya wouldn't be alive. Now let me finish the explanation of my plan. Now those two Welchek's wasn't so dumb as to spend a lot of time messin' around this place in broad daylight after murderin' a game warden. Or anybody else. So I figure they probably moved his truck so nobody'd see it from the highway. I suspect their truck was either in the barn or they jist drove in and caught Brian in the act of snoopin'. I doubt that possibility 'cause Brian would have heard them comin' and been on guard. I think Brian got surprised by them two. The one named Cory made a big fuss, when I got caught by them two ya-hoos, about me bein' a trespassin' snoop. Pissed him off real good."

"Then why didn't they shoot you?"

"The older one, Cory, wanted to blast me. But his brother, Todd,…seemed to be a couple of I.Q. points smarter, wouldn't let him. Todd seemed to kinda be the boss of the outfit. But Cory was gonna bump me off when he came to git me in the chicken coop. But I already told ya that part."

Hap relit his pipe and continued. "Now where was I?" Oh ya, after they parked Brian's truck out of sight they dragged him a ways and then probably had a discussion about what to do with the body. Takin' it someplace else would have been risky, so I'm guessin' they buried it close by someplace. My instinct tells me they carried it back in the woods further, dug a quick grave, and covered it up with grass and leaves so it'd be tough ta find. But 'cause the water table is close to the surface,...the grave had ta be shallow. I think. I hope."

"O.K. I'm following you so far. But how are we going to find it sitting here in the shade of the old pine trees?" Tom's face still had a puzzled look.

"Remember all them crows and ravens that was here when we drove up? Well, they ain't gone far. In fact, while we've bin talkin' a half dozen or more have sailed over us ta see if we left yet. They kin see my truck real plain, so they know we're still here somewhere. Crows are pretty smart and ravens are the Albert Einstein of the bird world."

"So?" The puzzled look was more pronounced.

"Here's where my plan may jist go sour. If the grave is a shallow one like I figured, well, some critter has already found where it is from the smell coming up through the freshly disturbed dirt. The rest of this is gonna be hard fer you to take, cousin. But I gotta tell ya, and warn ya, of what we might be lookin' at real soon."

"What in hell are you talking about? Put it to me straight." Tom was becoming frustrated at Hap's slowly developing explanation of "his plan."

"Tom, these woods are full of all kinds of critters that eat meat. If ya look at all these deer remains you'll see a good number of places where the wild predators have dined. But you already know that, you were born and raised up here. But let me run down the list to refresh your memory. We got skunks, coons, coyotes, wolves, bobcats, bears, and even a few cougars roamin' these woods. And any one of them would be more than happy to dig up some buried meat and fill their gut."

Tom's eyes grew wide as he finally realized what Hap was getting at! His cousin was suggesting that wild animals may be eating the remains of his son! He slowly shook his head and moaned, "No, no, not that on top of everything else! Oh God no, not that!"

Hap placed his hand on his cousin's arm and gave it a friendly squeeze. "Now I may be all wet on that last part, Tom. But we're gonna sit here a while and see if my idea has any merit. I warned ya this might be a tough assignment. If my plan works, and you don't want ta come with me to check it out,...I'll understand."

Tom turned his head to look Hap in the eye. "I'm still not clear on your so-called plan. Whatever it is,...and if it works to find Brian,...I'll be right behind you. I have to know. I must."

"If something has dug up the grave,...then them crows have spotted it. And 'cause they know we're still here in their favorite eatin' place,...well, they'll start congregatin' around where the grave is. And 'cause they're crows, they'll start fussin' and fightin' over what's there. And we'll hear it and head in that direction. And when we git close,...Sadie and Wolf will pick up the scent and lead us right to the spot. That's my plan."

Tom stared at his cousin in disbelief. He silently wondered if Hap was gone off the deep end. But he kept his thoughts to himself and simply nodded an O.K.

A half-hour passed. Hap kept pointing out more and more crows flying over the tops of the trees that shielded Hap's investigative unit from view. And then, faintly at first, but growing stronger by the minute, a chorus of cawing came drifting from deeper in the forest. Hap slowly got to his feet, picked up his dog's leashes, and whispered to his cousin, "It's time. Let's go."

Slowly easing their way though the thick underbrush, the cawing became clearer and clearer. One of the crows that served as a lookout was perched on the top of a tall tree. It spotted the human intruders and gave a sharp verbal warning. The sound of many flapping wings announced the flock's departure. But Hap and his companions were now less than a hundred yards from where the crows had re-grouped. Circling the area until they were down wind of the general area where the crows had been, Hap released his dogs. With noses uplifted and sniffing loudly, they made a beeline towards a thick stand of small balsam trees. Hap and Tom followed as quickly as they could.

Hap led the way into the interior of the thicket to find his two dogs sniffing the exposed and partially eaten remains of a human body. A body dressed in a tattered gray uniform, with a game warden's badge pinned on what was left of a jacket.

Chapter Seven: "Loose Ends"

Part One: "More Puzzle Pieces"

Dust was just blending into night when the body bag containing the remains of Conservation Officer Brian Matson were loaded into an ambulance for transport to the morgue. The grounds around the old farm on Highway 77 where jammed with official vehicles of all descriptions,……and one privately owned green Dodge Ram truck. All along the shoulders of the highway more cars were parked, as numerous curious citizens watched the spectacle before them and questioned each other as to what might be taking place. News and rumors travel rapidly in rural areas.

Upon leaving the scene of Hap Larson's latest discovery, the authorities in charge of the search for Officer Matson met in emergency session at their temporary nerve center at the Seney National Wildlife Refuge. The veteran woodsman, and recently self-appointed criminal investigator, had forced the authorities to take an entirely new view of the situation at hand. Besides becoming slightly embarrassed that a person with no criminal investigative training was stealing the show, so to speak, the leaders of the investigation now were faced with positive proof a murder had been committed. A possibility they had somehow refused to consider for the past four days.

Sheriff Ostermier, the chief overseer of the search operation, assigned several of his subordinates specific assignments, and instructed everyone who was participating in the case to meet in the Sheriff's Office in Newberry at nine a.m. tomorrow, the Sunday of Memorial Day Weekend. No one grumbled, and the meeting broke up near midnight.

The Air Canada DC 9 carrying Charles and Shirley Baldwin to Sault Ste. Marie touched down on the runway of Sault Ste. Marie International shortly after ten p.m. Saturday. They were successful in finding a room in what Charles later described as, "a half star establishment".

Things got worse the following morning, Sunday, when the couple attempted to rent a car to continue their journey to Newberry. Being Memorial Day Weekend, all available rental cars were rented! So, reluctantly, they hired a cab and began the final sixty-five miles of their trip.

Although not in the best of spirits, the couple arrived at the Newberry Truck Stop, Cafe and Convenience Center just before ten thirty a.m. A call to the Larson residence was successful in locating assistance. Edna answered the phone.

"Charles! I thought you and Shirley weren't coming until after the holiday."

"Well, we were able to get an earlier flight,...but the way things have been going; maybe we should have waited. But we're so anxious to start looking for a vacation retreat,...we just had to gamble and take the earlier flight. Now we're stuck here in Newberry without wheels." Charles sounded frustrated.

"Oh, I'll come and pick you up. Hap and his cousin Tom Matson,......I don't know if you know Tom and his wife Beverly,......well, Hap and Tom are in an important meeting at the Sheriff's Office. And don't ask me why! It's such a long and complicated story. You'll have to wait till we all get together and then we'll fill you in on what's been happening here. It's terrible. Where are you now?"

"We're having coffee and a sweet roll in the convenience store at the truck stop in Newberry."

"I'll be there in fifteen minutes."

Edna and Beverly got into Edna's '57 Nomad, turned taxi, and went to pick up their first fare.

The reunion between the Welchek Brothers nearly started out as a fight. Once the initial surprise at their unexpected meeting in a most unexpected location was over, Cory launched into his vile condemnation of his brother, which he had rehearsed while chained to an iron post in their chicken coop. Of course, Todd had no idea of what had transpired after his departure from their home, after their last fight over what to do with the bum they had caught in the basement of their pot farm. So Todd had no idea of why his brother was so pissed off.

Upon viewing Todd's torn and patched up face and neck, Cory's rage subsided quickly. The two then retreated into the cottage Todd was using as a temporary refuge from the law, and for the next hour the fugitives from justice filled each other in on the unfortunate chain of events that had befallen them.

The next order of business was to agree on a plan of action.

By mid morning on Sunday, news of the discovery of Officer Matson's body reached the press. Reporters and TV. news hounds began calling and visiting anyone who might be able to shed additional light on this extremely high interest news story. It wasn't long until the phone at the Larson residence was ringing off the hook.

Edna had just arrived home with Charles and Shirley Baldwin, in time to receive a call from the News Director from WSSM-TV in Sault Ste. Marie.

"Hello, is this the Eric Larson residence?"

"Yes, it is. Who's calling?"

"Walter Leopold from Channel 5 in Sault Ste. Marie. Is Mr. Larson there?"

"No, he isn't. He's at an important meeting and probably won't be home until sometime after twelve."

"We understand he was responsible for locating the body of Conservation Officer Brian Matson. Is that correct? And oh, to whom am I speaking?"

"I'm Mr. Larson's wife, Edna Larson. Uh,...yes, that's correct, my husband found the body late last evening."

"We'd like to interview him as soon as possible. Could I send a crew to your residence and have them wait for his return? Would you be so kind to allow that, Mrs. Larson?"

There was an awkward pause as Edna rapidly digested the request. She knew how much Hap hated talking to the news media,......but then again, he wouldn't listen to her advice and let the authorities handle the investigation. No, Mr. Sam Spade, Private Eye, had to show off and prove the "experts" were looking for Brian's remains in the wrong place! A cunning smile spread across Edna's face, as she answered, "No problem! Send out an interview crew. Here's how to find where we live."

Senator Randolph Redman, due to his political stature as being the senior-ranking member of the Michigan State Senate, had no difficulty keeping abreast of the ongoing search for Officer Matson. At the Senator's request, both Sheriff Ostermeir and Senior Warden Paul Vandenburg were updating the senator daily.

In turn, Senator Redman had passed on the disturbing information to his immediate superiors, Chief of Criminal Investigations for the State of Michigan, Corbet O'Keefe, in Lansing, and Kenneth Bradford in Washington D.C. The senator wisely used public pay phones to relay his information. Several, as Senator Redman put it; "solutions to our problem" were discussed with his two co-hearts in crime. After Senator Redman's latest update early Sunday morning, they agreed on a course of action. A course of action that needed to be completed ASAP!

Shortly before nine a.m., on a Sunday morning yet, everyone who had been invited or ordered to attend the meeting at Sheriff Ostermeir's office was assembled. The number in attendance was not large, but they were the key people in what now was a murder investigation, plus, a major poaching and marijuana investigation.

Besides Sheriff Ostermeir, Deputy Douglas Nordahl and two other deputies from Luce County, Jim Pearson and Vincent Palino were present. The list also included Chief Warden Paul Vandenburg, Warden Wayne Maki and Warden Phil Glasser. Representing the Federal Fish and Game authorities were the administrator of the Seney National Wildlife Refuge, Richard

Summers and Refuge Manager, Margaret Solvinski. Two new additions to the team had arrived in the wee hours of the morning, Special Agents Sherman Oaks and Terry McQuarie, representing the Federal Bureau of Investigation. And last but not least, private citizens Eric Larson and Tom Matson.

The meeting began with Bill Ostermeir introducing everyone to each other, then offering the committee to help themselves to hot coffee and fresh pastry. From there the meeting took on a much more serious tone.

The sheriff indicated he would be turning the leadership of the investigation over to the F.B.I. agents, Oaks and McQuarie, immediately after the conclusion of this meeting. The next order of business was a series of reports the sheriff had requested from those persons whom he had assigned to investigate certain specific aspects of the total investigation. Deputy Nordahl gave the first report.

"A complete search of the Welchek property and the truck owned by the two brothers, Cory and Todd yielded a considerable amount of information. We are sure the .223 caliber rifle we confiscated is the weapon that was used to kill Officer Matson. Two sets of fingerprints were lifted from the weapon and have been identified as belonging to Todd and Cory Welchek. Ballistic tests on the shell casings are in progress and the results should be known sometime today. Brian Matson's 9mm semi-automatic Glock pistol, and his Mossberg pump shotgun were recovered from the Welchek's house, which in my opinion, pretty well nailed down the identity of his killers. We also confirmed the marijuana found in the Welchek's garage was grown in the old farm on Highway 77. The blood sample found in the woods near the dump by Mr. Larson tested positive as human blood and it was type O, the same as Officer Matson's. DNA testing is in progress to determine for sure if it did come from the slain officer."

Jim Pearson spoke next. "The report from the coroner's office indicates Officer Matson was shot from behind with a high caliber bullet. The projectile entered the rear of his skull nearly in its center, passed through his brain and exited just above his nose, almost squarely between his eyes." Jim hesitated for several seconds and quietly added; "Brian probably never even heard the shot. Doc Schneider thinks death was instantaneous."

Vincent Palino continued. "The Welchek's phone records really didn't add much to our investigation. They didn't do much calling, nor were there many incoming calls. Most of the calls were local. but just to be safe, we're checking on all the numbers to see whom they called and who has been calling them. However, there were two numbers, which caught our interest. One is the number of a public phone in Menominee, Michigan that the brothers received calls from about once every two weeks. The other is a cell phone number from an area code here in the U.P. It only appeared on the phone records twice, but we're checking as to whom has that number.

Warden Maki volunteered to speak next. "The burned out truck was the one assigned to Officer Matson. We were successful in removing it from the wooded area where it was found. But of course, due to the complete destruction of the interior, as well as all the exterior paint being burned off, it offered no additional evidence."

Paul Vandenburg gave the last scheduled report. "For those of you who have witnessed the dump area near the old farm on 77, plus the interior of the barn, it doesn't take a rocket scientist to conclude a tremendous number of deer have been butchered, processed and stored at the site, at least for short periods of time. It is the unanimous opinion of every single one of my wardens that it would be IMPOSSIBLE for just two poachers to kill as many animals as the remains indicate have been processed at the farm. So,……it appears we have uncovered a huge poaching and distribution operation that encompasses an area much larger that a couple of counties here in the U.P.

Gentlemen, and you too Margaret, it looks like we've got a long investigative trail ahead of us."

There was an awkward pause. Then Special Agent McQuarie had a question. "Sheriff, just to satisfy my curiosity, why are those two civilians present at this meeting?", he asked, gesturing his head in the direction of Hap and Tom.

"Oh, excuse me Terry. I haven't had a chance to you tell you about Mr. Larson and his cousin Tom Matson." At the mention of the name "Matson", the two Special Agents stiffened, instantly realizing one of the civilians was probably Brian Matson's father. Sheriff Ostermeir continued. "Mr. Larson,……he prefers to be called Hap, has been the one individual who somehow was able to figure out the solution to Officer Matson's disappearance. It took him a little longer to convince us he was right. I'd suggest you have a talk with him about his investigative methods. They're quite unusual and unique. And I don't think there's a class that teaches what he knows and does. Mr. Matson is Brian Matson's father, and understandably has a great interest in what we are doing."

"No problem. I was just curious.", answered Special Agent McQuarie.

Sheriff Ostermier directed a question to Hap. "Do you have a few minutes after our meeting to discuss your findings and relate your story to our two Special Agents?"

"Sure, I guess I kin tell it one more time." Hap was always cooperative. Well, usually.

Bill looked around the room and had one more question. "Anybody else have anything to say or add before we adjourn and get down to locating those Welchek Brothers, and finding out whom else is involved in this mystery?"

Richard Summers spoke up. "Seeing as some of the poaching has been done on the property of a Federal Wildlife Refuge, I've called Washington and talked to the head of the Federal Fish and Game Department. The Deputy Director of the Department of Interior, Ken Bradford, said he'd send two Federal Wardens up here to give us a hand with the investigation."

With that, the meeting adjourned.

At about the same time Sheriff Ostermeir was adjourning the meeting in his office, a dark brown Buick Park Avenue was leaving Detroit. It was traveling north on Interstate 75, towards the Mackinaw Bridge and the Upper Peninsula beyond. There were two men in the car, Billy "The Bruiser" Kerletti and Tony "The Enforcer" Ramonni. They were heading north to carry out an important assignment!

Part Two: "The Cottage"

Hap and Tom returned to the Larson residence a little after eleven a.m. to discover another cousin, Charles, and his wife Shirley had arrived unexpectedly. Although Tom and Beverly had known about Charles and the Baldwin branch of the family tree, and visa versa, the two had never met. After Edna did the honors with introductions, Charles and Shirley received a detailed play by play account of the unbelievable chain of events that had taken place since Brian Matson disappeared five days earlier. The Baldwin's were stunned. And for the Larson's and the Matson's, it was difficult to believe so much had happened in such a short span of time.

"Hey Edna, let's whip up somethin' fer lunch. I'm starving and I bet our guests could stand some grub."

At that moment a van drove into the yard amidst a chorus of barking dogs. Hap looked out the window and saw large letters on the side of the van proclaiming; "WSSM, Channel 5, Sault Ste. Marie, MI". Hap looked disgusted. "Now look at this. The media hounds jist arrived."

"Oh Hap darling," cooed an innocent sounding Edna, "I forgot to tell you the TV station called and I set up an interview for you. I know how much a famous detective like you enjoys being interviewed."

"Hap looked at his wife and thought of several replies he would have liked to make, but with guests in the house he laughed politely and accepted his fate.

Forty five minutes later the van departed. The good news was that Edna had ample time to prepare a mouth watering lunch.

After everyone had had their fill of thick, yummy beef stew, several kinds of sandwiches and homemade pie for desert, Hap invited everyone outside for a tour of the beautiful grounds surrounding the Larson Homestead. He turned all five of his sled dogs loose from their kennel and allowed them to roam freely. Hap was feeling guilty he had not been able to pay as much attention to his beloved dogs as usual.

The tour group walked to the dock below the Larson home, and watched Sadie retrieve sticks tossed into the waters of the mighty Tahquamenon River. Once that routine was completed, Edna had a suggestion.

"Hap darling." Hap knew any mushy adjective following his name meant Edna wanted something." "I've got a good idea!" There was a pause as Hap narrowed his eyes and looked suspiciously at his wife. "Why don't you take Tom and Charles out fishing on the river? You haven't done much fishing lately,...and the relaxation would be good medicine for all of you, seeing as what we all have been going through lately. And,...and,......I know you could catch enough fish for a nice fish fry this evening. You could cook our evening meal outdoors on the deck. Wouldn't that be nice?" Edna looked at her guests for a show of support. By the looks on their faces the verdict was unanimous.

Hap's face lit up in a grin. "By golly Edna, fer once ya got a good idea! Why didn't I think of doin' that?"

"Hap, darling, Once in a while I AM smarter than you."

"Dream on honeybun, dream on! I'll round up some fishin' poles and grab my tackle box. Tom,...Charles,...how about bailin' out the boat, git the oars and motor out of the shed over there and we'll git ta catchin' our supper."

Edna winked at Shirley and Beverly as they began walking up the path towards the house. When they were out of hearing range from their husbands, Edna whispered, "As soon as they leave, I'll drive us to town. There's some wonderful quaint little shops chucked full of women's things in Newberry."

Memorial Day dawned sunny and warm. Hap remarked a miracle had occurred. There hadn't been a drop of rain for the entire holiday weekend!

Edna prepared a gut filling breakfast, although all her guests agreed they were still full from all the fresh fish, French fries, beans, homemade bread and salads they had consumed the past evening. Hap also reminded them they had neglected to mention the pie and ice cream for desert.

Today was a day the Baldwin's had looked forward to for many weeks. They were going to meet with a real estate agent and look at several pieces of property that might suit their taste as a vacation retreat. Charles and Shirley had invited Hap, Edna, Tom and Beverly to go with them, but Tom and Beverly declined. They needed to return to Manistique and make final plans with a funeral director for their son's funeral, which was scheduled for Tuesday. Hap and Edna accepted the Baldwin's invitation, and would act as chauffeurs.

Cory and Todd Welchek discussed various plans and ideas of how they would escape capture, from what by now must have escalated into a major manhunt. There was no doubt the authorities had already found their stash of marijuana in the garage, plus the freezer containing the butchered remains of seven deer they had poached nearly a week ago. The trespasser, they had been duped into believing was simply a wandering bum, had certainly ratted on them. After all, he led a deputy sheriff right to their private property, and Cory had been arrested. And they surmised the bum had given the deputy a description of their truck, which led to the officer looking for Todd at The Howling Beagle. The brothers were indeed fortunate to have eluded imprisonment up to this point. Several times Cory restated his resolve to, as he put it, "get even with that son of a bitch and make him wish he was never born."

Later that evening, after the brothers had consumed the last of the beer and liquor, they turned on the cottage's TV set and watched the evening news. The lead story was an interview with a man named Eric "Hap" Larson. The ten-minute segment featured his story of how he had located the remains of the slain Conservation Officer, Brian Matson. Todd and Cory sat and listened in stunned silence. The "bum in the basement" had surfaced once again, and discovered what would certainly point an accusing finger of guilt directly at the Welchek brothers!

At the conclusion of the news segment, Cory's rage was instant. "That snoopin' son of a bitch! Now he's really got us in hot water. Now the cops will know we're the ones who shot that damn snoopin' warden." Cory shook his fist at the TV set and made a promise. "Now I know who you are! And I'm gonna git even with you MR. SMART ASS LARSON! Boy am I gonna git even!"

By early Monday morning Cory and Todd had agreed on a plan. They were becoming more and more nervous about continuing to stay at the cottage. What if the owners suddenly appeared? After all, it was Memorial Day Weekend. Several times boats containing anglers entered the bay in front of the cottage to do some fishing. One group of fishermen actually came ashore to relieve the pressure in their bladders. And one of the men walked around the cottage, admiring its design and secluded location!

Besides all that, the food supply was nearly exhausted, and the once well stocked liquor cabinet was empty. Just as dawn was breaking the two felons departed, leaving their temporary hide out looking like a well used pigpen.

The prospective buyers and their chauffeurs arrived at the office of "North Country Realty" in Newberry at nine a.m. Audrey Meschik, one of the sales representatives, was eager to begin showing the Baldwin's the company's extensive selection of vacation properties. The foursome were ushered into a small office and for the next hour Charles and Shirley poured through piles of photos and descriptions of numerous seasonal and year around dwellings. The couple was finally successful in narrowing their choices down to three very nice and somewhat secluded cottages. Then all five individuals piled into a spacious Chevy Tahoe and headed out to inspect the chosen properties.

Their first stop was at a fairly new log home that overlooked Lake Superior between Deer Park and Grand Marais. Although the view of "Old Gitche Gumee" was breathtakingly beautiful, the building was set high above the water without easy access to the beach. Neither Shirley nor Charles felt it was what they were looking for.

The second piece of property was twenty miles south of Newberry on the west shore of Millecoquins Lake. This too was a nicely kept year around home, handsomely done in rough cedar siding. The beach area was lovely, but being located on the west side of the lake it would not afford much direct sunlight during the late afternoon and early evening hours during spring, summer, and fall. Charles and Shirley didn't rule it out entirely, but wanted to see additional offerings.

The third cottage was located on the northwest corner of Manistique Lake. This too was a fairly new log home, with a stunning view of the lake. It looked to be just what the couple was looking for,...except there were neighbors on both sides of the property, and both Charles and Shirley were looking for a bit more privacy. They made a decision to return to the real estate office and look at the remainder of the property listings one more time.

Audrey followed the driveway to the highway, turned east on H-44, and suddenly remembered something. Turning her head to look at her prospective buyers she had a suggestion. "Oh, I just remembered something. A couple of miles further is a piece of property that JUST came on the market. It's tucked away in a small bay on the northeast corner of the lake you just looked at, Manistique Lake. The husband of the couple that owned the property passed away this past winter and the widow decided to sell it. We just got the listing on Friday and haven't had time to take pictures or make up a descriptive sheet. But I do remember the fire number, 5454 H-44. I don't have a key with me, but we can stop by and let you have a look around the grounds. If it's something you might like, we can get the key from the office and come back. Are you interested in stopping?"

Charles and Shirley looked at each other, shrugged and answered, "Sure, why not?"

The sun was just beginning to kiss the trees on the west shore of Manistique Lake "Good Morning" when Cory knocked on the back door of April Ravovich's living quarters at The Howling Beagle. Cory knocked several times before they heard

April stirring. A sleepy sounding voice inside asked, "Who the hell is pounding on my door at this hour of the day?" The voice definitely had a ring of irritation.

"It's Cory and Todd, Cory and Todd Welchek.", came a whispered reply.

April unlocked the door, opened it a crack and asked a second question. "What the hell do you two want this early? I ain't in the mood to go to bed with either one of you,......if that's what you're looking for!" And then as her sleep drugged eyes focused on Todd's scabbed and patched up face, she whistled and asked, "Who beat the hell out of you?"

"Never mind what happened to my face,......I had a little accident. We're on the run from the law. You remember that cop that came looking for me Friday night? He arrested Cory later that night. But then he wrecked his squad car avoiding a deer on H-33 and Cory got away. Now we probably got every cop and game warden in Michigan looking for us." Todd and Cory had already decided to admit to no one the fact they had killed Brian Matson, so Todd only confessed to the things April already was aware of. Judging from the look on her face, she hadn't watched the evening news. "By now the cops have found all our pot plants and a bunch of the venison we had stored at our place. We need someplace to hide out until we can figure out how to get to hell away from here."

"Well, you ain't staying with me! The cops know you two hang out here and sooner or later they'll be coming here to look. I don't need any cops snooping around my bar. Ain't good for business."

"No, we didn't mean to ask you to let us stay with you in the bar. But how about that old run down cabin by the lakeshore? The one the previous owners used to rent. We'll just be hiding out here for a day or two. Then we'll go someplace else, but we don't know where yet. We need time to think, time to make a plan. Come on April, we've been good customers. We've supplied you with good grass,......and venison to mix with your burgers. Have a heart."

"O.K. But just for a couple of days. If the cops show up,...get you asses out of here and fast. I don't want no trouble with the cops. I've seen more squad cars cruising up and down the road out front in the past couple of days than I normally see in a month! The door to the shack is open. But the damn place is a mess. But then again it'll probably look just like home to you two."

Todd and Cory had found a new temporary hiding place.

Audrey slowed the Tahoe and turned right at fire number 5454-H-44. A narrow, winding driveway several hundred yards in length ended abruptly in a small, secluded clearing. An old, but seemingly well kept vertical half log cottage overlooked a peaceful bay, from which it's mirrored surface reflected a royal blue spring sky laced with fleecy white cumulous clouds. Charles and Audrey both sucked in their breath at viewing the beautiful cottage situated perfectly in the center of the tranquil and serene setting.

"I want it!", exclaimed Shirley, before Audrey's Tahoe even came to a stop.

"Now this is what we're looking for!", added Charles.

The passengers quickly piled out of the vehicle and began circling the cottage, ooohhhing and aauuuing as they went. An inspection of the beachfront area resulted in similar verbal sounds of approval. A boat house situated on the shoreline was unlocked, and contained a vintage Thompson mahogany inboard run about, a canoe, and a sixteen foot fully equipped fishing boat. Under a tarp next to the boathouse was a fairly new pontoon boat.

"I can't wait to see the inside!" bubbled Shirley. "Let's go get the key!"

But Hap's all encompassing gaze had already spotted something that didn't look quite right. He was inspecting a window, which had its screen leaning against the cabin wall, rather than set firmly in place within the window casing. He pushed up on the bottom portion of the sliding window and it opened. "Hey, I kin crawl in this window that was left open and unlock the front door. We don't need no key!" Hap grinned at the four onlookers, boosted himself up, and slid through the open window.

Seconds later the front door opened and a startled looking Hap Larson announced, "Holdy Shit, wait till ya see the inside of this place!"

Part Three: "Closure"

The mess inside the cottage was substantial. The group of onlookers stood just inside the doorway in open-mouthed silence and stared at the spectacle before them. Beer cans; liquor bottles, soup cans, used paper plates and an assortment of other forms of garbage littered the floor, tables and furniture. Hap broke the silence.

"Whoever did this, it's recent. Real recent." He scratched his head in thought, and then a sly look took control of his facial expression. "Say Edna,...ain't this real close to where that Welchek asshole,......oh, pardon me Miss Meschik, I git excited once in a while and let my language git away from me. That Todd Welchek,...asshole," Hap couldn't resist. "tried ta steal yer car last Friday night?"

"Why yes,...where that happened is just a short distance further from where we turned off the highway."

"Well then, I've got a good idea who made this mess. We gotta call the sheriff."

Audrey came to the rescue. "I've got a cell phone right here in my pocket. Do you know the number?"

Minutes later two squad cars were heading south out of Newberry towards 5454-H-44 at Manistique Lake.

The sheriff and three of his staff spent nearly two hours at the cottage searching for clues. Fingerprints were found in abundance and it appeared as though more than one person had been living in the cottage for several days. When the group was finished putting all the pieces of the puzzle together, there was unanimous consent the mess had most likely been created by the now infamous Welchek brothers.

Before leaving, Audrey assured the Baldwin's she would see to it that the cottage would be completely cleaned and sanitized. Charles and Shirley assured Audrey they would make an offer to buy the property, and then set up an appointment with Audrey to meet at the realty office on Wednesday afternoon at one thirty.

Charles had one more suggestion. "Audrey, if you have a "sold" sign in your Tahoe, you might as well put it up at the end of the driveway." Audrey had several.

By Tuesday morning the miracle that Hap had suggested was taking place came to an end. Rain was falling steadily from solid gray skies that stretched unbroken from horizon to horizon. As Hap was putting on his one and only suit, he grumbled, "Perfect day for a funeral."

The church in Manistique was packed! Relatives representing both sides of the Matson family tree had arrived in great numbers, most of which Hap did not even know existed. There was a large contingency of Conservation Officers from all over the State of Michigan, as well as other law enforcement personnel from cities, counties and townships.

For obvious reasons, the lengthy church service was held with the casket closed. The incessant rain created a royal mess at the graveside ceremony, and although there were an abundance of umbrellas, there weren't enough to keep everybody dry. Hap brought along his yellow rubber rain suit, which although it kept him from getting soaked, Edna complained and looked embarrassed. Several times she whispered to her husband, "No one wears one of those at a funeral!"

Hap answered, "I do."

Back in the church basement after the burial, the usual luncheon was served. Hap and Edna were introduced to numerous, as Hap put it later, "shirttail relatives". The slain officer's wife and her two small children spent nearly a half-hour talking to and getting to know "The Larson's from Newberry".

Dianne Matson sincerely thanked the couple for all their assistance in helping to bring closure to the horror she had experienced after her husband's disappearance.

After saying good-bye, and giving hugs and handshakes to the young widow and her children, Hap made a promise. "Me and Edna ain't done yet. We're gonna do all we kin ta bring them killers ta justice. I won't rest till they're both either in jail or six feet under." Hap was a man of his word.

The drive home from Manistique to Newberry was drenched in silence. The rain continued. Hap dropped Charles and Shirley off at their motel, and by mid afternoon Hap and Edna were safe and sound back at their home. Both felt and looked tired, and a rainy afternoon was perfect for taking a well-deserved nap. But first Hap asked Edna if she'd be interested in, as he put it, "a little mid afternooner".

Edna winked, and issued a challenge, "Race you to the bedroom!"

Cory and Todd were becoming more and more frustrated with what was definitely a rapidly deteriorating situation.

Although they talked about many different schemes that might allow them to flee to some distant location to avoid capture, predictably, the two couldn't agree on a plan of action.

The rain on Tuesday proved the old cabin in which they were staying leaked. Badly! The small amount of food that was left in the cottage they vacated had been taken with them to their new hide out, but by noon on Tuesday it was gone. The tiny dilapidated cabin had a wood stove for heat, but fearing any smoke coming from the stovepipe might give away their presence to the police, they were forced to endure the chilly dampness. And worst of all, they were nearly broke. Their combined net worth stood at twelve dollars and thirty-eight cents.

Shortly after noon Todd looked out one of the small dirty windows and noted no one was presently at The Howling Beagle. His frustration and hunger prompted a decision. "Cory, I'm going up to the bar and bum something to eat from April. At least she should be willing to give some of our venison back to us." Cory failed to see any humor in Todd's comment.

April was smoking a joint and sipping a warm glass of beer when Cory arrived. His plea for food was accepted. As the owner was packing some left over 'burgers, fries and slices of pizza in a small box, Todd brought April up to date on what had happened to Cory and himself since his hasty evacuation from April's bedroom last Friday. April was visibly upset upon hearing Todd's tale of woe, not so much because she felt sorry for the Welchek's, but feared the authorities might snoop around and discover the various illegal aspects of what really went on inside The Howling Beagle.

Todd bought a six pack of beer and was about to head back to the dreary cabin when the sound of a vehicle caused him to quickly peek out a rain streaked front window. "Whew!", he exclaimed. "For a minute there I thought it might be the cops. It looks like a couple of tourists. Big new Buick and two guys all decked out in suits. They're probably lost and looking for directions."

The door swung open and the newcomers hesitated briefly to allow their eyes to adjust to the dim light inside the bar. The one with a pock marked face had a question. "Can either of you tell me where we can find the Welchek brothers?"

Chapter Eight: The Noose Tightens

Part One: "Stake Outs"

Special Agents Oaks and McQuarie wasted no time in forming a plan of action and putting it into motion. Sheriff Bill Ostermeir called his counterpart in Menominee County, Sheriff Ted Humbolt, and devised a plan to monitor the pay phone in the city of Menominee from where the calls to the Welchek brothers originated. Sheriff Humbolt, in turn, met with the Chief of Police for Menominee city. The chief instructed one of his officers to install a hidden video camera trained on the public phone that was being used to call the Welchek's. Hopefully, the identity of the caller or callers could be determined. Eyebrows were raised back in Newberry when it was learned the phone, which was now under surveillance, was less than a block from a small meat packing facility.

Two of Bill Ostermier's deputies were assigned the task of checking on the identity of all the person's who's phone numbers appeared on the Welchek's phone records. The cell phone number was quickly traced to the office of Senator Randolph Redman, but it was but one of four such phones used by the senator's office staff.

During the next several days additional progress was made in building a watertight case against the Welchek's.

Ballistic tests on the .223 casings confirmed all five had been fired from the weapon owned by the two brothers.

DNA testing proved the dried blood discovered by Hap Larson near the "deer remains dump" was that of Officer Brian Matson.

Upon checking as to whom owned the old farm on Highway 77, the mystery deepened. The tax bills were being paid through a blind trust in Washington D.C.! The trust was named, "Friends of the Environment", and the address was a post office box number. Discovering who specifically owned the property, and also might be involved in the illegal activities that had transpired there, would be a major challenge facing the investigators. It would take additional time to follow that trail to its source.

An attempt was made to locate a bank where Cory and/or Todd Welchek had an account. No banking records of any kind had been located in their home when the authorities searched it, nor did they discover a checkbook. None of the local banks had any records of the Welchek's ever having an account of any kind. Personnel at the phone and electric companies indicated the brothers paid their monthly bills with postal or bank money orders. It appeared the Welchek's marijuana and venison operation was "strictly a cash deal".

But all in all, it was a beginning. Still, many puzzling mysteries remained. Who were the real brains of the illegal operations? Who else was involved in the poaching? How many other basements were concealing pot gardens, or might conceal labs producing other illegal drugs? Were there any "middlemen" distributing the drugs and venison? How, when and where was it being transported? And at the moment, the biggest question……where were the Welchek brothers hiding?

For several moments after the stranger asked for information about the whereabouts of the Welchek brothers, the inside of The Howling Beagle became as quiet as a tomb. Todd looked at April and April looked at Todd, neither knowing what to say or who the two men were that had asked the question. Todd swallowed hard and found his voice.

"Well, hey,...we ain't seen neither one for a few days now. It was sometime last week when they last stopped in for a beer, wasn't it April? April was grinding out her reefer on the floor and simply nodded her head in agreement to Todd's question. "You might try looking for them at their house. It's the first driveway south of here. Take a left off the main road. Their name is on a mailbox." Todd's hands were trembling and a knot was forming in his stomach.

The second man spoke. "We already tried their place. The whole house, garage and some other old building out back are all surrounded with yellow crime scene tape." What the hell are the cops after them for? Did they murder somebody or what?" Both men chuckled at the joke, not knowing how well they had assessed the situation.

Todd could feel his knees getting weak. "Boy I'm not sure. I live on the other side of the lake. I don't go out much and I haven't heard a thing. Was there a black Ford pickup by their house?"

The one with the pock marked face replied. "Nope, no vehicle of any type,...except an old tractor that didn't look like it had been used for half a century. Where else do they hang out? And by the way, if you live on the other side of the lake, how did you get here? Our car is the only one in the parking lot."

Todd looked at April again, wishing she would take over the conversation. April was chewing gum and filing her nails. "I came by boat. I got a boat down at the beach. You guys are asking the wrong person, I really don't know the Welchek's too good. I've seen them a couple of times here and there,...but I got no idea about their habits. Maybe the cops caught 'um doin' something. Maybe they're in the cooler someplace."

The two men paused and looked at each other, and Todd's sixth sense told him the strangers weren't buying his story. The knot in his stomach continued to grow. "O.K. thanks anyway. We'll ask around someplace else. It's real important that we find them. There's something important we have to give them."

With that the two mystery men turned and left the building. Todd breathed a sigh of relief and then moved to a front window and watched the strangers get into their car and drive off. "Now who in hell do you think those two were April? Todd took a cigarette from his dirty shirt pocket and lit it with trembling hands. "Didn't strike me as being cops. At first I thought maybe they was. And why in hell are they looking for me and Cory? And what is it they want to give us? I never saw either one of 'um before."

"Maybe they heard you two sell something they want. They looked the type. They certainly weren't from around here. Nobody in these parts dresses like that or drives a car like they were driving. Beats me who they might be." April was very happy she wasn't the one they were looking for, unless they wanted something expensive she could provide for them in her bedroom.

"Thanks for the grub,......sweetheart. I gotta go tell Cory about those two guys lookin' for us. Something's fishy about those two. A couple of mean asses if you ask me." April didn't answer or comment and Todd took his box of food and ran through the rain to the old cabin by the lake.

The driver of the dark brown Buick Park Avenue pulled over to the side of the road as soon as The Howling Beagle disappeared from sight in the rear view mirror. The two men conversed for several minutes while looking at two photographs that had been supplied to them by Corbet O'Keefe. The one named Billy got out of the car, opened the trunk and took out a plastic poncho and a gun case. He quickly donned the poncho and then removed a sawed off semi automatic shotgun from the case, slipped five rounds of twelve gauge double "0" buckshot into the magazine, levered one shell into the chamber, closed the trunk and slipped into the woods. Tony, the driver of the vehicle, pulled away and disappeared around a curve.

Part Two: "Bang, Bang, You're Dead"

Billy Kerletti had made several dozen "hits" in his long distinguished career serving "The Mob", but never had he been thrust into quite this type of environment before. Usually, all he and his accomplish had to do was drive by someone walking on a sidewalk and pepper them with buckshot or machine gun bullets. Another simple hit was to blow away a victim while they were relaxing on a park bench or perhaps while they were dining in a secluded booth of a dimly lit restaurant. One of the most satisfying hits was to use a high powered rifle with a scope and pop somebody when they stepped out of their house. An extra added thrill often accompanied a hit like that if the guy's wife and kids were there to see the guy get smacked. The most strenuous effort might include busting down a door and splitting someone's head open with a baseball bat. But attempting to navigate a tangled wooded area in a soaking rain in order to get in range for a hit was an entirely new experience. But the pay was good and this assignment would soon be successfully completed. How smart could a couple of north wood's hicks be anyway?

Todd's hurried tale describing his barroom encounter with two strangers immediately ignited Cory's fear and anger. And while pacing the floor of the small, cold, damp cabin, Cory characteristically vented his deepest feelings.

"Christ sakes, Todd, why the hell did ya have to go up to the bar anyway? "I suppose you were going to try getting a free lay out of April! DAMN! What did ya tell those two guys? Are you sure they wasn't cops, or some kind of Federal Agents,……or whatever? Now what we gonna do? We can't keep running and hiding out in vacant cabins forever!" Cory wasn't very good at making sensible choices.

"God damn it Cory,…don't piss and moan at me. I went to the bar to get us some food. I was so hungry I could have eaten the asshole out of a skunk! At least I did something more than sulk and whine, like you've been doing lately. Remember, you're the stupid asshole that killed the warden. We should have just laid low till he left the farm and then cleared out and told Redman and whoever the rest of his pals are to shove the whole operation up their ass. I knew sooner or later we'd be the ones to get our balls in a noose."

Cory sat down in a rickety chair and held his head in his hands. Todd's furious rebuttal had deflated him somewhat and his anger towards his brother changed to feeling sorry for himself,…and his brother. "It's that Larson asshole who really screwed us up. He's the one to blame. If you'd have let me have my way, he'd be out in the swamp next to that damn snoopy warden and our troubles would never had started. But no,……you thought he was harmless. Well, what do you think now,…brother dear?"

Within several minutes Bill reached the shore of Manistique Lake. He turned left and eased his way along the heavily wooded shore line for another few minutes until he was able to see The Howling Beagle and a tiny run down cabin near the shoreline. He remained hidden behind a bushy cedar tree, a scant thirty yards from the buildings, and watched the grounds for another several minutes. All was quiet except for the incessant sound of rain falling and a low moaning of the wind through the branches of the trees. He was about to slip out of the shelter of the forest and make a dash for the bar where he and Tony had identified one of their intended victims. Just then the door of the small cabin opened.

Todd Welchek appeared and quickly walked a few feet from the cabin, unzipped his pants and turned to urinate on the grass. Bill "The Bruiser" Kerletti calmly raised his twelve-gauge shotgun, centered the bead on Todd's back, and squeezed the trigger.

The impact of twelve lead balls, each being the diameter of a .30 caliber bullet, struck with awesome and deadly power. Todd's lifeless body was propelled forward, his right hand still clutching his penis, and crumpled in a heap on the muddy, rain drenched ground. The hit man, not realizing his second contracted victim was inside the cabin, slowly moved forward to make sure his shot had completed it's task. For a man of his skill and experience, it was a foolhardy move.

At the sound of the shotgun's blast, Cory leaped to his feet and grabbed the 9-mm pistol he had taken from Deputy Nordahl. He peeked through a corner of the dust-covered window next to the cabin door. What he saw made his blood run cold. His brother's body, oozing blood, was sprawled on the ground in front of the cabin. A husky looking man dressed in a green plastic poncho and carrying a sawed off shotgun was heading towards the cabin.

Cory's mind raced! What the hell was happening? Am I having a nightmare? The reality of the moment brought his mind back into focus and his instinct for survival took control. Cory waited until the unknown gunman had stopped over his brother's still form, then quickly aimed the pistol at the man's head and fired right through the dirty window!

Cory's aim was perfect. The bullet struck the mystery assailant just in front of his right ear and exited just behind his left ear. Bill "The Bruiser" Kerletti was dead before his body toppled and fell on top of Todd Welchek. The Mob had lost one of their finest. And Cory had lost his only close kin.

Meanwhile, in The Howling Beagle, April also heard the shotgun blast. Not knowing from which direction the sound had come, she quickly went from window to window on all four walls of the bar looking for who had fired a gun. She was mystified as to why someone would be shooting so close to her place of business on a rainy Tuesday afternoon in May, when no hunting seasons were open. Looking out a window facing the lake, her unspoken questions were answered.

Her first view was of a man wearing a green rain poncho walking towards her lakeside cabin holding some sort of firearm.

Next she saw the body of someone sprawled on the ground just outside the cabin door. When the man with the gun reached the prostrate form of the person on the ground, a burst of broken glass erupted from the cabin window, immediately followed by a muffled gunshot. The man in the poncho jerked violently, as a small cloud of material exploded from the side of his head, and then he fell on top of the man sprawled in front of the cabin. But there was more action to follow.

Cory grabbed his coat and hat and burst from the cabin like the very Devil was chasing him. At first April wasn't sure who it was, but as the fleeing individual ran towards her bar, she recognized him to be Cory Welchek. Cory ran straight to April's red Jeep Cherokee. He jerked open the door, and quickly looked to see if the key was in the ignition. April knew it was, as like most folks who lived in the U.P. she never removed it. Cory jumped behind the wheel, slammed the car's door, started the engine and spun the rear wheels as he roared around the bar and turned left unto Highway H-33.

For several minutes April stared off into space, her mind churning in total disbelief as to what she had witnessed. Then moving quickly she picked up her phone and dialed "911".

Within forty-five minutes there were nearly as many vehicles in The Howling Beagle's parking lot as would normally be parked there on a Friday night. But none had brought paying customers to April Ravovich's place of business. An accounting of who had been summoned by April's frantic call to 911 included two squad cars from the Luce County Sheriff's office, a non-descript Plymouth sedan bearing Federal Department of Justice license plates, one police cruiser owned by the State Highway Patrol, two ambulances, one fire truck and a search and rescue team from Manistique.

Sheriff Bill Ostermeir and Deputy Jim Pearson had arrived first. After viewing the two corpses next to the cabin by the lake, the sheriff had questioned the owner of The Howling Beagle. April stated that Todd and Cory Welchek had suddenly entered her bar, threatened her with a gun, and demanded food and money. She described them as being very nervous and very dirty looking, as though they had been living out in the woods somewhere.

Her version of what happened continued by claiming two male strangers drove up in a large brown sedan and entered the bar while she was preparing a box of leftover food for the Welchek's. The four then went outside and walked to the cabin by the lake. They all entered the cabin and remained inside for about five minutes. Then one of the strangers returned to his car, and drove off.

April then stated that suddenly Todd and the remaining stranger came out of the cabin and appeared to be having some sort of a violent argument. The stranger pulled a gun out from under his rain poncho, causing Todd to turn and run, but the man shot him in the back at point blank range. Then another shot was fired from inside the cabin and the man who had just shot Todd fell on top of him.

At that point Cory Welchek ran out of the cottage, took April's Jeep and left, turning north on H-33.

Sheriff Ostermeir asked several more questions about the stranger who had driven off prior to the shootout, while Deputy Pearson finished recording April's testimony in his spiral notebook.

It was nearly dark before the authorities finished additional investigations in and around the cabin, in the bar itself, as well as asking April to retell her version of what had happened several more times. The two bodies were loaded in the ambulances and sent to the morgue for further study by the coroner. And last but not least, the entire area was sealed off with more yellow plastic crime scene tape.

The Howling Beagle would be closed to the public for several days.

Part Three: "Twists and Turns"

After dropping off his partner, Tony "The Enforcer" Ramonni drove north on H-33 for several miles pulled over to the side of the road and pretended to be looking at a road map. His efforts were not necessary, as not one single vehicle passed his location during his forty five-minute wait.

Looking at his watch for the tenth time, he noted the agreed upon time had elapsed. Turning his car around he hurried back to The Howling Beagle to pick up Bill Kerletti, who by this time would have completed his hit on one of the Welchek brothers. The two had also agreed that should the sleazy looking blond bartender be a witness to the hit, she too would be eliminated.

Tony had almost reached his destination when a red Jeep Cherokee came streaking down the highway towards him. Tony wondered why the driver was in such a hurry.

Upon reaching The Howling Beagle, Tony expected his companion would quickly appear, jump in the car and report that half of their mission had been completed. But all seemed quiet at the bar. Tony parked his Buick just off the shoulder of the highway and kept looking at the bar, expecting Bill to appear at any second. But then, through one of the front windows, he saw someone moving around in the bar. It was the blond bartender, and she was talking to someone on a cordless phone. A warning signal flashed through Tony's mind. Something was wrong!

Easing his vehicle forward slightly, Tony was able to see past the building that housed the bar. Perhaps Bill was standing in the covered entryway out of the rain and hadn't seen or heard his partner arrive. Beyond the Howling Beagle he could see a small cabin nestled at the shore of a large lake. He remembered seeing the cabin when he and Bill had entered the bar an hour earlier. But this time his view also included what appeared to be two bodies; one sprawled on top of another, lying in front of the building. And one was wearing a green rain poncho!

Tony stepped on the accelerator and sped south on H-33.

Senator Redman had been a busy man the past few days. Although he detected a few cracks beginning to appear in his world, he was confident he had enough mortar and glue to make the necessary repairs, although as he put it, "things aren't going to be normal for a few weeks, possibly a few months." He never even considered the possibility of "never again".

Using pay phones and several different cell phones, the senator was forced to make a considerable number of calls. His first call was to an extremely important cog in his wheel of illegal operations that lived in Menominee, Michigan. Next, there were calls to Stephenson, Sagola, Paulding, Steuben, Republic, McLoads Corner and Bessemer, all Michigan communities. Then came calls to the network in Wisconsin. Mountain, Alvin, Sayner, Park Falls, Cable, Mellen and Saxon. The message was the same; "Shut down all operations until further notice. We've got a problem!"

The only variation in the message was the one heard by his contact in Menominee. The order declared; "Run the route one more time and pick up any merchandise presently stored at your normal pick up points. Deliver the goods to the usual destination. But skip the old farm in Michigan on Highway 77."

Greed can often contribute to ones downfall.

Two days after the surveillance camera was installed to monitor the pay phone in Menominee, the tape was removed and examined. Although a number of persons had been photographed using the phone, the tape clearly identified one individual who spent nearly an hour making calls on one occasion and two additional fifteen minute conversations, all within a five hour period. The police recognized the caller as Ron Waltman, owner of "North Woods Meats", a small meat processing and distribution plant less than a block from the public phone.

Special Agent McQuarie was notified of the findings and four plain clothed Michigan Conservation Officers manning unmarked State Patrol vehicles, plus two Federal Wildlife Officers who had just arrived to aid in the poaching investigations, were staked out at the plant in pairs on four hours shifts. Their orders were to keep a twenty four-hour watch on the processing plant and note any suspicious activity. It was further ordered that should any refrigerated trucks belonging to North Woods Meats leave the city of Menominee, the vehicle should be followed.

On Thursday, a large refrigerated truck, bearing no markings of any kind, exited North Woods Meats and left Menominee headed northwest into Wisconsin. A non-descript maroon sedan with two occupants inside began following the truck at a safe distance.

Wednesday morning dawned gray and dreary, but the rain had finally ended. Small breaks in the clouds to the west promised the sun would probably be making an appearance shortly. By nine thirty the skies had cleared, and a cool, dry northwest breeze began drying the surface moisture left over from the nearly twenty-four hours of rain that had fallen on Tuesday and into early Wednesday morning.

Charles called Hap from his motel room shortly after seven a.m. and invited his cousin and Edna to join the Baldwin's for breakfast at The Pub and Grub in Newberry. By eight thirty the Larson's and the Baldwin's were fairly well stuffed with pancakes, bacon, eggs, hash browns, toast, coffee and orange juice. As Hap put it, "somehow I jist lost my appetite." Edna added, "The food was almost as good as my cooking". It was Edna's way of complimenting a fine meal. The remainder of the day loomed ahead.

"Hey", began Hap, "what time you two gotta meet Audrey ta make an offer on that property at Manistique Lake?"

"Our appointment is at one thirty this afternoon,…isn't it Shirley?" Charles' wife nodded in the affirmative. "Why do you ask Hap?"

"Well seein' as we're all retired old farts, with nothin' really to do,…except what we wanna do,…let's all take a little sight seein' trip this mornin'. It' won't take too long, and I'll git ya back ta the real estate office on time fer yer meetin' with Audrey."

"Sight seeing? What U.P. treasure do you want to show us now?"

"Jist up Highway 123 apiece is the Upper Falls of the Tahquamenon River. You know,…the river that runs through me an' Edna's place. She's a dandy! Biggest waterfall east of the Mississippi,…except Niagara Falls. It's one of the premiere attractions in the U.P. Ya gotta see it to believe it Charles! Ain't that right Edna?"

Edna enthusiastically agreed with her husband, and several minutes latter the four seniors were headed north on 123 for a sight seeing adventure. Looking forward through the window of the topper was a black Labrador Retriever with a wagging tail.

Cory Welchek's rapid exodus from The Howling Beagle came to a temporary halt on an old two rut logging road several miles north of where he had stolen April's Jeep. His only reason for stopping at his present location was to organize his thoughts and decide what he should do next. He remembered that Todd had been the one who usually did most of the planning. But now Todd was gone. Now he was all alone. Now all decisions were his to make! And decision making had never been one of Cory's strong points.

Cory sat behind the wheel and simply stared out the windshield for nearly a half-hour. He played and replayed the seemingly unbelievable chain of events that had happened so suddenly, and ended so quickly, back at the little cabin. Cory wanted to become angry, he always felt good when he became angry. But in his present emotional state he simply felt numb. For the moment at least, anger was not an emotion he was able to generate.

Finally, his mind began to form a plan of action. The first thing he had to do, and do quickly, was get rid of April's red Jeep! By now she had surely called the sheriff reporting the theft, and there were few red Jeeps in the area. And Cory was equally sure April had also reported the shootout. But even as his mind raced, Cory did not yet realize the seriousness of his situation and the depth of his dilemma. But he did realize that even where he was now located in a somewhat remote area on an old road that rarely saw a vehicle, a search plane could easily spot a red Jeep. Next, he had to risk returning to his home and retrieve several items of vast importance. After that he'd head for another hide out, and he had just the perfect spot in mind. From there he'd make final plans to carry out the promise he made to himself and his now departed brother. Cory Welchek would gain great pleasure extracting revenge from Mr. Eric Sever Larson!

Special Agents Oaks and McQuarie made an appointment and met with Senator Redman at his office in Escanaba. The main subject of discussion was centered on a cell phone number registered to the senator's office. The agents were interested in finding out who might be responsible for sending or receiving phone messages from two brothers named Welchek, who lived near Curtis, Michigan.

Senator Redman quickly explained he recently discovered that particular phone had been misplaced or stolen by person or persons unknown. When he discovered the phone was missing, but he was still receiving bills from the provider, he had ordered his personal secretary to cancel the contract.

However, the senator was good enough to give the agents a name of a former employee who had worked for the senator, but had been fired for drinking on the job, plus was suspected of also using drugs. The senator suggested it might be that disgruntled former employee who had taken the phone and was somehow connected with the Welchek brothers,……whoever they were.

The four sightseers reached the parking area where persons coming to view the Upper Falls of the mighty Tahquamenon River parked their vehicles and began the quarter mile walk to the falls. Even at that distance the distinct roar of falling water could faintly be heard.

The well maintained and well used trail meandered through a magnificent mature forest of beech, maple, elm, basswood, yellow birch and a smattering of other hardwood species. Spring flowers, such as trillium, marsh marigolds, woods violets and arbutus added mingled colors and scents to the beautiful spring setting. Mother Nature had provided a wonderful introduction to the spectacle that lay ahead.

Later, heading back to Newberry in Hap's truck. Charles and Shirley couldn't stop talking about how surprised they were to see such a beautiful and monstrous waterfall in Upper Michigan. "It's every bit as breathtaking as the American Falls at Niagara. It was awesome!" Shirley had summed up the experience for everyone.

By two fifteen the Baldwin's had made an offer on the property at Manistique Lake. Audrey then called the owner and received verbal acceptance of the offer. After the paperwork had been signed, and all the "i's" dotted and "t's" crossed, Charles wrote a check containing six figures. The deal was completed.

As soon as the required forms were sent to and recorded by the proper governmental agencies, the Baldwin's would be official taxpayers of Luce County, Michigan!

Many months of fun and relaxation for the Larson's and the Baldwin's loomed ahead!

Chapter Nine: Traveling a Twisting Trail

Part One: "Country Road, Take Me Home"

For Federal Wildlife Officers, Carl Noone and Ralph Rossi, their three-day adventure following a refrigerated truck across parts of two states was without a doubt the longest "tailing assignment" either officer had ever experienced. The twisting trail they covered took them through some of the mid-west's most magnificent rural areas, all of which neither officer had ever visited.

The "tailing" of the refrigerated truck was fairly simple for the two veteran Federal Officers. However, when the driver of the truck and his assistant stopped to either unload or load cargo, generally it was impossible for the officers to park in a location to view exactly which was taking place nor identify what was being loaded or unloaded. The addresses of the places where the truck stopped were recorded in a notebook, as well as on videotape. Some stops took place at grocery stores, or other places of business, in small towns or villages. Other times the truck would stop at restaurants or private residences. Some stops were made at locations removed from the main highways on secondary roads, making it impossible for the tailing officers to see where the truck had stopped. But each day information on their whereabouts, and a brief verbal account of what was taking place, was phoned to the Luce County Sheriff's Office.

At the end of each day the occupants of the truck would stop for the night at a cheap motel. The tailing officers simply slept in their car, each taking a four-hour watch while the other curled up in the rear seat and tried to get some sleep. It was a boring assignment, but a necessary one. The groundwork was being completed for a much larger investigation, once all the stopping points along the route were established as well as the truck's final destination. The evil web of mystery was beginning to unravel.

Cory Welchek was successful in getting in a few hours of much needed sleep in the rear of April Ravovich's Jeep, after mentally completing plans for his next course of action. It was nearing midnight when he left his wooded retreat and turned the red Jeep south on H-33. As he approached The Howling Beagle he turned off the headlights, allowed his eyes to adjust to the night's blackness, and slowly maneuvered the vehicle behind the bar. He quietly eased the car door closed, and quickly headed south on foot. Cory had decided to return April's Jeep, as his tiny conscience had bothered him for stealing something from someone who had been somewhat of a friend. And friends were something the Welchek brothers had in very small numbers.

The rain had finally stopped, but the sky was still solidly overcast, making travel by foot without the aid of a flashlight very difficult. Upon reaching the driveway leading to his home, Cory turned left unto familiar territory. As he navigated the quarter mile long driveway, his memory recalled several significant links with the past.

He recalled the crushing memory of his father's disappearance when he and his brother Todd were in their early teens. Mr. Welchek drove out of the yard one morning and never returned. Nor was he ever heard from again! From then on Cory and Todd lived with their mother, up until she died nearly fifteen years earlier. The brothers inherited the property, debt free, which allowed them to live a very frugal life style.

Nine years ago, while getting drunk one Friday evening at The Howling Beagle, Todd and Cory happened to meet Senator Redman. That was several years before April Ravovich purchased the property. The senator was looking for someone to replace a local poacher who had been working in the senator's complex illegal operation. The poacher's carelessness had resulted in a fatal self-inflicted gunshot wound during one of his nighttime poaching sessions. The Welchek brothers took his place and quickly became the most efficient deer poachers among the more than thirty in the senator's employ.

Cory's mind switched gears and he resumed thinking about why he had risked returning to the only home he had ever known. And after tonight, he would never see his home again. He quickly began putting phase two of his present plan into action.

Making his way through the crime scene tape, Cory entered his home and flipped on a light in the kitchen. From a closet in the hall he removed a large canvas backpack, called a Duluth Pack, returned to the kitchen and partially filled the pack with canned goods. Next he went into the bathroom and took a quick shower, gathered up some personal items and changed his filthy clothing for some clean ones.

Looking in the bathroom mirror, Cory saw someone staring back at him that at first he did not recognize. The man had a week's growth of heavy beard and a mustache. His overly long stringy hair was twisted and matted. The red rimmed eyes looked tired and bloodshot, and the wrinkles around the mouth and eyes were much deeper than he had remembered. The brow was imbedded with furrows, which his mother once called "worry lines". Cory had never sported a beard or mustache, but considering the present set of circumstances, growing a crop of hair on his face sounded like a good idea. To complete his new facial appearance, he used a pair of scissors and chopped off all the hair on his head. Then after lathering the stubble he shaved his head bald.

From his bedroom he removed additional socks, pants, shirts, a wool blanket, and a few other assorted items which were placed in the pack with the canned goods.

Cory looked in another closet where the brothers had stored their small collection of firearms and ammunition, but as expected, the police had removed them. A quadrangle map of Luce County, a large hunting knife, a compass and a flashlight were added to the store of supplies in the pack.

Satisfied he had secured everything he would need during the next phase of his plan; Cory turned out the lights, exited the house and walked to the garage.

Taking a shovel from a barrel filled with assorted tools, he began to dig in a corner of the garage's dirt floor. A few inches under the surface of the floor his shovel struck a metal object. Cory quickly removed a military ammunition box and opened the watertight cover. The beam of his flashlight revealed a small notebook and a stack of paper currency; both secured with rubber bands. He stuffed the notebook in his backpack and shoved the wad of bills into a pocket of his pants.

Before leaving the garage he located a five-gallon container of gasoline. Cory sprinkled a small amount of the liquid on each interior wall of the garage, and ignited it. The flames licked hungrily at the dry lumber and spread quickly. Next, he circled his home and splashed gasoline on the exterior walls all around the house. After tossing the empty red plastic container through the open door of the house, Cory struck a match and ignited the volatile fluid.

With a resounding "whoosh", the flames quickly followed the trail of gasoline around the perimeter of the building, and within minutes both the house and the garage were engulfed in flames. Cory walked to the edge of the woods that surrounded his home, looked back at the roaring inferno, blew a kiss at the blazing buildings, and vanished into the darkened forest.

Phase two of his plans had been completed.

As Tony Ramonni sped south on H-33 towards U.S. Highway 2, his mind asked many questions, but gave few answers in return. He turned east on 2 and drove until he found a small motel overlooking Lake Michigan near the little community of Epoufette. He rented a room, then drove to a convenience store where he filled up with gas, bought several pre-made sandwiches, some potato chips, and a bottle of scotch.

Returning to his small motel room, he closed the window blinds, locked the door, and poured himself a glass of liquor. As he munched his cold and somewhat tasteless dinner his mind tried to imagine what had gone wrong. From the brief view of the scene he had witnessed near the small cabin next to the bar where he and Billy had found one of their contracted victims, Tony was sure one of the bodies had been that of his partner. But that was all he was sure of.

Who was the second person? Hopefully it was the Welchek brother he and Billy had identified in the bar. Were both Billy and the second person dead, or were they simply badly wounded? How much had the blond bartender been able to tell the authorities? Had she been able to give a good description of the car he was driving? What should he do next? All-important questions, but for the moment, none had answers.

By nine p.m. the bottle of scotch was three quarters empty. Tony turned out the light in his motel room and wearily fell into bed. As the room began to spin, just before he became sick to his stomach, he realized he still had to call his boss. But that would have to wait until morning.

Federal Marshalls in Washington D.C. were making some progress in tracing the "paper trail" in an attempt to discover, "who owns and pays the taxes on the old farm property on Michigan Highway 77?" Strangely, the money, which was sent to Luce County to pay the property tax bill each year, arrived in the form of a money order. And for the past fourteen years each money order had been drawn on a different bank or post office!

The bills for the farm's electricity and propane fuel were likewise sent to the same address, as were the property tax bills. They too were paid with bank or postal money orders.

Efforts to locate an organization called "Friends of the Environment" had so far failed. The search continued.

Part Two: "Roads to Nowhere"

Sheriff Ostermeir, plus most other members of the investigative unit were frustrated. The events that had recently taken place at The Howling Beagle created more questions than they answered. As Deputy Nordahl put it, "now we've got more puzzle pieces than ever, and trying to find pieces that fit are already like looking for the proverbial needle in a haystack."

The shootout at The Howling Beagle had solved one mystery. The question, "where WERE the Welchek brothers?", had been answered. Now the question was, "where IS Cory Welchek?" But additional questions needed answers. The already muddied waters of the investigations had become even more clouded.

The corpse with the green rain poncho and the sawed off shotgun had been identified. Fingerprints taken from the dead man indicated he was William Vito Kerletti, a long time criminal who had served time in several penal institutions. His life of crime began at age nine in the streets of Detroit. Stealing hubcaps had escalated to breaking into vending machines, then car theft, robbing a savings and loan, and finally landing a job as an "enforcer" and hit man with the nationally syndicated "The Mob, Detroit Branch". Since then he had been sought as a prime suspect in numerous mob related executions, but so far the police had been unable to obtain enough evidence against him to warrant an indictment by a Grand Jury.

It was evident Billy Kerletti had shot Todd Welchek. But why? Someone must have given the order, or "put out a contract", as the current vocabulary labeled the procedure. But who? The shotgun, a Browning A-5 semi-automatic twelve gauge, had been stolen from a sporting goods store in Detroit nearly five years earlier. A simple check of its serial number proved that point, which came as no surprise. After all, criminals don't buy guns, they steal them. So much for any help from the much heralded "Federal Gun Registration" efforts.

It was also very evident April Ravovich had lied about Todd being "shot in the back at point blank range." Yes, he had been shot in the back, but certainly not at point blank range. The distance between the buckshot pellets in his back was much too far apart to have been fired at point blank range. And only eight pellets had actually struck the target. Four pellets had missed their intended victim and were found imbedded in the side of the cabin. This would suggest the shot that killed Todd Welchek had been made from a distance of at least twenty or thirty yards. Why did Ms Ravovich lie?

Who was the fourth person? The one April indicated had left the cabin prior to the shooting and, as she put it, "driven off". Her description of the vehicle was also very vague. All she could remember was the color being "kinda dark brown". Sheriff Ostermeir was convinced April's account of the incident was far from the truth. Was she somehow involved in the murders?

More mysteries surrounded the disappearance of Cory Welchek,……again! Was he the person who had fired the fatal bullet through Billy Kerletti's skull? What weapon was used? If Cory had been the triggerman, then the gun was probably Deputy Nordahl's missing 9mm Glock. The bullet that had passed through Kerletti's head had yet to be found.

Where had Cory fled with April's Jeep? And why did he return it a few hours later? April stated she did not hear the vehicle when it was returned, nor did she see Cory,…or whoever returned it. Was she lying about this also?

Sheriff Ostermier was still deep in thought as he tapped his pencil on top of his desk when his secretary buzzed his office to inform her boss he had a call on line two.

"Hello Bill. This is Deputy Pearson. I drove into the Welchek property to see if there was any evidence of anyone being around the place since we put it off limits." There was a pause. "Well, somebody was fooling around the property." Another pause. "The house and garage have been burned to the ground!"

Senator Redman was becoming more and more uneasy concerning the ongoing investigations pertaining to the murder of Conservation Officer Matson, the apparent wide spread poaching operation, and the "marijuana farm", as Sheriff Ostermeir referenced it. The arrival of federal agents and federal wildlife officers indicated the local authorities had received re-enforcements of the highest caliber.

Although no longer receiving daily updates from the sheriff's department, from time to time the senator was fed some current information. But one bit of news was being withheld from not only the senator, but from everyone except those directly involved with one particular aspect of the investigation. And that was the "tailing operation" presently underway in Wisconsin and Michigan.

Federal agent Oaks raised a red flag concerning the obvious "over interest" in the case by Senator Randolph Redman. Agent Oaks conferred with Sheriff Ostermeir and convinced him to reduce the amount of pertinent information being relayed to the senator. As Agent Oaks put it, "It's quite unusual for someone so apparently far removed from this type of investigation to be so overly concerned about it's progress."

Coupled with the fact that a cell phone number registered to the senator had turned up on the Welchek's phone records, perhaps someone in the senator's inner circle of assistants or friends were somehow involved in part or all of the aspects of the case.

The individual whom the senator had suggested might be the person who had used the cell phone to communicate with the Welchek's had been located and questioned. The story the investigators received from the senator's former employee was quite different from that given by the senator, concerning the cell phone in question and the reasons why the employee no longer worked for the senator. According to the testimony given by the senator's x-employee, he had become disenchanted with the senator's overall "credibility" and his questionable bookkeeping procedures. The former employee claimed he had not been fired, but had handed in his resignation. The individual was presently working for a nationally known income tax preparation and consulting firm.

After speaking with the senator's former employee Sheriff Ostermeir stated, "Looks like we just opened another whole can of worms."

The cracks in Senator Redman's once secure world where widening.

After burning down his home and garage, Cory Welchek spent the next two days and nights laying low in a remote, thickly wooded area several miles north of where he once lived. He built a shelter out of saplings and boughs, and although the mosquitoes were quite bothersome, the quiet of the forest allowed him to fine-tune his immediate plans.

Foremost, he needed to obtain a vehicle. Next, he would find shelter and seclusion in something better than a crude hut in a balsam thicket. And thirdly, he'd take his good natured time locating the exact location of where Eric Larson lived and finalize a plan to, as Cory often mumbled to himself, "make that son of a bitch pay dearly for being responsible all the grief and suffering he caused me and my brother!"

Tony Ramonni awoke with a splitting headache. He located a bottle of aspirin among the other basic items in his overnight case and swallowed three of the pain reducing pills. After showering, shaving, and brushing the leftover taste of scotch and vomit from his mouth, he sat on his bed and replayed the events of the previous day.

During his career working for the mob in Detroit, there had been several jobs that had not come off as planned. But this hit, one that originally seemed so simple to complete had become a nightmare. He recalled how he and his former partner, Billy Kerletti, while driving north from Detroit had joked, "this job is gonna be a piece of cake!" And now the cake had crumbled!

Not really wanting to, but knowing he had to, Tony picked up his cell phone and dialed a number in Detroit. The conversation with his immediate boss was considerably less than pleasant. Upon hearing of Billy's death, and the fact only one of the two contracted "hits" had been made, Tony's boss went ballistic!

Tony was forced to listen for several minutes to his boss ranting and raving, and then cringed when he heard his new set of instructions.

"Get your sorry ass back where that other guy lives,…find the son of a bitch,…and fulfill our contract! And don't let yerself get caught before he's shut up for good. We've got big money coming in on this deal and we intend to complete the assignment and collect! If you screw up,……well,…you know what comes next! Now get moving before the coppers catch that dumb asshole and he spills his guts! And don't call me whining again. Yer supposed to be a professional,……act like one!"

Tony checked out of the motel and headed his car west on U.S. 2.

Part Three: "Good Bye's and Hello's"

For all members of the Matson Family, the ordeal created by Brian's murder continued. Final closure was impossible with one of the murderers still on the loose. For the grandparents, Dewey and Betty, the loss was crushing. Grandpa Dewey had been one of the proudest persons on earth when his favorite grandchild pinned on the badge of a conservation warden, following in the footsteps of his grandpa. At Dewey's age, as well as his wife, life offered few pleasures for the two octogenarians, and what had been their biggest pleasure was now resting under a granite monument in the Manistique cemetery.

For Brian's parents, Tom and Beverly, the loss of their only son was likewise devastating. But there was little or nothing they could do to lesson the grief, except allow time to partially heal the deep, festering wound Brian's death had created. Although certain aspects of their required journey to Tom's hometown in Michigan had been pleasant, the time had come for them to return to their home in Florida. A farewell party was planned prior to their departure.

Hap and Edna invited Tom, Beverly, and Tom's parents, Dewey and Betty, to spend a day at the Larson homestead near Newberry for a day of relaxing and feasting upon some of Hap's outdoor cuisine and Edna's deserts. Edna thought it would also be a nice gesture to invite the Baldwin's to attend. Edna reminded Hap that his cousin from Canada, and his wife, would be flying back to their home in Quebec very soon. The couple needed to gather some additional necessary items before returning to their new seasonal residence for the remainder of, as Shirley had put it, "the warm months". A call to the Baldwin's new residence at Manistique Lake resulted in a sincere acceptance of the invitation.

And so it was, on a glorious spring morning, the first of June to be exact, the party commenced.

First to arrive were Charles and Shirley in their, as Charles put it, "brand new used Chevy S-10 SUV." Now that the Baldwin's had become, as Hap put it, "transplanted Yoopers", they had purchased a fairly new vehicle from "Newberry Pre-owned Vehicles". Shirley brought a tossed salad and some fresh baked biscuits to compliment whatever, as Edna put it, "The Outdoor Gourmet" might cook up on his grille.

A half-hour later the delegates from the Matson side of the family arrived and, as Hap put it, "the farewell bash began".

As with all life's pleasant experiences, the day evaporated much too quickly. But everyone genuinely had a wonderful time. The senior Matson's reminisced about, as Dewey and Betty put it, "the good old days", relating numerous events and situations the younger party goers were unaware of.

Sitting on the Larson's deck, overlooking the beautiful Tahquamenon River as it's waters gurgled slowly eastward towards the big lake the Indians called "Gitche Gumee", the entire assembled group, as Edna mentioned to Hap later, "really got to know each other".

The master outdoor chef professionally grilled three different species of fish fillets, using three different recipes, while a massive skillet of potatoes and onions rings browned to perfection. The third entree consisted of a bubbling cast iron kettle filled with home made baked beans, smothered with crisp bacon, brown sugar and molasses. Edna topped off the meal with her specialties, homemade blueberry, raspberry and blackberry pies,......served with mounds of vanilla ice cream. No one was hungry when they pried themselves away from the picnic table!

By four in the afternoon the party began to wind down. Hugs, kisses and handshakes were exchanged between everyone, and then Hap and Edna waved good-bye from their front porch as the visitor's vehicles disappeared down the Larson's driveway.

"Now that was a real nice time, wasn't it Edna? I'm glad I got the idea ta have a party and invite all them folks over ta our house fer a feast."

Edna wrinkled her brow, then smiled and agreed with her husband. "Yes it was! You sure have some nice relatives, dear. I wish my children and grandchildren lived closer. We haven't seen them since our wedding last December. I'm going to give Colleen a call."

Just as Hap and Edna stepped inside their living room the phone rang. Edna picked up the receiver on the second ring.

"Hello." There was a pause. "Oh my goodness, I was just going to call YOU! Makes one believe there might be something to that ESP theory. Oh Colleen, it's so nice to hear your voice,...how are my grandkids?"

Hap went back out on the deck overlooking the river, packed his corn cob pipe full of Bond Street, ignited the bowl and settled into his hammock. "This is going to be a long phone conversation", he muttered to himself.

Edna and her daughter, Colleen, chatted for nearly an hour. It was what Hap would later capsule as "typical women's gab". Upon ending the conversation, Edna hurried to the outside deck, which overlooked the river to tell Hap the wonderful news she had received. Edna was very excited.

"Oh Hap darling", she began, Colleen and the grandkids are coming to stay with us for a few weeks. Isn't that..........." Edna was going to end her sentence with "wonderful?", but she stopped to stare at her husband reclining in his hammock. Hap's eyes were closed and the sound of deep sleep snoring was his reply.

Edna's would have to wait another hour or so to deliver her exciting news.

Chapter Ten: "Visitations"

Part One: "Deceptions"

On the second morning after burning his home and garage, Cory Welchek emerged from his wooded seclusion and began walking north on highway H-33. Shouldering a large packsack and sporting a new facial appearance, he relied on a hunch any locals passing by would not recognize him and assume he was just one of many "summer time wanderers" who often appeared on the highways of the U.P during the summer months. But his luck turned out even better than he expected. The driver of a logging truck stopped and gave him a lift to Newberry.

Two blocks off the main street Cory discovered what he was looking for. At the end of a driveway was parked a rust infested, gray colored Honda sedan with a "For Sale" sign displayed on the windshield. And the price was reasonable. Within fifteen minutes Cory had taken a short "demonstration ride", paid the owner five hundred dollars in cash, and departed.

Before leaving town he made a stop at a mini-market. Cory filled his vehicle with gas, purchased a quantity of food and beer that filled several large bags, plus two newspapers published in the U.P. From there he drove a few miles east of town, turned north on one of the numerous seldom used logging roads, and spent the remainder of the day drinking beer, munching snacks, and reading the papers.

Cory was impressed at how much space the newspapers devoted to the ongoing manhunt for Cory Welchek. The copywriters went into great detail about the mystery surrounding the shoot out at The Howling Beagle, and the inability of the authorities to locate the missing Welchek brother. There were even photos of the man who was being accused of killing Officer Matson and a second individual from Detroit. But what Cory was hoping might be in the paper wasn't. Nothing was mentioned about a man named Eric Larson, or where he lived.

It was nearing two thirty a.m. when Cory returned to Newberry. His first stop was at a public phone booth where he tore a page out of the phone book that included all the local residents named "Larson". Next he drove to a residential area, parked his car on a side street, and with a screwdriver in hand located a parked vehicle that sported a valid Michigan license plate. He quickly removed the plate, returned to his car, and once again left town. Cory's mission had been completed.

After leaving his motel room in Epoufette, Tony Ramonni drove west on U.S. 2, turned north on H-33 and began searching his brain on how he might find the missing Welchek brother. He realized there was a strong possibility the man he was looking for had already slipped out of the area and might be hundreds of miles away. As he slowly drove north, he met two different squad cars. Evidently the police were still looking for the same man he was.

Tony planned on visiting the Welchek's property one more time on a chance the man he sought might have returned home. He realized it was indeed a long shot, but with no leads or information to go on, long shots and hunches were all Tony had to rely on.

When he reached the entrance to the Welchek's driveway, he found it blocked by wooden barriers and an abundance of yellow crime scene tape.

A few minutes later he passed The Howling Beagle. Yet another police car was parked in the parking lot, and one officer could be seen prowling around the small cabin by the lake. Not knowing what to do next, Tony continued north to highway 28, turned west and stopped at a cafe in Newberry for breakfast.

A half dozen people who appeared to be locals were gathered around a table drinking coffee and munching pastry. All conversation ceased as Tony entered the dining area and took a seat at a corner table. Six pairs of eyes scanned the stranger who had just entered the cafe. Satisfied the newcomer was evidently a tourist, the conversation resumed.

After a waitress filled Tony's cup with hot, black coffee and taken his breakfast order, he picked up a newspaper lying on the next table and began scanning the local news columns. Trying to look interested in the paper, Tony tuned his ears to the local gossip-taking place at the other occupied table. The talk was centered on the three murders that had occurred during the past few days and the ongoing investigations. Where Tony lived, murders were a common daily occurrence, to which few persons paid any attention. But in rural areas, like the U.P, murders were rare, and certain to be the main topic for discussion when one occurred. And now citizens of the surrounding area had three murders to talk about!

Tony turned to page four and there was what he was looking for! A recent photo of the man he desperately needed to locate! "Maybe, just maybe", he thought, "my luck is going to change!"

After finishing his breakfast and three cups of coffee, Tony walked to the cash register to pay his bill. The local conversation again ceased. After the waitress gave Tony his change, the stranger asked her a question.

"Say Miss, I just got into town from down state. The newspaper I work for sent me up here to get some first hand information about the murder spree that's hit your neighborhood. What I'm looking for is someone who might be able to give me information that would make a good article for our down state readers. Do you have any suggestions as to who might be able to help me out with some details about the murders and the scope of the investigations?"

The waitress paused as though trying to think of a suitable answer. "Have you talked to the people in the sheriff's office? It's just down the street a few blocks next to the courthouse."

"No, I haven't. But generally all the cops,...er, I mean police,...will tell reporters from out of town are what the local papers have already written. I'd like to talk to a citizen of the community. Someone who knows what's going on. I'll even pay for an interview if I can get some good material for a story."

Now there were six other people in the cafe listening to a conversation!

The waitress looked at the table filled with locals and asked for assistance. "What do you say boys,...can any of you help this gentleman out? I'm SURE you all heard what he had to say."

All six of the men at the table looked at each other as if each was waiting for someone else to say something. Herb Whitney, one of Hap's friends, decided to become the group's spokesman. "Ya mister. I know just the guy you need to talk to. His name is Hap Larson. He's a friend of mine and he knows lot's about what's goin' on. He's the guy who discovered the poaching operation at the old Coskey Farm south of here on 77. He's also the guy who found the body of the game warden who got murdered. Besides that, he got captured by one of the guys who everybody thinks shot the warden, then he escaped and got the sheriff and his boys headed in the right direction. It's quite some story. Old Hap's a real friendly guy. He'll probably be willing to give ya a story."

"Well, thanks for the tip. Where does this friend of yours live?"

"Here,...I'll draw ya a map on this napkin. It's easy to find his place. Ya can't miss it."

Tony left the cafe and rented a room at the "Up North Motel", on the outskirts of Newberry. Ten minutes later he was heading north towards a log home overlooking the Tahquamenon River. Tony's luck had indeed changed!

For federal wardens Carl Noone and Ralph Rossi, their "tailing assignment" ended in Michigan's Lower Peninsula just across the Mackinaw Bridge in Mackinaw City. The refrigerated truck they had deceptively followed for nearly four days ended its journey at the same type of business establishment as where it had started its journey. On the surface, "Mackinaw Meats, Retail and

Wholesale, Inc." appeared to be just another of your basic small meat processing plants.

The officers were able to position themselves in such a manner, which allowed them to zoom in with their video camera and record the entire unloading operation. By rough count it appeared that somewhere in the neighborhood of one hundred or more deer carcasses were transferred from the truck into the processing plant.

Before heading back to the investigation center in Luce County, the wardens noted a sign displayed on the door to the plant's main entrance. Bold red letters proclaimed; "HELP WANTED".

The time had come to plant a "mole" in the establishment known as "Mackinaw Meats, Retail and Wholesale, Inc".

Part Two: "Destinations"

Following the map Herb Whitney had drawn; Tony Ramonni arrived at the Larson's home shortly after ten a.m. The Larson's dogs began barking at the sound of an approaching vehicle, alerting Hap and Edna that someone was going to arrive shortly. Hap and Sadie had already emerged from the house and was standing on the front deck before Tony's car came to a stop.

Smiling, and attempting to look and act like a reporter, Tony began his deception. "Hello! I'm looking for a gentleman named Hap Larson. Could that be you, sir?"

"Yep,…I'm him. What can I do fer ya?" Edna appeared in the doorway behind her husband.

Tony reached the steps leading to the deck, stretched out his right hand in greeting, and answered Hap's inquiry. "I'm Harold Scofield from down state. I'm a reporter for a newspaper and I'm up north here looking for a story. You know how we newspaper hounds are always looking for a story". Tony ended his introduction with a chuckle.

Hap hesitated briefly before taking Tony's outstretched hand and gave it a firm, but short shake. The veteran woodsman continued a visual inspection of his visitor with his usual conservative suspicion. "What kinda story ya lookin' fer, and how did ya find where I live? responded Hap.

"Well,...I was having breakfast in a little cafe in Newberry and I inquired of my waitress if she might know anyone locally who could give me some information about the illegal poaching and the seemingly related murders that are being investigated in this area. The downstate press has been getting bits and pieces of information, but not enough hard facts to produce a comprehensive story. So my boss sent me up here to see if I could dig up enough information to produce a worthwhile story. A friend of yours who was also in the cafe, a Herb Whitney, volunteered your name as someone who might be willing to fill me in on the entire situation". Tony kept smiling.

"What paper do ya work for?", asked Hap, keeping his visitor on the defensive and allowing him more time to evaluate the newcomer's intentions.

"Oh it's one of the smaller papers in Detroit. You probably never heard of it." answered Tony, not expecting to be grilled so professionally by what looked to be just some ordinary country hick.

"Try me. Ya might be surprised what I've heard of", Hap answered, his voice coated in ice and his eyes narrowing to slits.

"Ah,...it's the Detroit Morning Star. Like I said,...a fairly small paper. But our management is very progressive minded and our circulation is growing with leaps and bounds. And getting a good story about the mysteries surrounding the situation up here would make us look as good as the big well-known papers." Tony was starting to beg.

"Fer bein' from a small newspaper, they sure gave ya a fancy car ta drive around in. Looks like a brand spankin' new Buick Park Avenue ta me." Hap's gaze kept boring into Tony's face.

"Oh,...no,...that's not a company car,...it's my personal vehicle. It's the first expensive car I ever bought. The payments are terrible, but what to heck,...we only go around once in this old world. The paper pays me mileage, so I make enough to pay for my gas". Tony laughed nervously and hoped his explanation would be acceptable.

"Have ya talked to our sheriff about what's goin' on? He'd be better able to tell ya the facts than I could." Hap really didn't like reporters, and this stranger certainly didn't look or sound like any reporter Hap had ever known. And just last year, Hap had rubbed elbows with lots of reporters!

"No,...no, I haven't talked to the sheriff's department yet. Usually the authorities only give out a very watered down version anyway. I understand,...after talking to your friend, Herb,...that you have been one of what might be called,...stars,...in the investigations. Mr. Whitney gave me a brief outline of your involvement as being the person who discovered the poaching operation and also responsible for locating the body of the slain game warden. Herb said you'd be a good person to talk to".

Edna couldn't remain silent any longer. "Hap, why don't you invite our visitor inside and tell him about your experiences. I could tell him about mine too. This young man has come a long ways to get a story." Edna referred to anyone under fifty as "young". "We've nothing planned this morning. Colleen and the children aren't arriving in Sault Ste. Marie until six this evening."

Hap hitched up his pants and jerked his thumb in the direction of their front door and said, "Ah what the heck,...come on in. We might as well tell what we know one more time." Hap never surrendered without a fight.

For the next hour Hap and Edna fielded questions from the reporter who claimed to represent the Detroit Morning Star, never suspecting that none of what they said would ever appear in print. At least not in the Detroit Morning Star. Hap continued to be skeptical of the man who claimed to be a reporter, and strangely, many of Harold Scofield's questions centered on the chief murder suspect, Cory Welchek. Questions like, "How well did you know the Welchek brothers?" "Do they have any relatives living in the area?" Who are some of the Welchek's friends?" And, "Where do you think the one who is still at large might be hiding out?"

Naturally, Hap and Edna were unable to supply any concrete answers to the questions the reporter asked about the Welchek's. By the time the interview concluded, there was very little information scribbled on the reporter's notepad. Thanking the couple for their time, Harold Scofield got in his car and quickly departed, leaving Hap and Edna looking at each other with questioning looks on their faces.

As the brown Buick disappeared over a hill and out of sight, Hap had one final comment. "If that guy was really a newspaper reporter, then I'm American's newest sex symbol!

Edna put her arms around her husband and whispered in his ear, "I don't have to leave for the airport until four thirty. How about taking your wife to bed and practice being American's newest sex symbol.

Hap gently rubbed his red headed wife in a sensuous area and grinned saying, "Best offer I've had since my relatives left."

Just as Tony Ramonni began to descend the first hill in the Larson's driveway, which would put him out of sight of the Larson's home, he spotted a rusty, gray colored Honda parked at the bottom of the hill. A man carrying a pair of binoculars had just gotten out of the car and was walking up the hill towards the Larson's home. Tony slowed slightly and took a close look at the individual. His baldhead appeared to be recently shaven and his face contained a thick, but short crop of dark whiskers and a mustache.

After passing the parked vehicle Tony looked in his rear view mirror and noted the man had turned and trained his binoculars on Tony's car. "Strange acting bird", thought Tony, "but he's not the guy I'm looking for. Must be a friend or neighbor of the two hicks I just left."

Cory Welchek watched as the brown Buick Park Avenue disappeared around a bend in the Larson's driveway. A ripple of fear, mixed with anger, rumbled through his body. "I'll be damned", whispered Cory to himself, "that's the same make, model and color of the car Todd saw at April's bar just before he got shot!" Cory's mind began to spin. Pieces of the puzzle apparently began falling into place. "That guy driving the Buick must be a pal of the one who shot my brother. The one I killed seconds later! What's he doing here at the Larson guy's house? The two of them must be in on this together,...that asshole Larson must have told those two guys where we might be hiding out!" Cory's thoughts made sense, but little did he know how far off the mark his thinking was.

Continuing to the top of the hill, Cory nestled down behind a bushy balsam tree and spent several minutes scanning the Larson home with his binoculars. All was quiet and no one was moving about outside, nor was anyone visible inside the house, from what he could see through the windows.

Next he noted two vehicles parked next to the house. A green Dodge pickup truck and a copper colored '57 Chevy Nomad Wagon! Cory lowered his binoculars and thought for a second or two. Then he looked at the Chevy again. "That's the car!", Cory whispered to himself again. "That's the car Todd tried to take from some red headed woman when her two dogs chewed hell out of him! She must be married to, or living with, that Larson asshole!"

Cory's spirits soared! Now he could settle two scores at one time. Now he would make two troublemakers pay for their mistake of pissing off Cory Welchek. After glassing the area one more time, Cory retreated down the hill to his car, turned it around, and departed. He had seen enough to make a final plan on how he would take reprisals on two of the people he hated. And maybe, just maybe, he'd also get a chance to give the guy driving the Buick a taste of "Welchek Justice"!

Edna returned from Sault Ste. Marie a little past eight p.m. Her station wagon was loaded to capacity with suitcases, bags, boxes and her daughter, Colleen, plus Edna's three grandchildren, Gwen, Scott, and Carla. Within minutes, the quiet household that Hap had been enjoying during the early evening hours was filled with joyous conversation and laughter.

The grandchildren somewhat reluctantly gave their new grandpa brief kisses of welcome on Hap's bewhiskered cheek before hauling all their luggage up into the loft area, which was the location of the "guest room". Although quite small, the bedroom in the loft contained a queen-sized bed and two single sized bunk beds, all which would do nicely to house the grandchildren. Colleen would have the spare bedroom downstairs all to herself.

Hap expected he might have to feed his newly arrived guests, but Edna had stopped at a fast food establishment in Sault ste. Marie and filled her daughter and grandkid's bellies with burgers, fries, onion rings, soda and shakes.

The welcome party lasted until nearly midnight, as Hap and Edna received mountains of information about what was happening in the lives of their guests. Hap, being a recent newcomer into Edna's side of the family, was presented with nearly complete biographies from each of the grandchildren.

Gwen, the oldest at fourteen, was in eighth grade. Her deep reddish colored hair clearly indicated some of grandma's genes had been successfully transferred to another generation. Edna extracted an old photo album and located a picture of her when she was a teenager. The resemblance between grandmother and grandchild was striking. Gwen was an honor roll student, and deeply involved in volleyball, basketball, softball and music. Hap had already noted her obvious physical coordination by simply watching her movements.

Scott, twelve, and in sixth grade was the next in line. According to Colleen, her son was "the spitting image" of his father Andrew. As with most boys his age, Scott's report card was somewhat below what his scholastic abilities indicated his grades should be, but besides football and hockey, his intent interest in fishing and hunting took too much of his time. Grandpa Hap took an immediate liking to Scott.

Carla, the baby of the family, was in fourth grade and nine years old,……and slightly spoiled. Her features definitely resembled those of her mother, sprouting dish water blond hair and a slightly upturned nose. At the moment her interests included lots of reading, watching TV, and talking to friends on the phone. Grade wise, she claimed to be maintaining a B+ average, although her mother suggested B- might be more realistic.

Colleen's husband Andrew, a Methodist minister, would be arriving in two weeks and spend but a few days visiting with his wife's relation. His church only granted him two weeks of vacation time and he had opted to use but one week. Week two was already planned with reservations for the entire family at Disney World in Florida.

By one a.m. the Larson house finally quieted down as sleep overtook the weary travelers and their hosts.

Several weeks of fun and relaxation loomed ahead.

Part Three: "Mixed Intentions"

Everyone but Hap slept until mid-morning. The old woodsman was up and about a little after six a.m. Glorious sunlight was streaming through the kitchen windows as he loaded the automatic coffee maker with water and fresh coffee grounds. He reflected on how different his life had become since retiring from over three decades of trapping in Quebec's wilderness, romancing Edna, and their eventual move back to Michigan, getting married, and taking up residence in Hap's boyhood home. As the coffee began to perk, Hap grinned as he remembered how many years he had brewed his coffee or tea in a large tin can with a wire handle. How times had changed!

After filling an insulated coffee mug with the hot brew, he went out side and fed his six dogs. For the next hour he took a walk along a trail that overlooked the river and allowed his dogs to romp and roam the pristine forest that bordered the stream. The solitude and beauty that accompanied just being out of doors in a remote area was something Hap always enjoyed and looked forward to. And having his beloved dogs as companions made those walks in the wild all the more enjoyable.

Returning to his house, Hap noted all was still quiet. Not wanting to wake anyone up just yet, he and his four legged friends continued their outside adventures by walking along the driveway. At the bottom of the first hill Hap suddenly stopped and studied some indentations in the soft sand. His eyes clearly detected that someone had parked a vehicle in the somewhat soft soil at the bottom of the hill, and then turned it around and departed. Only the tracks of Edna's Nomad had crossed the other tracks, so Hap knew whoever had stopped in his driveway for whatever reason had done so after the individual claiming to be a reporter had left. He also noted the tires left imprints that were very narrow and the width of the axels were less than that of a full sized vehicle.

Further investigation of the spot where the vehicle had pulled to the side of the driveway and stopped showed that one person had gotten out of the vehicle, walked off the driveway and returned. Hap thought possibly someone had chosen his property to dispose of a bag of garbage or the like, but a short search of the area turned up nothing. Puzzled, but not concerned, he continued walking to the end of his driveway, and then returned to his home. When he and the dogs arrived, Edna was cooking breakfast and their guests were anxiously awaiting their morning feast. And having worked up a good appetite himself, Hap was eager to join them.

Having finally located Hap Larson's residence, Cory Welchek's next move included moving to a location not too far removed from his intended victims. His plan was to spend some additional time spying on, as Cory put it, "That Larson asshole and that red headed squeeze he lives with". Cory had already organized a plan of action against the Larson's which would cause as much pain and suffering as possible before death put them out of their misery. But he needed to know more about their daily and nightly routines in order to plan exactly when he would strike.

Cory had given much thought as to where he could hide out and remain safe from being detected by the police. His mind kept returning to the secluded cottage at Manistique Lake where he and Todd had spent several days before they decided to move to the small cabin at The Howling Beagle. He decided he would return to the cottage, and if no one was there, he could hide his car in the garage and once again use the facility as a hide out until his appetite for revenge was satisfied.

He parked his car well out of sight of the cottage and walked along its driveway until the cottage came into view. All was quiet, no vehicle was present, and all the window shades were drawn. Returning to his Honda, he drove into the yard and gave the buildings a closer inspection. Both doors to the cottage were locked, as well as the garage. Someone had been here since he and Todd vacated the property!

The bedroom window, which Todd had been able to open and gain entry to the cottage, was likewise locked. The screen door on the screened in front porch was unlocked. After locating a large rock, Cory entered the porch and busted a small windowpane in the front door. Then reaching in and unlocked the latch, he entered the house.

It was immediately noticeable that someone had completely cleaned up the mess that he and Todd had created when the two brothers had used the cottage as a hide out. Checking the refrigerator and freezer, Cory discovered a number of items had been purchased to replace what he and Todd had consumed. He concluded the owners must have spent the Memorial Day Weekend at their cottage, then returned to their permanent home,...wherever that might be.

Although he felt somewhat uneasy about remaining at the cottage, he really had no other idea where he might hide out. And surely he thought, staying there for just a few days would not be overly risky.

A set of keys were discovered in one of the cupboard drawers, which included the keys to the house and the padlock on the garage. Cory drove his car into the garage, and returned to the cottage for a nap. God, he was tired!

After the breakfast dishes had been washed and the kitchen tidied up, Edna had a suggestion. "Hap, let's take Colleen and the children to the cottage Charles and Shirley purchased and show them around. The children could take their swimming suits and take a dip. I promised Shirley I'd do some additional cleaning while they were gone so the cottage would be all spick and span when they return and settle in for the summer."

Hap frowned. "I got a better idea. Why don't you gals go to the cottage and me and Scott will stay here and do a little fishin' on the river. The smallies should be startin' ta git active and I jist bet Scottie would love ta do battle with a few of them whoppers."

Edna attempted to compromise. "You could use the fishing boat at the cottage and go fishing on Manistique Lake. Don't you want to come with us?"

Hap's face switched to a grin. "No, not really. I don't know much about Manistique Lake. It's too dang big. Gits real rough if the wind blows. Plus I know this river. I know Scottie and me kin catch some fish and have some good ole peace and quiet at the same time. I suspect by now some of those summer home owners who vacation on the lake got their jet skis and speed boats cranked up and them things and fishin' jist don't mix too good. You women folk go ta the cottage,......me and Scottie will stay here an' fish the river."

Edna attempted to look upset, but failed miserably. Colleen came to Hap's defense. "Mom, I think Grandpa Larson is right. Let's us girls go and do our thing and the two boys can go fishing and do that male bonding thing."

Edna shrugged and gave in. "You're right daughter dear. If we make old grumpy go with us he'll ruin everyone's day." Edna winked at her husband, opened the front door, and whisked "the women folk" out and into her car.

Hap and Scott waved good-bye from the front deck. As the Nomad disappeared over the hill, Hap looked at his fishing buddy and said, "Now I hope ya took that all in son. That's how ya deal with women when they try ta git ya ta do something ya don't wanna do. And it ain't gonna be long before you'll need ta know that kinda stuff. Let's go catch some fish! Hap liked to brag a bit about his ability to manipulate his wife,...when she was out of earshot.

Cory arose early and spent the early morning hours looking closely at a quadrangle map which contained detailed information concerning the topography of the area around the Larson property northeast of Newberry. He happily noted there was an unimproved two rut logging road, which meandered east from Highway 123 and ended at the base of a high hill almost directly across the Tahquamenon River from the Larson's home. It was a promising location from which he might be able to spy on his two intended victims and develop a plan for his final retribution. The area needed to be investigated, and there was no time like the present to do so. The longer the delay in carrying his plan to completion, the greater the risk he might be caught. By nine thirty a.m. he was once again heading towards Newberry armed with a map and binoculars.

Part Four: "Disturbing Evidence"

Edna and her three companions chatted excitedly about how much they were going to enjoy the day together at the Baldwin's cottage on Manistique Lake. What definitely was a delightful spring morning promised a delightful spring day would follow. Gwen and Carla were especially excited at the prospect of spending a day swimming, canoeing and just roaming around the lakeshore exploring some new surroundings. Colleen and Edna were excited just to be able to be together and experience, as Edna put it, "Mom and daughter chitchat".

There was little morning traffic, which was the norm anywhere in Michigan's U.P. during early June, or actually during most any month, so the 27 mile drive from the Larson's home to the cottage at the lake seemed to take less time than usual. Little or no attention was paid to the few vehicles they met, including a gray, rust infested gray Honda sedan containing but one passenger.

But the occupant of the Honda noticed the vintage '57 Chevy Nomad. Most anyone's eyes would be attracted to such a classic automobile driving on a nearly deserted highway. Cory carefully scanned the interior of the Nomad as the two vehicles passed each other. The driver was that red headed woman who lived with Cory's sworn enemy, Hap Larson. A younger blond woman occupied the front passenger's seat and two young girls filled the real seat.

Cory watched in his rear view mirror until the vehicle disappeared from sight. "Looks like that asshole Larson and his squeeze got some company", mumbled Cory to himself. "Tough shit for them if they're in the wrong place at the wrong time when I git even with that bastard and his live in broad, or whoever that red headed bitch is." Cory smiled just thinking about his plan to "get even".

Hap and Scott enjoyed a spectacular morning of fishing on the mighty Tahquamenon River. Scott beamed with excitement as he caught several nice sized small mouth bass, two northern pike and an undersized musky, plus eight or ten smaller bass and pike. Hap simply rowed the boat, and gave Scott instructions on how to cast and where to cast. All three of the biggest bass were taken from a rocky area where the river's current swirled and eddied around some large boulders. The two biggest pike were coaxed out from under the tangled remains of an old beaver house, and the musky was lured from its shaded ambush location beneath a thick patch of lily pads. Hap released all the bass, the small pike and the undersized musky, but kept the two large pike, which contained enough tasty fillets to feed, as Hap put it, "The whole crew fer supper tonight."

Besides the action packed fish catching adventure, Scott was treated to numerous sideshows, which were pointed out by his guide, Grandpa Hap. "Hey Scottie, look up near the top of that old white pine over on yer left. See them two mature bald eagles eyeballin' us? They're hopin' we release a fish and it croaks. When it dies and floats ta the surface, there'll be a mad scramble ta see which one gits to it first."

And Lady Luck smiled on the "guide" and his young angler. A small pike inhaled Scott's lure, causing the hooks to rip loose it's gills. Hap tried valiantly to revive the fish, but it had lost too much blood. Within a few minutes after being released the dying pike began thrashing on the river's surface, as its life quickly ebbed away. And just like Grandpa predicted, both majestic eagles swooped down in an attempt to retrieve some brunch. The larger of the two won the race, scooped up the dead pike in its talons, and departed into the depths of the forest to feast on fresh fish flesh. The smaller eagle returned to the crown of the ancient pine to continue a game of waiting.

All Scott could say was, "Wow, that was awesome grandpa!"

In addition to the "eagle show", Scott witnessed an osprey drive from a dizzying height and plunge into the river to snatch a small fish from the water. Several painted turtles and a massive snapping turtle were seen sunning themselves on shore side logs. A doe and her twin fawns quietly came to the river for a drink, and for a few minutes dined on lush grass at the water's edge. Numerous varieties of songbirds serenaded their passage, and colorful wild flowers dotted the riverbank. Several times Grandpa Larson reinforced one of his favorite concepts by saying, "All this wildlife stuff is what really makes a fishin' er huntin' trip worth while. Catchin' some fish or shootin' something is simply a bonus. Ya probably don't quite agree with me now,...but when yer older,...well, you'll understand."

What the two anglers did not see was a distant figure crouching behind a busy tree on a high hill that was also watching the show with a pair of binoculars.

Upon arriving at Charles and Shirley's cottage, Carla and Gwen made a mad dash for the lakeshore. Having donned their swimming suits prior to departing for the lake, they were overly eager to go for a dip. Grandma Edna attempted to stem the stampede towards the water by yelling after the departing children, "Wait, let me show you around inside the cottage before you go swimming!"

Carla yelled back over her shoulder, "No Grandma, we want to go swimming first!" And upon running the full length of the dock, both girls jumped into the water with a resounding "splash".

Edna and Colleen walked to the lakeshore and sat down on a wooden bench to watch the two girls frolic in the clear water. "Those girls of mine really love the out of doors and swimming is one of their favorite activities", said a smiling Colleen. "I'm so lucky to have such healthy and energetic kids."

Edna smiled and added, "And I'm lucky to have such a wonderful daughter who has given me three wonderful grandchildren."

The swimming activity lasted for nearly an hour and finally degenerated into a giggling session as the two sisters threw wet sand and clumps of mud at each other. Colleen called a halt to the friendly war ordering the girls to come ashore and dry off with grandma's towels. Next, Gwen and Carla needed to explore the boathouse.

Once inside the building the girl's attention centered upon the canoe, which was resting upside down on one of the walkways. "Can we take a ride in the canoe?", begged Gwen.

Edna looked at her daughter and shrugging her shoulders said, "Why not! We did come here today to have some fun. The cottage cleaning can come later."

Each girl was fitted with a life jacket, and within a few minutes the two were zig zagging around the bay. Their mother gave strict orders they were not to paddle beyond the boundary of the small bay where the cottage was located. Upon hearing the rule, the girls offered a mild protest, but accepted the terms when grandma seconded the order. Another hour evaporated as the girls circled the bay twice and then completed a detailed investigation of the shallow shoreline.

Discoveries included several spawning beds that contained bass in the act of laying eggs, numerous frogs, a garter snake, and several varieties of butterflies. The sisters were having a delightful, fun filled morning.

Finally tiring of their water adventures, the girls paddled the canoe into the boathouse. With mom and grandma assisting, the canoe was returned to its proper resting-place, the paddles were hung on the wall next to the life vests, and it was time to receive a guided tour of the cottage.

The foursome slowly walked around the cottage inspecting the exterior, and after Edna unlocked the back door the tour began. The back door entered into the kitchen area. Next, an arched doorway led to a combination living room / dining room, which faced the lake. The front door opened into a large screened in porch containing padded metal deck chairs and an eight foot swinging wooden bench seat with a back rest suspended from the ceiling with chains. There was also a ping pong table.

As the group was about to re-enter the living area of the cottage, Gwen noticed one of the windowpanes in the front door was missing. Closer investigation clearly indicated the window had been broken, as sharp pieces of broken glass jutted out all around the window frame. Edna's brow wrinkled in thought as she recalled the mess that had been discovered when she, Hap and the Baldwin's first visited the cottage with the realtor, Audrey Meschik. At that time entry into the cottage had been gained through one of the bedroom windows, which had been carelessly left unlocked. It was obvious someone had once again trespassed and illegally entered the building!

A red flag of warning flashed through Edna's brain!

Continuing a careful search of the cottage's interior uncovered more evidence someone had recently spent time there. The bed in the master bedroom had been slept in and not made up. Edna knew Shirley Baldwin would never leave a bed unmade. On top of the bedroom dresser rested a large backpack containing some assorted canned goods, a wool blanket and several additional items. Returning to the kitchen, Edna opened the refrigerator to discover, among other things, four six packs of beer. Next to the refrigerator was a garbage container half filled with empty beer cans. Charles and Shirley rarely drank beer. Edna's warning signal changed to "danger". She remembered the numerous beer cans and liquor bottles scattered throughout the cottage after the earlier break in. Edna also remembered it was highly suspected the Welchek brothers had been the cottage's illegal occupants!

Trying not to allow her growing apprehension to show, Edna commanded Colleen and the grandchildren to exit the building and return to the car. Edna's explanation was simple, "We must leave here at once,...something is very wrong!" All three looked questioningly at Edna, but responded to her order and exited the cottage through the back door.

As they neared Edna's car, the sound of another vehicle approaching reached their ears. Heading down the driveway towards them was a rust infested, gray colored Honda.

Chapter Eleven: Bad News, Good News

Part One: "Abduction"

Hap and Scott returned to the dock shortly before noon. Grandpa Larson gave his student a comprehensive lesson on how to clean northern pike and end up with succulent fillets that were bone free. After thoroughly rinsing the fillets in the river, the two anglers walked up the hill to the Larson homestead, and after sealing their dinner's main course in zip lock bags, placed the contents in the refrigerator.

"Well Scottie, what would ya like ta do next. Hard tellin' when them females will come draggin' themselves home. Wouldn't surprise me none if they ended up in town doin' some shoppin' in all them fancy gift shops. Shoppin' is women's favorite pastime ya know. They'll go shoppin' not even knowin' what there're shoppin' fer. Men can't figger why women shop that way and it's one of the great unsolved mysteries of the universe. Beats me why ya'd wanna wear out a pair of shoes walkin' the sidewalks lookin' at stuff in stores without knowin' what yer lookin' fer and then maybe not buy nothin' atall. You like shoppin' Scottie?" Hap was finished with his sermon on women and shopping.

"No not really. I like to go to sporting goods stores though. I love looking at all the fishing rods, guns, camping equipment and all the other out door stuff they sell. Some day I hope to have enough money to buy some of those things."

"How about you and me go outside and do some plinkin' with my .22? You like to shoot?"

"OH YEA! I love shooting. Dad takes me to the rifle range once in a while and we shoot his .22.

"O.K. then, you git some tin cans out of the recycle box next to my garbage containers, set them up against that big pile of sand next to the garage, and I'll git the gun and some shells."

Hap was just loading his .22 rifle when he heard the phone ring inside the house. "Hey Scottie, run inside real quick and see who's callin'. Find out who it is and tell 'um I'll call back later,......unless it's important."

Scott bolted for the door and reached the phone as it began its sixth ring. A few seconds passed before Scott yelled for his grandpa. "Grandpa Hap, come quick! My mom's on the phone and needs to talk to you. She said something really bad has happened at the lake!"

Before Hap even reached the steps leading up the deck, a large knot had formed in the pit of his stomach!

Edna's premonition of impending danger was well founded. Before the gray Honda came to a complete halt, the driver side door was opening to reveal a man pointing a pistol at them. Edna, Colleen and the two girls froze in place, with widening eyes and puzzled looks on their faces. But their facial expressions soon changed from one of puzzlement to one of fear and terror!

As the bald man with a scrubby beard and mustache slammed his car door, an evil smile spread across his lips. "Well, well, well, what have we here? What are you doing trespassing on my property?", demanded the intruder.

For several seconds no one answered. But then as Edna's Irish temper began to flare, anger replaced her initial feeling of fear. "I don't know who you are or who in hell you think you are, but YOU'RE the one who's trespassing! This property belongs to one of MY relatives and WE have permission to be here. YOU DON'T! NOW GET BACK IN YOUR RUST BUCKET AND GET OUT OF HERE!" Lightning bolts began to snap from Edna's blue eyes. "AND PUT AWAY THAT GUN! YOU'RE SCARING MY GRANDDAUGHTERS!"

Edna's outburst caught Cory off guard, and for several seconds he searched for the appropriate words to re-establish his superiority and control of the situation. "You shut up your mouth, WOMAN, or I'll shut it up for you,...PERMANENTLY!" It was then Cory Welchek noticed Edna's car. "Well I'll be damned! Yer that woman who let her dogs chew hell out of my brother a while back! Yer the bitch who lives with that asshole, Hap Larson. You two are the ones responsible for causing me and my brother all the grief we've been put through. DID YOU KNOW MY BROTHER IS DEAD? SOME SON OF A BITCH SHOT HIM AND IT'S ALL YOU AND THAT LARSON ASSHOLE'S FAULT!" Cory leveled his pistol at Edna's head with a hand that quivered with rage.

Edna refused to back off, even as she suddenly realized who it was that was threatening her. Edna's words hissed from her mouth as she rebutted the stranger's accusations. "You are out of your mind Mister! You and your brother made your own bed, and now own up to what you are. You're a common criminal, admit it! And quit trying to blame your stupidity on someone else. You two were the ones who murdered that young game warden, Brian Matson. You are the ones who were slaughtering dozens of deer illegally. You were the ones who were growing pot........."

Cory suddenly lunged forward and slapped Edna across the face with a tremendous backhand swat. The impact knocked Edna to the ground, causing a trickle of blood to exit both corners of her mouth. "I WARNED YOU, BITCH,...NOW KEEP YOUR MOUTH SHUT OR I'LL BLOW YOUR DAMN HEAD OFF!"

Colleen fell to her knees at her mother's side and shielded Edna's body with her own. "Oh please", Colleen begged, "don't kill my mother! Why are you doing this to us? We haven't done anything to you. Please,......just leave and let us be!"

Cory's breathing was coming in short, violent bursts and his face and neck had turned beet red. "Don't you start tryin' to tell me what to do,......or I'll blow your head off too. Get up,...both of you. I've got some plans for your bitch of a mother,......and that bearded asshole she lives with."

Edna got to her feet and spit the blood from her mouth into Cory's face. "You're going to be one sorry bastard for what you just did to me MISTER WELCHEK!"

Cory drew back his fist as though to strike Edna again, then hesitated and grabbed her by one arm and pushed the barrel of his pistol under her chin. Get in my car,...bitch." Cory opened the back door and shoved Edna into the back seat. Then turning to face Colleen and her two daughters, he studied them for several seconds. Walking forward he grabbed Gwen by the hair and fiendishly gloated, "Think I'll take this little cutie along too. A little more insurance never hurts. Plus, if I get bored or can't sleep, she might be downright entertaining!"

Gwen screamed and kicked Cory in the shins, but her bare feet made no impression on the angry felon. Colleen pleaded once more. "No, no, not my daughter too. Why are you doing this? Where are you taking my mother and daughter? PLEEEEASE, let them go. We won't tell anyone!"

Cory shoved Gwen into the front seat of his Honda, slammed the door and pointed the gun at Carla. Looking at Colleen, Cory gave an order. New get your ass in that cabin and bring me that packsack on the dresser in the big bedroom. And also bring all the beer that's in the frig. I'll wait right here, but don't drag your ass. Make it snappy, I ain't got all day.

Within two minutes Colleen returned with the items Cory had demanded. He placed the items in the car's trunk, then got behind the wheel and started the engine. Before leaving he gave Colleen and Carla two orders. "Tell that Larson asshole I'll be callin' him. Tell him I've got a deal for him he can't afford to pass up. And don't bother callin' the cops."

The terrified mother and daughter watched as the abductor and his victims disappeared from sight down the driveway. Colleen's mind swirled with fear and a feeling that what had just taken place really couldn't have happened. Then, realizing she had to act quickly, Colleen re-entered the cottage and dialed the Larson's phone number.

Once underway, Cory pointed his pistol at Gwen, who was huddled against the passenger side door and sobbing. Then turning to give Edna a hateful, threatening look, said, "We're not going very far. I've found a place nice and secluded where the three of us can hide out until I call that Larson asshole and tell him what I want. So just sit tight, bitch, or I'll put a hole in your granddaughter's pretty little head."

Edna had no choice but to glare back and obey.

Part Two: "Aerial Search"

Before Hap reached the phone several horrifying scenarios flashed through his mind. One or both of the girls had drowned. The cottage burned down. Someone had gotten seriously injured. But he was totally unprepared for the terrifying news Colleen relayed to him. Through choking sobs she blurted out a disjointed version of what had taken place at the cottage. When the name "Welchek" reached his ears, the knot in Hap's stomach doubled in size!

When Colleen finished pouring out her tale of horror, Hap instructed her to get into Edna's car and drive to the sheriff's office in Newberry as quickly as possible. He ended with; "I'll meet ya there".

Next, Hap quickly dialed the number of the sheriff's office. Bill Ostermeirer's secretary answered the phone.
"Hello. This is Hap Larson. I've got a serious emergency on my hands. Is Bill there?"

"No, he's out somewhere with Special Agent Oaks investigating a tip we received from someone as to the whereabouts of Cory Welchek. Deputy Nordahl is here. Would you like to speak with him?"

"Ya, he'll do. Put him on the line."

"One moment Mr. Larson, I'll ring his office."

Doug Nordahl picked up the phone on the second ring. "Hey Hap, what's up? The secretary said you have some sort of an emergency?"

"Worse than that Doug. We got real problems."

Hap quickly filled the deputy in on the unbelievable news he received from Colleen. Deputy Nordahl listened in stunned silence. When Hap finished his tale of horror, the officer had already decided upon a plan of action.

"I'll radio Bill. If he's not in his squad I'll get him on his cell phone. I'll get the O.K. to call in our pilot who flies our search plane and we'll begin an aerial search. In the meantime I'll have our dispatcher contact all available squads already on the road and have them set up roadblocks in case that son of a bitch tries to make a run for it. At least we know he's still in the area, although I'd rather not know he's here and have Edna and your granddaughter safe and sound."

"I'm gonna be at yer office in a few minutes. Tell yer people in the squads I'm gonna be breakin' the speed limit a tad. I wanna go up in the plane with yer pilot, I've got good eyes and I wanna help."

"We don't allow lay persons in our plane,……but you've been such a help to us already,……O.K., I'll clear it with Bill. I think he'll agree you'd be an asset to have up in the air. I'll see you in a few minutes. Don't drive too recklessly."

Within moments Hap and Scott were leaving a trail of dust behind them as Hap raced his pickup towards Newberry.

Cory turned right on H-44, then swung his car south on H-33. A mile north of the tiny village of Curtis he turned east on a two-rut road, which looked as though not more than two or three vehicles had used it in the past several years. A mile and a half later, after dodging numerous water filled pot holes and bouncing over large rocks hidden by the lush spring grass and weeds, Cory turned left again unto an even less traveled trail, which was blocked by a metal gate with a "No Trespassing" sign attached.

"Hey bitch in the back seat. Get out and open the gate. And don't try any funny stuff or you'll be digging a grave for your lovely granddaughter."

Edna noticed a chain and padlock had once secured the gate to an iron post, but the padlock contained a bullet hole that looked to have been of recent origin. Once the gate was opened, Cory drove beyond it, stopped, and told Edna to close it again. Getting back in the vehicle Edna couldn't resist a verbal stab at her captor.

Oh Mr. Welchek,......aren't we trespassing? Isn't that against the law?"

Cory looked in the rear view mirror and glared at a glaring Edna. "Yer a real smart-ass,...ain't ya bitch?.

Edna pushed her luck a bit further. "Why yes, I would guess my ass has more brains than your ugly head."

Cory slammed on the brakes, and turned to face his heckler as he pointed his pistol at Edna's head. "Keep it up bitch,...keep it up. Enjoy your little verbal shots while you can,...'cause you ain't got much time left. And when I'm done messin' with you and that asshole you live with, you'll both be begging for death!"

Edna extended her middle finger and shoved it in the barrel of Cory's pistol. "Up yours, dipshit."

Cory swore and continued driving.

A few hundred yards beyond the gate was a tiny hunting shack buried in a dense stand of balsam, spruce and cedar. Holding the gun, Cory instructed Edna and Gwen to carry his belongings into the shack. Next he removed a roll of duct tape from his pack and ordered Gwen to tape Edna's hands together. Next, Edna was placed in a wooden chair and could only watch as Gwen tearfully taped her ankles to the front chair legs and then wound tape around her grandmother's body and the back of the chair. Within three minutes Edna was securely restrained and helpless.

Cory then taped Gwen's hands together and used a length of hemp rope to tie her securely into another wooden chair. His work completed, Cory smiled an evil smile, opened a beer and flopped down in a moth eaten overstuffed chair. "Well ladies, let's all relax and get some much needed rest. Tomorrow I've got some work to do."

It was nearing two in the afternoon before the Piper Cub cleared the treetops at the end of the runway and made a slow turn towards the southwest. Two of the three occupants were focusing binoculars and cleaning the lens. The pilot, Hugh Mancini, told his passengers to put on their earphones, then adjusted the radio and ran a quick test of the internal communications system. Next, he quickly studied a map spread out between himself and his front seat passenger, Hap Larson, and traced a route on the map with his index finger. Hap nodded in a sign of understanding and began testing his vision out of the window on the plane's right side. Deputy Doug Nordahl occupied a rear seat behind the pilot and would be responsible to scanning the land below out the left side of the plane.

Upon reaching an altitude of one thousand feet, Hugh leveled it off and gave his observers a "thumbs up" signal for the search to begin. The plane's air speed was slowed to the minimum necessary for it to remain aloft, which gave the observers the maximum amount of time to scan as much territory below for a gray colored Honda.

The first leg of their journey began at Seney where the junctions of highways 28 and 77 are located. Turning south, the plane followed a compass bearing to the coast of Lake Michigan. Then Hugh swung east for a half mile, then turned north, and followed another compass bearing back to highway 28. This pattern continued well into late afternoon. Net result,......nothing!

By the time their fuel supply was beginning to run low the trio had only covered half the territory between highway 77 and highway H-33, the area where it was suspected Cory Welchek may be hiding out with his captives.

The earphone crackled as the pilot spoke. "I'm heading back to base. We'll refuel and get right back up, as we'll have enough good daylight for one or two more passes. Once the evening sun starts casting long shadows, it makes things that are located in forested areas difficult to see. And you can bet our quarry is hunkered down in a dense thicket." With that, Hugh headed the plane northeast towards the airport north of Newberry.

Cory drank three beers, went outside and emptied his bladder, then checked his captive's bonds and sprawled on one of the bunks and took a two-hour snooze. Edna waited until Cory's snores indicated he was in deep sleep and then tried to wiggle free of her restraining tape. It was no use. She thought of tipping her chair over in an attempt to break the old rickety piece of furniture, but she knew that would produce too much noise and awaken their jailer.

In soft tones Edna tried to convince Gwen somehow someone would find the shack and free them from their prison. By the expression on Gwen's face, Edna knew her words had failed to achieve her goal. Gwen said little and sobbed softly off and on. The afternoon dragged.

Cory awoke from his slumber about five p.m. and began consuming another beer. Half way through his third swallow the distant sound of an airplane reached everyone's ears. Cory walked out of the shack and looked skyward, protected from view by a bushy cedar. A small single engine plane passed high overhead on a northeasterly course. Cory finished his beer, tossed the can into the brush, and returned to the shack and opened another beer.

As the plane crossed over highway H-33, Doug glassed the cottages on the shoreline of a small lake located just south of Manistique Lake. Of the few vehicles he could see, none were gray and none looked to be compact cars like a Honda.

Hap continued to scan the thickly forested area on his side of the plane. Afternoon shadows were already distorting visibility. Just as he was about to put down his binoculars and wipe his watering eyes, a faint glint of something reflecting sunlight caught his eye. He looked again. Nothing.

Hap turned on his microphone and commented; "Thought fer a second I saw something glimmer down there in one of those thickets."

Hugh answered. "I could swing around so you could take another look, but we'd be pushing our luck more than I care too. We're getting pretty low on gas and I want to make dang sure we don't come up short and have to put her down on a highway. The boss frowns on that kind of stuff." Hugh chuckled a bit. "I did that once and besides me crapping my shorts, I put three cars and a truck in the ditch."

"Yer the captain. But after we gas up let's make another pass or two over this area. I really thought I spied something that reflected sunlight."

"O.K. with me Hap. We'll be back here in about an hour. Won't be much light, but I'll fly a bit lower and we'll have a look."

Between five and six o'clock Cory consumed three more beers and ate a bag of corn puffs. Edna asked if she and Gwen might have a drink of water and something to eat, plus be released from their chairs to answer a much needed nature call.

He reluctantly agreed first releasing Gwen and allowing her to exit the shack to urinate, after a stern warning. "You can walk outside till I tell you to stop. Then drop your drawers and do your thing. Don't make a run for the woods or I'll fill your grandma full of holes. When you're back in the shack I'll give you a glass of water and a piece of bread."

Gwen obeyed, and Cory took great pleasure watching as an embarrassed teenager emptied her bladder by the side of the shack. Back inside, she quickly consumed a glass of water and a piece of stale three-day-old white bread.

Cory re-taped and retied Gwen, but this time she was tied hand and foot on one of the bunk beds. Next Edna was cut free and the nature call procedure was repeated. Cory waited until Edna had squatted to relieve herself and then gave out with a "wolf whistle" to let her know he was watching the performance.

When Edna returned to the shack, Cory couldn't resist making a crude comment. "Hey bitch, not too bad an ass for an old lady."

Edna scowled and shot back, "At least my ass is where it's supposed to be. You, Mr. Welchek are ALL ass!"

Cory laughed sadistically and replied, "You'll be calling me worse names than that before I'm done with you and that Larson asshole. I was gonna be nice and tie you to a bed like your lovely granddaughter. But seeing as you keep shootin' off that smart assed mouth of yours,......you're gonna spend the night back in your chair."

Edna received a glass of water and one piece of dry bread, as had Gwen. Then she sat down on the wooden chair and prepared herself to once again be taped tight. While Cory was wrapping her in duct tape, she gave her captor another verbal jab. "And you, Mr. Welchek, will eventually eternally burn in Hell."

Cory laughed, opened another beer and plopped down in the cabin's only comfortable chair. Within twenty minutes his alcohol soaked mind caused him to drift off to sleep again.

Refueling the Piper Cub took longer than expected, as the fuel truck was gassing up another plane when the trio of searchers arrived at the airport. Finally, at six twenty p.m. Hugh once again lifted the Cub off the runway.

The lengthening shadows indeed made viewing the ground difficult. The shaded areas looked exactly like solidly wooded areas. Hap was deeply depressed as his mind kept imagining all types of horrible things that Cory Welchek might be doing to Edna and Gwen.

Within a few minutes the plane was over the general area where Hap had detected what he thought was a glint of reflected sunlight off something tucked away in a densely wooded thicket. Hugh made several passes over the area, reducing the plane's altitude with each pass. During the descent the pilot would cut the motor and allow the plane to glide, further reducing its speed to allow his passengers more time to scan the forest floor below.

On the fourth pass over the area Hap caught a brief glimpse of a light colored vehicle parked next to a small shack! At first he wasn't sure he had actually seen what he though he saw. He turned on his mike. "Hey, there it is! I saw a car down there next to an old shack! Jist got a quick look, but it sure enough looked like a light colored car of some sort! Take her back up Hugh and make one more pass. I hope whoever is down there doesn't catch on to what this plane is doing up here."

On the next pass Hap's eyes recorded details of the area surrounding the location of the car and the shack. He clearly noted a faint break in the trees that extended from highway H-33 eastward towards the thicket where he had seen the car and shack. This indicated some sort of an unimproved road existed below the plane. Immediately, Hap's mind began forming a plan.

Below, in the shack, Edna and Gwen listened to the sound of a plane circling in the sky above them. Cory continued to snore, unaware that someone had spotted his hideout. Someone who was preparing a plan.

Upon returning to the airport, Deputy Nordahl drove Hap to the sheriff's office. For the next hour Sheriff Ostermier, Hap, and three deputies discussed and finalized a plan of action to locate the vehicle and shack Hap had discovered during the aerial search.

A computer check indicated the land and the shack was owned by a local hunting club which generally only used the shack during Michigan's sixteen day deer season in November. Quadrangle maps pinpointed the "unimproved jeep trail" that passed just south of where the shack was situated.

Although everyone was anxious to investigate the old shack as quickly as possible, after discussing the situation it was agreed they should wait until daylight. To venture into the unknown in the dark would possibly be too risky. The vehicles used to transport the search team would have to use their headlights and the lights might tip off the kidnapper. And knowing how unstable Cory Welchek was,......who knows what he might do to his captives. It was a difficult decision, but the "attack team" would wait until daybreak to head out.

It was agreed that a team made up of Luce County Deputies, led by Sheriff Ostermier, plus several conservation officers led by Chief Warden Paul Vandenburg would meet in Newberry at six a.m. and finalize their plans as to how they would ease into position and surround the shack. If Cory Welchek and his abductees were there, this time there would be no escape.

Hap arrived home well after dark and filled Colleen, Scott and Carla in on the details of the search and the plans that were made to converge on the suspected hide out where Cory Welchek may be holding Edna and Gwen prisoner.

After finally going to bed, Hap found sleep impossible to find. He tossed and turned and tried to extinguish the reoccurring thoughts of what Cory might be doing to his wife and granddaughter. To make matters worse, Hap was not satisfied with the plan that had been formulated at the sheriff's office. Cory Welchek was a desperate man. A highly dangerous and unstable man. Should the shack actually be his hideout, and should he suddenly be confronted and surrounded by a large armed force,......the list of possible consequences was frightening!

It was nearing midnight when Hap quietly slid out of bed, dressed, and scribbled a short note, which he left on the kitchen table. Exiting the house, he spoke quietly to his dogs to prevent them from barking, removed Wolf and Sadie from their kennel and loaded them in his truck. He checked under the front seat to make sure his .44 was there, and then with the lights off, Hap drove slowly down his driveway until he was well away from his home. Reaching the highway he turned on his headlights and sped towards a seldom-used two-rut road which led east off highway H-33.

Chapter Twelve: Coming Into Focus

Part One: "Untangling A Tangled Web"

Special Agent Terry McQuarie drew what is known as "the short straw". It was he who had been selected,...no ordered is the correct term, to apply for work at "Mackinaw Meats, Retail & Wholesale, inc.".
In other words, Terry McQuarie assumed a false identity and became the investigation team's "mole".

The Bureau in Washington D.C. had acted quickly to supply Special Agent McQuarie with "proper identification" to satisfy his soon to be new employer that the well-mannered and well-educated applicant was actually who his driver's license said he was, Zachary Novak.

"Zachary Novak" had lived in numerous localities around the country, working at numerous jobs ranging from menial minimum wage "no-brainers" to mid level management. And twice he had served short sentences in prison for selling marijuana.

Zachary's interview went well, as he smoothly and seemingly honestly answered a host of questions, which were asked of him by the owner of the company, David LaMar,......including admitting to having served jail time. Zachary had been extremely convincing with all his answers asked during the interview, and within a half-hour he was hired. David had his new employee fill out a time card, and the "Help Wanted" sign on the front door was removed. Zack was put to work that same day, in the meat grinding and packaging department.

With a little luck mixed in with the special agent's investigative skills, the destinations of the illegal "finished product" would be known in a few weeks. Possibly even less time.

The continued "sleuthing" by Sheriff Ostermier and his deputies, along with the able assistance of Special Agent Sherman Oaks, had likewise began to pay dividends. One of the many tips the authorities received finally paid off. Most of the so-called "hot tips" turned out to be dead end streets, but a former loyal customer of The Howling Beagle dropped a bombshell.

It had all begun with what at the time seemed to be "just another well-meaning citizen" calling in to relay what they perceived to be a "hot tip". Calls came into the sheriff's office daily from citizens suggesting they might know something that would aid the police in their ongoing investigations related to what the newspapers, radio and TV reporters were referring to as "The Dilemma in Luce County".

The caller failed to identify himself to Deputy Vincent Palino, who was receiving incoming calls at the time. But the information the caller supplied was presented in a very sincere manner. The individual on the line indicated he had been a frequent customer at The Howling Beagle up until about a month ago. He stopped going to the bar after two drunken brothers named Welchek made a pass at his girlfriend, which included the use of vulgar, suggestive language and sexual harassment. The unidentified called claimed to have attempted to protect his date, but his efforts resulted in being dragged outside and badly beaten. Furthermore, the caller said he had opted not to file a complaint with the sheriff's office because the two brothers had described what they would do to him and his girlfriend if he "squealed".

The most interesting bit of information came near the end of the call when the informer told the deputy that besides beer, booze and 'burgers, Audrey Ravovich also served illegally obtained venison, reefer, some type of white powder, and accepted money for sex after hours. The final kicker that really caused the deputy to raise his eyebrows was a statement that "some big shot politician named Redman often came in the bar, bought everyone drinks, and stayed overnight with the owner."

The following morning Sheriff Ostermier sent a deputy to The Howling Beagle to remove the crime scene tape and inform the owner, April Ravovich, she could re-open her bar for business. What the deputy did not tell April was even more important.

On yet another front, continued investigation into Senator Redman's phone records revealed numerous calls had been made to a phone number in Lansing, Michigan and another in Washington, D.C. The Lansing phone number in question was registered to Corbet O'Keefe, who was the appointed head of Michigan's Criminal Investigation Department. The Washington D.C. number belonged to Kenneth Bradford, a Deputy Secretary of the Department of Interior.

Some of the missing links were beginning to connect!

Chief Warden Paul Vandenburg opened yet another "can of worms". The more he digested the accumulating evidence pertaining to the apparent wide spread network of poaching, the more he began to suspect the complex operation might be even more widespread than just the geographical areas of Michigan's Upper Peninsula and Northern Wisconsin.

He turned his staff "computer expert" loose, and instructed her to begin communicating with wildlife officials from numerous other states having good populations of big game animals, inquiring if they too were experiencing a large degree of poaching. The information that began piling up was astonishing!

Wildlife officials from Pennsylvania, Texas, Maine, New Mexico, Wyoming, Colorado, Montana, and a host of other states, sent replies and statistics pertaining to poaching and suspected poaching activities in their respective states! Nationwide, besides deer, poachers were killing hundreds, and perhaps thousands, of elk, moose, mountain goats, wild sheep, and even wild turkeys! It appeared organized poaching had become a National epidemic!

Armed with this disturbing information, Warden Vandenburg flew to Washington D.C. and met with the head of our nation's Federal Wildlife Officers and the boss of the National Park System Rangers. The outcome of that meeting resulted in the formation of a "National Hot Line and Information Screening Network". Its function would be to coordinate all the ongoing investigations into the obvious widespread poaching situations nationwide, and share that information with the state's agencies. As Warden Vandenburg put it, "We all need to be on the same page!"

Upon returning to his office in Escanaba, Chief Warden Vandenburg sat at his desk for nearly an hour thinking about all the unbelievable events that had recently taken place, and were still taking place. All of which was a direct result of Brian Matson being murdered. He ended his thoughts by whispering quietly to himself, "Brian, I sure wish you could see what was under the tip of that iceberg you discovered!" And then a strange feeling rippled through his body, creating goose bumps on his arms and causing him to think one more thought. "Maybe you do know Brian, maybe you do!"

The day following the re-opening of The Howling Beagle, Sheriff Ostermier met with Circuit Judge Wendell Montgomery and applied for a search warrant. The request was granted.

Next, the sheriff instructed Deputy Jim Pearson to discretely set up a surveillance camera near The Howling Beagle's parking lot to discover and monitor who patronized the bar.

Bill Ostermier was becoming more and more convinced that April Ravovick knew a lot more about the illegal activities, which were under investigation, than she had originally led the authorities to believe. And the sheriff was out to prove his suspicions were correct!

Part Two: "Smile, You're on Hidden Camera"

Actually, Senator Randolph Redman hadn't planned on taking a minor detour while driving from his home in Escanaba to the State Capitol at Lansing. He had enjoyed the long Memorial Day Weekend, all two weeks of it. But the State Legislature would be back in session on Monday, and seeing as he was the senior member AND Speaker of the State Senate, as Senator Redman put it, "duty calls." He left his home about ten p.m. Sunday night and planned to drive straight through to Lansing. He'd easily be there for the nine a.m. opening bell of a short special session to help the governor pass a budget bill.

He had vowed to stay away from The Howling Beagle, but as he neared the intersection of U.S. 2 and H-33, an overpowering urge to violate his vow came over him. There were several "urges", which caused him to slow his dark blue Ford Explorer and turn north on H-33 towards April's bar.

One urge was to talk to April and see if she had heard any current news concerning the ongoing investigations into the poaching scandal, and as the press phrased it, "marijuana factory on highway 77", plus the search for Cory Welchek, the prime suspect in the murder of Officer Matson. "God", he thought, "I wish somebody would kill that stupid asshole, or maybe he'll kill himself." But Randolph knew that was probably too much to hope for.

Urge two concerned finding answers to another troubling question, "Where is Toni Ramonni?" It seemed as though he had dropped off the face of the earth. "The Boys" in Detroit had not heard a word from him since his phone call from a motel in Epoufette right after Billy Kerletti got waxed. The Mob assumed he had contracted a severe case of "cold feet" and fled to some distant undisclosed location. The senator and his associates had put up a considerable sum of money to have the Welchek brothers "liquidated", and only half the job had been completed. It was possible April had heard something about Tony's whereabouts or possibly even knew where he was hiding or hanging out. It was also highly possible that Tony had even banged April a few times.

Urge three was more basic. He was horny and April only charged twenty-five dollars for a "quickie".

The digital clock on the Explorer's instrument panel recorded the time as being eleven thirty three p.m. when the senator eased to a stop next to April's red Jeep Cherokee behind her bar. The parking lot was empty and the neon beer signs in the front windows were turned off.

Randolph got out of his vehicle, walked to the back door and knocked three times. As he waited for any sound from within signifying April had heard his knock; the words to one of Tony Orlando's old classics came to mind. "Knock three times on the ceiling if you want me". The throbbing bulge in the senator's shorts reminded him what he badly needed.

The door unexpectedly opened a crack and April whispered, "Who's there?"

"It's your ever lovin' senator and I'm lookin' for some lovin'!"

The door swung open, April's hand appeared, grabbed the senator in the crotch, and pulled her customer inside.

The video camera was well camouflaged, equipped with a zoom lens and a motion sensor devise, which automatically turned itself on, and off. The camera recorded everything, including the arrival of the Ford Explorer and it's license number, the senator walking to the door and knocking, and the grab in the crotch. And then with a faint "click" it turned itself off.

Cory Welchek awoke from his second "nap" shortly after seven p.m. Bad news greeted him. Upon picking up his last six pack of beer, he discovered there was but one can remaining! A major emergency had occurred! He popped the tab and guzzled half the can in three gulps, whipped the foam from the bristles of his scruffy beard, and belched.

Edna glared at her captive and asked, "Did you get any on you?"

Not "getting it", Cory glared back and asked, "Get any what on me, bitch?"

"That sound you just made,…you did throw up on yourself, didn't you?" Edna smirked, knowing full well her comment would irritate her alcoholic abductor.

"Real funny, bitch, real funny. Enjoy your smart assed remarks while you can! Because what I got planned for you and you know who ain't gonna be funny!"

Cory finished his beer, flung the can into a corner of the one room shack, and began to pace the floor. After several minutes of pacing and thinking he dragged Edna, and the chair to which she was duct taped, to a four by four post that was located in the middle of the room. The post had been installed years earlier to support a badly sagging roof. Using a stout hemp rope he tied his helpless captive and the chair she was seated in securely to the post.

Next he checked Gwen's restraints and made several minor adjustments. For a moment Edna thought he might be getting ready to do something terrible with Gwen, but Cory had other plans, at least for the time being.

"I'm going to leave you two lovely females alone for a spell. I need to take a quick trip to town and buy some supplies and make a phone call. Don't go anywhere or do anything that'll get ya into trouble while I'm gone". Cory laughed an evil laugh as he exited the shack.

Edna and Gwen breathed a sigh of relief as they heard the Honda's motor start up and listened until it's sound slowly faded in the distance. Twilight was waning and soon the world would be dark, including the inside of their prison. Spring peepers began a spring time chorus from a nearby swamp. Mourning doves cooed a sweet goodnight to each other. A pair of whippoorwills discussed their nightly hunting plan. And a pack of coyotes announced the beginning of a chase. Somehow all of these normal evening sounds added to the already dismal attitude of the two captives.

But then a new terror began. Inside the shack the hum of mosquitoes announced more predators were on the prowl. They soon located exposed portions of Edna's and Gwen's skin. Dozens of the despicable creatures began to feast. And there was no possible way to swat them. A new form of torture had begun.

The time was eight forty five p.m.

Cory took his time driving to the Quik Mart in Newberry, making sure he drove well within the speed limits which were posted along his route. With all the squad cars in the area, he was already playing a dangerous game just driving to town. And getting stopped for a speeding violation was certainly something he needed to avoid at all costs.

Passing The Howling Beagle, he noted it was once again open for business, as the neon beer lights were on and a half dozen pick up trucks occupied the parking lot. Cory considered stopping to buy some beer, but quickly cancelled the thought. He'd be less conspicuous doing his shopping in Newberry.

There were only two vehicles parked in front of the Quik Mart. Cory remained in his car until the customers inside the store had finished shopping and left. He felt it wise to take as few chances as necessary. Cory entered the store at nine twenty eight p.m.

Several blocks from the Quick Mart Tony Ramonni turned off the TV set in his motel room and decided to have a bit of scotch on the rocks. His frustration at not being able to locate the individual he was supposed to dispose of had grown steadily with each passing day, as had the amount of scotch he consumed. Continuing to assume the role of a newspaper reporter from "down state", he had "interviewed" numerous citizens of the surrounding area in an attempt to find a lead that would direct him to his intended victim. All attempts had been in vain.

Tony filled a glass with ice from the room's small refrigerator and attempted to pour several fingers of scotch into the glass from the darkly colored bottle. Only one dribble of liquid escaped the bottle, indicating it was empty. Toni slammed the empty bottle into a trash container, grabbed his car keys and headed for the Quik Mart.

The time was nine twenty nine p.m.

Cory was in the process of selecting several twelve packs of generic beer when the headlights of a car flickered through the store windows announcing the arrival of another customer. A rather husky male, who appeared to be in his mid forties, entered and almost immediately began talking to the check out clerk. Cory couldn't help but hear the entire conversation.

"Hello, how are you this evening?", greeted the newcomer.

"O.K. I guess. It's been a slow night. I'm bored.", answered the young clerk.

"I'm Harold Schofield. I'm a reporter for a downstate newspaper on assignment up here attempting to gain some newsworthy information about the murders your area has recently experienced. I know there is usually little serious crime in these rural areas, and our downstate readers like to read about something different than all the problems in the larger metropolitan areas of our state."

The clerk stared blankly at the reporter as if trying to conger up some sort of reply. None was forthcoming.

"Could I ask a few questions? I mean, would you allow me a short interview? I'd even use your name in the paper,……if it's all right with you."

"Gee,…wow! Sure thing Mister. I've never had my name in any newspaper. Go ahead,…ask away!"

"Well, I know it's a long shot, but the editor of my paper has offered me quite a large sum of money if I could somehow find and interview the suspected killer of that game warden,……ah,…Brian Matson. I realize the police have not been able to find the suspect,……ah, what is his name,……oh yes, Cory Welchek. Do you know who he is?"

"Ah, naw. But I've heard about him and his brother. I guess they were a couple of real tough cookies. Got into a lot of trouble I've been told. But I've never met either one of them. Can't help you out there, Mister Schofield."

"Well then, do you know if the Welchek's had any relatives living in the area? If I could find someone who knows them well, or is related to them,...I might be able to get a good story without actually locating the suspect."

"Nope, can't help you there either. Actually I moved to Newberry fairly recently and ain't too well acquainted with many people yet. Sorry."

"Well, thanks for your time anyway. I need to buy a few items as long as I'm here. My little refrigerator in the motel just down the street doesn't hold much, and it looks like I'll be hanging around Newberry for at least a few more days."

Cory waited until the man who claimed to be a reporter walked to the liquor display before he went to the check out counter. After paying for his beer and a bag filled with snacks and junk food, he quickly exited the store.

Hidden within the cigarette display above the check out counter, a surveillance camera silently recorded the image of each customer.

Cory walked to his car and was placing his purchases in the trunk of his Honda, when his gaze fell upon the vehicle which belonged to the man still in the store. Cory's eyes opened wide as he realized it was the brown Buick Park Avenue which he had seen leaving the Larson's residence. Also, it was most likely the same one his brother Todd had described which was driven by the two strangers who came looking for the Welchek brothers at The Howling Beagle just before Todd was killed! The fear and anger he had felt in the store upon hearing the reporter was looking for Cory Welchek instantly turned to blind rage.

Cory started his car, drove out onto the street and parked with his lights off, watching the convenience store he had just left. Shortly the man who drove the Buick Park Avenue appeared, put a shopping bag on the front seat, and drove out of the store's parking lot. The Buick turned left. Cory waited several seconds and then, with his car lights still turned off, followed the Buick at a safe distance. Three blocks down the street the driver of the Buick turned into the parking lot of a small motel. Cory stopped one block short of the motel and waited until the man he now hated as much as Hap Larson disappeared into unit number three.

Part Three: "Hit and Miss"

Cory quietly got out of his car, and opened the trunk. From his Duluth Pack he removed a large hunting knife, protected by a leather sheath. He carefully placed it in his back pocket, then removed the 9-mm pistol from his belt and checked the chamber to make sure a live round was present. He tucked the pistol back into his belt, pulled his shirt tails out of his pants to conceal the weapons, and made his way to the doorway of unit three of the small motel.

Inside, Tony Ramonni had wasted no time in filling his glass with scotch. The first swallow burned as the one hundred proof liquid slid down his throat into his nearly empty stomach. He gritted his teeth and took a second swallow. There was a knock at the door.

Tony put down his glass and grabbed his .357 Smith & Wesson from the nightstand. "Who's there?", he questioned.

From outside came a weak voice. "The clerk from the convenience store. I overcharged you when I gave you your change and need to give you some addition money."

Tony was suspicious. "How'd ya know where I'm staying?"

"When you were asking me about the murders, you told me you were staying at a small motel just down the street. And this is the only motel in the neighborhood. I saw what kind of car you were driving when you left the store, so I ran after you to give you the correct change. My register wouldn't balance if I overcharged somebody."

Tony remembered that part of the conversation. "God he thought, these country hicks are just too damned honest." Tony put his revolver under his pillow, unlocked the door and opened it.

As soon as the door opened a crack Cory gave it an inward shove with all his strength. The ploy worked perfectly, sending Tony backwards sprawling on the floor. Cory was inside in a moment, gun in hand and trained on the prostrate hit man. Tony's face reflected shock and fear.

"I hear yer lookin' for Cory Welchek. Well, ya found him! Who the hell are you mister and why are you so interested in finding me?" Cory cocked the hammer on his semi-automatic and thrust the gun against Tony's head. "Ya better start talkin' real quick or your brains are gonna be splattered all over this floor!"

Tony had been on the delivery end of a gun before, but never had the opportunity to be on the receiving end. It was not a pleasant sensation. "I'm,...I'm...a reporter. A reporter from down state. I'm just up here looking for a good story. Honest. Put that gun away, you're scaring hell out me! I'm just a reporter!"

"Reporter my ass! You and your pal are the ones who came lookin' for me and my brother Todd at that bar over on Manistique Lake. REMEMBER? My brother told me all about you two assholes JUST BEFORE YOUR BUDDY FILLED HIM FULL OF BUCKSHOT!"

Tony's eyes grew wide and his heart leaped into his throat. "No,...no,...there must be some mistake," he croaked, "I don't know what you're talking about. Really, I'm just a reporter........."

Before Tony could finish his lie, Cory stood up and delivered a vicious kick to Tony's face. His head snapped back, hitting the floor with a resounding "thud", and blood gushed from his mouth. Tony moaned clutching his face then rolled over on his stomach and spit several of his blood-covered teeth out on the floor. Cory delivered another kick, this time square in Tony's ribs. A slight "cracking" sound indicated several were broken. Cory's rage intensified.

Leaping on top of his crippled victim, Cory next planted both knees in the middle of Tony's back, knocking the wind out of his lungs. With his free hand he grabbed Tony's hair and jerked his head backwards, as he hissed, "This 'ill teach ya not to go snoopin' around in Cory Welchek's business!"

Cory released his grip on Tony's hair and quickly extracted his hunting knife from its protecting leather sheath. Raising the weapon he plunged the eight-inch blade into Tony's back. Tony tried to scream, but still gasping for breath, no sound except a slight gurgling of blood escaped his mouth. Cory withdrew the knife and plunged it into his victim's back again,……and again,……and again,……and again. Later, the coroner would count fourteen stab wounds.

After the third or forth thrust of the knife, Tony's body stopped twitching. One of the most feared "Hit Men" from the Detroit Syndicate had discovered the meaning of the phrase, "What goes around, comes around." The hit man had been hit.

Slowly Cory's rage began to ebb. His breathing was rapid and the excitement of the act had caused his heart rate to race. Cory walked into the bathroom and washed the blood off his hands and knife. His pants and shirt were spattered with blood, but he hardly noticed. Next he made a quick inspection of the room, removed Tony's wallet from his rear pants pocket, removed the money, grabbed the bottle of scotch, and closed the motel room door behind him. Softly whistling, "That's The Way I Like It, Uh Huh", he nonchalantly strolled to his Honda.

The time was nine thirty seven p.m.

Cory had one more chore on his list that needed to be completed before he returned to the old deer-hunting shack where he had left his two female prisoners. He needed to find a pay phone and give Hap Larson a call. Cory knew by now his sworn enemy would probably be worried to death about what was happening to his red headed squeeze and her granddaughter. He smiled inwardly as he envisioned the emotional pain "that Larson asshole" must be experiencing. Cory felt good. Cory would take great delight in ordering Mr. Larson to meet him at a remote location, ALONE, and detailing what would be done repeatedly to the two female captives if he did not follow orders. What he would not tell Hap Larson was what Cory Welchek had planned to be Mr. Larson's "punishment" for being such a "troublemaker". Cory felt even better.

As he began to leave the area where he had parked his car before murdering the man in the motel room, Cory noticed the car was not handling normally. He stopped on the deserted street and got out to investigate. The right front tire was flat. Very flat. He swore. Getting back in the car he slowly drove to a service station just a few blocks from the convenience store. It was closed for the night. Cory swore again, got out of his car and opened the trunk to remove the spare tire and the jack. Fate struck a second blow. The old bald spare was also flat. Cory swore again, louder this time and kicked his car. The jolt stung his foot. He swore again, and his rage was returning.

He slammed the trunk cover and drove his crippled vehicle out of sight behind the service station. He needed to think. His current situation had put an enormous crimp in his plans. But thinking and making new plans was not one of Cory Welchek's strong points.

Suddenly he remembered the brown Buick Park Avenue back at the motel. He'd return to the scene of the crime, get the car keys, and drive away in luxury. Cory's rage subsided and he silently praised himself for solving his dilemma so quickly.

He walked the seven blocks to the motel, only to discover the automatic dead bolt had not been locked in the "open" position when he exited the motel after murdering the room's occupant. Cursing himself, Cory returned to his immobilized Honda, as his rage again inched upward.

For the next hour Cory sat in his car trying to come up with an alternate plan of action which would put his original plan back on target. While he sat he sipped scotch and washed it down with beer. No seemingly workable plan of action was forthcoming. The sipping and drinking continued. By eleven p.m. Cory Welchek was sound asleep in a drunken stupor.

It was a little past twelve thirty when Hap turned his truck off highway H-33, extinguished the headlights, and began inching his way down the dark seldom used "two rut" road he had discovered from the window of the sheriff's search plane. Just a few yards into his bold journey he was forced to stop and allow his eyes to adjust to the near total darkness.

Although there was a sizable sliver of moon present, a brisk southwest wind sent thick, dark, foreboding clouds scurrying across the sky, obscuring what little moonlight could have been available. Driving down the unfamiliar trail would have to be accomplished as much by the "feel of the wheel" as by sight. Progress was terribly slow, and Hap was seized with a nearly uncontrollable desire to reach the old shack quickly. He just had to find out if his hunch was right. And for the hundredth time he said a silent prayer he'd arrive in time to prevent something unthinkable happening to his loved ones.

His emotions were interspersed with waves of fear and anger, as his imagination supplied him with various visions of what Cory might have done, or might be doing, to his captives. And he made a silent vow, should Cory Welchek harm Edna or Gwen in any way, Cory Welchek would be leaving the shack in a body bag!

Several times Hap was forced to stop quickly and back up, when the front wheels of his truck nearly rolled off the narrow road and into swampy, muck filled potholes.

Because of such poor visibility, he nearly drove by the turn off, which he assumed led to the old shack he had viewed from the air. He cautiously got out of his truck and risked turning on his flashlight to examine the wheel tracks, which turned left off the trail he had been following. A muddy bare spot in one track clearly indicated a vehicle with narrow tires and very little tread had traveled the old road very recently. Hap's heart rate increased a tad. Hap removed his .44 magnum and shoulder holster from under the front seat, put Wolf on a lease, commanded Sadie to "heel", turned off his flashlight, and began following the two track to whatever might be at the end of the trail.

The time was one twelve a.m.

Cory awoke a few minutes before one thirty a.m. to the sound of sirens blaring. It took a few seconds for his alcohol-clouded brain to comprehend what was taking place and also remember where he was. He stumbled out of his car fearing the sirens might be announcing the police were closing in on him. Much to his relief he saw a fire truck and an ambulance speeding down the street in front of the gas station behind which he was hiding.

The fresh air slowly began to clear his head somewhat, but the throbbing pain caused by the over consumption of scotch and beer continued. He leaned back against his car and became fearful that if he stayed where he was until daybreak, the chances someone might find him and become suspicious of his intentions would increase greatly. That in turn might get him into serious trouble. Cory's mind screamed at him to somehow find a way to get out of town.

A large pile of tires and rims that were piled behind the service station caught his attention. It was worth a look. Digging through the pile of old tires Cory located several with rims that looked as though they might fit the hub of his vehicle. Once again he opened his trunk, took out the jack, and in ten minutes had removed his flat tire.

None of the rims matched perfectly, but one nearly matched. If he could break off two of the threaded studs on his hub, it looked as though the rim and tire might fit. Despite the noise it caused, he whacked one of the studs with his tire iron. It took three solid smacks before it snapped off. Cory stopped, listened for the sound of anyone that might be coming to investigate. The only thing he heard was the wind moaning in the tree tops which bordered the street. Four more whacks were required to snap off stud number two. The substitute tire and rim just barely slipped on the two remaining studs. Cory tightened the two lug nuts as tight as he could and ten minutes later he was carefully heading out of Newberry, bound for an old deer hunting shack east of highway H-33.

Hap's progress on the overgrown two track was slow and deliberate. The evergreens through which the old road meandered were tall and thick. The poor visibility, which had hindered his travel since he left highway H-33, became poorer still. Not knowing exactly how far it was to the old shack made him fearful he might blunder into it and alert the kidnapper to his presence.

The overcast had intensified and the wind was gradually gaining strength. The low moaning of the wind through the crowns of the trees had increased to a dull whine. "Good", thought Hap, "any noise I might make will be masked by the wind." Two minutes later the rain began.

As expected, Hap came within just a few feet of the old shack before he was aware of its location. He froze in his tracks and a lump began to form in his throat. Several assorted fears rippled through his mind as he pondered his next move. "What if the abductor is outside the shack,......just waiting for someone to attempt rescuing his prisoners? What if this very moment his weapon is trained on me? What if I'm too late? What if........" Hap shook his head and commanded himself to stop thinking negative thoughts. And just then Sadie let out a soft whimper.

Hap kneeled down and clamped one hand over her muzzle and drew his .44 from its holster. He strained his eyes to detect whatever it was that Sadie had detected. He could feel her nose twitching and heard the soft sound of air being inhaled and exhaled as she continued to test the air currents. Hap knew full well she had detected some sort of scent that had aroused her interest. But what?

High above, the cloud shrouded sky opened briefly, allowing the subdued light of the moon to slightly illuminate the cabin and the area around it. The slight increase in visibility only lasted for several seconds but it was long enough for Hap to make out the door to the shack and one other vital piece of evidence. No vehicle was parked anywhere around the shack!

Hap's anticipation evaporated in an instant. He was too late! Cory Welchek had departed. He cursed himself for not coming sooner. And then a new fear leaped into his mind. What was it Sadie had scented? Oh God no! Had Cory killed his captives and fled after seeing the plane circling the area? Was it the smell of death that Sadie had detected? He fought back the tears and approached the shack.

Inside, Edna and Gwen had been drifting in and out of fitful sleep. Both were mentally and physically exhausted by their ordeal. The swarms of mosquitoes had stopped feasting on their blood sometime before midnight, although neither had any concept of time. Discomfort, pain, hunger and thirst were their only companions. The darkness of night and apprehension as to what else lay in store for them when their kidnapper returned only heightened their terror and fear.

And then Edna heard a footstep and the sound of toenails clicking on the wooden steps outside the door.

Hap and his canine companions eased up to the door and paused briefly. He unsnapped the leash from Wolf's collar, cocked the hammer on his .44, and kicked the shack's door open.

Sadie and Wolf leaped inside as Hap flicked on his flashlight and swung his weapon in an arc around the cabin's interior. The beam of light settled on the prostrate form of someone tied to the four posts that supported a crude bunk bed in one corner of the room. To his right, Hap heard Sadie whining. He swung the beam of his flashlight towards the sound and saw a sight that made his heart skip several beats! Tied securely to a chair, which was in turn tied to a support post, was the love of his life! And she was alive!

Edna squinted as the bright, piercing beam of the flashlight flooded her eyes. Next she felt two large furry animals rub against her legs and warm, wet tongues began licking her bare ankles. For several seconds bewilderment was her main emotion, but then she heard a voice she was beginning to think she would never hear again!

"Edna,……oh my God,…are you all right? Hap was kneeling beside her holding her head between his loving hands.

All her pent up fear and dread suddenly were released and Edna began crying so hard she could barely speak. "Oh Hap darling,…sniff, sniff, sniff,…you did come! I just knew you'd find us! But,……how,…how did you?"

"I'll tell ya later, first let me git ya outta this chair."

Hap had already extracted his knife and was slashing through the bindings that had been used to restrain her. Within seconds Edna was free. The couple embarrassed briefly and then they rushed to where Gwen was bound to the bunk and Hap quickly cut through the ropes that been used to cruelly secure her spread-eagle.

The barbaric ordeal was over.

"Are you two really O.K.?", asked a skeptical Hap. "Did that son of a bitch do,……ah,……do anything to ya? Did he……"

Edna hugged her husband and interrupted his question. "No Hap, he didn't. But I think he was planning to,…to,……rape Gwen when he returned from wherever he went." Suddenly Edna's fear returned. "Hap, we've got to get out of here. NOW!

He'll be coming back sooner or later and we've got to get out of here!"

Hap agreed, and quickly led his freed prisoners down the trail to his truck. Seconds later Hap was pushing his truck to the limit heading west down the muddy two track towards the highway. Heavy rain continued to fall.

A little more than a half-hour later Hap was escorting Edna and Gwen into the Urgent Care department of the Newberry Medical Center. Both seemed to be basically physically sound, except for some minor scrapes and scratches on their wrists and ankles, which had been caused by the restraining ropes and tape used by their abductor to immobilize them. Also, the areas of skin, upon which the hoards of mosquitoes had feasted, were swollen and covered with hundreds of bites. Both were also somewhat dehydrated and starving. A trip to the vending machines for liquids and munchies took the edge off Edna's and Gwen's thirst and hunger.

As the two patients were being attended to by the doctor and nurse on duty, Hap made a hurried call to the Sheriff's Office. He hastily informed the dispatcher of his harrowing adventure and the fact he had found and freed the two victims who had been kidnapped. Hap's final suggestion was for the dispatcher to notify Bill Ostermeir and have him organize a team of deputies to get to the old hunting shack as quickly as possible. Cory Welchek was certain to return to it sooner or later and wouldn't stay around long after he discovered his two prisoners had been set free.

Within ten minutes Sheriff Ostermier arrived at the Medical Center. He was not happy!

"God damn it Hap,……what in hell did you do? Here we had made plans to surround that old hunting shack at daybreak and you go off on a tangent like you're 007 or Dick Tracey and screw up the whole detail!" The sheriff's face and neck were red.

"Now hold on one dang minute, Bill. Peek in that examination room across the hall and take a look at my results. Don't look like I screwed up nuthin'. Look's a lot like I jist mighta saved a couple women folk from the clutches of a dirty asshole who was bound to do somthin' worse than he already did to 'um. And yer idea of chargin' in at daybreak with a whole army could very well have set that maniac off and he mighta done somethin' worse than jist tiein' 'um up and scarin' the bejesus outta 'um." Hap's face and neck were red.

Sheriff Ostermier took off his hat and slumped down in a chair. Normal color began returning to his face.
Shaking his head and presenting a tiny grin he replied. "Sorry Hap for blowing up at you. But you aren't the law around here,......in case you didn't know that. I guess I'm getting a bit testy and frustrated at our inability to corral Cory Welchek. I thought just maybe we had him cornered and we'd put much of this case in the "solved" file. But seeing as he wasn't at the shack,......well, maybe he got cold feet and finally decided to clear out of the area and crawl off somewhere else and hide."

"Don't think so, Bill. Edna told me he left the shack about dusk and said he had to go to town for a few items. I would guess the town he was talkin' about would be Newberry. Nuthin' else close by. He ran outta beer, so I suppose that was one of the items he went for. Why he didn't come back sooner is anybody's guess. But at least now we've got a good description of the car he's drivin' and Edna, bless her beatin' heart, was smart enough to memorize the license number. I don't remember what it was, but you kin go ask her as soon as Doc Meyers gits done tendin' ta all her mosquito bites."

"Well, I did take your suggestion that we send some deputy's back to the shack to wait and see if Cory shows up. They should be well on their way by now. I told them to keep in radio contact with my office to keep me abreast of what happens. If anything. I still think it's possible our pigeon flew the coop."

Within a few minutes Edna and Gwen finished having their bites and minor injuries attended to and were released from the Urgent Care facility. Sheriff Ostermier questioned both former prisoners for several minutes, all the while taking notes. After a sincere statement as to his relief that Edna and Gwen were once again safe and sound, he headed back to his office. The time was three fifty one a.m.

Chapter Thirteen: Springing The Trap

Part One: "Tap, Tap, We're Listening!"

David LaMar, owner of "Mackinaw Meats, Retail & Wholesale, inc." was absolutely delighted with his new employee, Zachary Novak. He was intelligent, reported to work on time sober, was willing to work overtime and weekends without demanding overtime pay, and had a delightful sense of humor, which kept the other employees relaxed and laughing. Zachary was also very resourceful!

Within three days after being hired to work at the meat processing plant, which processed, packaged, and distributed the loads of "poached venison", various law enforcement agencies realized just how resourceful the new employee was! Special Agent McQuarie, alias Zachary Novak, had tapped all the company phones, and "bugged" the offices of the owner and his secretary. In addition, all six of the refrigerated delivery trucks had been rigged with a device known as "Star Sat" which tracked each vehicle via satellite. Suffice it to say the "twisting trail" was beginning to straighten out.

Although it would take several weeks, possible a tad longer, state and federal law enforcement officials would be in a position to begin rounding up dozens and perhaps hundreds of individuals connected with the vast poaching operation. And with a bit of professional "questioning", some of those arrested and charged with various crimes were sure to break down and name names of those at the head of the illegal organization.

Another positive bit of news included the fact that the newly organized "National Poaching Hotline and Information Screening Network", which Chief Warden Paul Vandenburg had helped organize, was likewise beginning to produce substantial numbers of tips, information and most importantly, evidence. Optimism was running high within the organizations charged with the task of protecting the nation's natural resources, that stemming the tide of rampant poaching was slowly becoming a reality.

The blood stained body of Tony Ramonni was not discovered until two days after he had been murdered. An elderly lady, who did the room cleaning for the owner of the small hotel where the Detroit hit man had been staying, finally rang an alarm bell after realizing the renter's vehicle had not been moved for two days. She convinced the motel owner to use his pass key to investigate unit three in order to satisfy her suspicion that "something is wrong". Upon opening the door to unit three, they immediately discovered just how wrong something was!

Sheriff Ostermier and the county coroner had never viewed a crime scene that indicated such rage had been present during the completion of the brutal murder. At first the investigative team suspected more than one person would have needed to be present in order to inflict such brutal and numerous wounds and injuries to the victim. However, as the investigators continued to examine the crime scene, but one set of bloody footprints could be found on the floor of the motel room. And with the tremendous amount of blood that had seeped from the victim's body, it would have been nearly impossible for anyone in the room to avoid stepping in blood and leaving a tell tale shoeprint.

At first robbery seemed to be the motive for the crime. A wallet that belonged to the victim, one Anthony Roberto Rammoni, was laying on the floor, minus the money that had surely been in it. But after searching the room and finding several hundred dollars tucked into a pair of clean socks in the top dresser drawer, and a very valuable and expensive .357 Smith & Wesson nickel plated revolver hidden under a pillow, robbery no longer appeared to be the major motive for the murder. Dusting for fingerprints turned up numerous clear impressions.

The victim's driver's license indicated he was from Detroit. And it didn't take Sheriff Ostermeir but several seconds to remember the man who had shot Todd Welchek, and in turn probably had been shot by Cory Welchek, one William Vito Kerletti, was also from Detroit. Questioned after the shootings at her bar, April Ravovich testified two strangers driving a dark colored sedan had visited her bar shortly before the double murders had occurred. It certainly looked like the pieces of THAT puzzle had finally come together. At least the circumstantial evidence pointed to the fact that the two men from Detroit who were looking for the Welchek brothers were now both dead. Suspicion quickly grew in the minds of the investigating officers that the same man had killed both of the men from Detroit. Who else could it be but Cory Welchek?

But larger questions remained. Who had sent Billy Kerletti and Tony Ramonni here in the first place? Obviously someone had sent them here to find and kill the Welchek brothers. And who was paying the bill to have the brother's hit? Billy's criminal background had already been substantiated, and it was becoming more apparent Tony Ramonni was his partner. And Sheriff Ostermier knew full well, "birds of a feather flock together." It was time to involve Special Agent Oaks,...again.

After leaving the automated surveillance camera in place at The Howling Beagle for three days, Deputy Jim Pearson removed the disk and replaced it with a clean one. This was done well after the bar had closed for the night and the owner was sound asleep.

Upon viewing the tape, Sheriff Ostermeir was ecstatic! "I'm becoming more and more convinced our dear Senator Redman isn't the square shooting, upstanding public servant he pretends to be. I've got a hunch he's up to his neck in much more than just being an important elected official."

The three deputies present in the room nodded in agreement.

"Well boys, look's like the time is right to bring Ms Ravovich in for a good old fashioned round of interrogation. And there's no time better than the present. Doug, get the search warrant from my secretary and meet me out in the yard. I'll drive squad number two. Jim and Vincent, you take squad number three. Let's roll!"

Thirty minutes later Bill Ostermier was knocking on The Howling Beagle's front door.

Back in the Sheriff's Office, Special Agent Sherman Oaks was doing his homework. Lab reports on the fingerprints obtained from the motel room where Tony Ramonni had been savagely killed arrived by fax. There were no surprises. There were several unidentified prints, plus positive I.D.'s of "Anthony Romonni and Cory Welchek. Tony's criminal record was nearly a carbon copy of the report he had revived on William Kerletti. Both had been career criminals with suspected connections to "The Mob". This evidence re-enforced his hunch that someone had contracted the mob to have the Welchek brothers killed. And the only conclusion as to who may have paid for the contract would be whoever was the mastermind of the local poaching and illegal drug operation. From the additional evidence that had been collected, Agent Oaks suspected that person appeared to be the Senior Senator of the Michigan State Legislature!

The report from the coroner placed the time of death to have occurred sometime during the early evening hour's two days before the body had been discovered. Zeroing in on the approximate time frame was an important factor.

Item two concerned the license plate numbers Edna Larson had supplied to the authorities. The number matched a tan 1995 Pontiac owned by Theodore E. Webber of Newberry. Mr. Webber had reported his license plate had been stolen a few days earlier. This made it apparent the authorities main suspect in three of the four murders had been roaming the streets of Newberry right under their noses! And that pissed off Agent Oaks considerably!

Leaving the Sheriff's Office, Agent Oaks began driving around the neighborhood where Mr. Webber lived. The investigator noticed the motel where Tony Ramonni had been killed was only two blocks from the Webber residence. Agent Oaks also noted a convenience store was also in the neighborhood. He pulled into its parking lot, walked into the store and asked to see the manager.

As Cory Welchek headed his wounded Honda south, planning to return to the old hunting shack as quickly as possible, little did he know his evil plans were rapidly beginning to unravel. The spare tire he had stolen from the service station in Newberry, and only being secured by two lug nuts, was causing his vehicle to shimmy, ever at low speeds. Cory cursed his bad luck but his mind kept telling him his prisoners were bound securely and would still be right where he had left them. A few minutes one way or the other would make little difference. One minor set back in his plan, the phone call to Hap Larson that couldn't be completed due to the problem with a flat tire, could be made later. A few hours one way or another was of little consequence. Retribution would be forthcoming and he smiled inwardly at the prospect of watching Hap Larson suffer before he died. Less than a mile further, Cory's plan took a detour.

Rounding a slight curve on H-33, just a few miles north of The Howling Beagle, the right front wheel of Cory's vehicle dropped into a large pothole in the pavement. The sudden jar caused the two remaining lug nuts to sheer completely off the hub. The wheel, now separated from the hub, rolled off the highway and down a steep embankment, coming to rest in a low, swampy area. The sudden and unexpected jolt tore the steering wheel out of Cory's grip. The aging Honda veered sharply to the right and followed the wheel down the steep grade, landing with a loud, squishy "plop" in muddy wetlands.

Part Two: "Let's Make A Deal"

April Ravovich arrived at the Sheriff's Office a little after ten a.m. and was escorted into the interrogation room. Deputy Nordahl removed the handcuffs from April's wrists and gesturing towards a straight back chair and gruffly ordered her to "sit down". Present in the room besides Deputy Nordahl and Sheriff Ostermier, was a female jailor who was operating a tape recorder and a video recorder.

April's naturally pasty white face was outlined in fear and her hands trembled uncontrollably. The search team's early arrival at her bar had found the owner of The Howling Beagle still in bed, and the arrest had denied her the ability to give herself "a morning fix".

The subsequent search of the bar and April's living quarters quickly resulted in the discovery of several illegal items the authorities had already suspected were present. Evidence above and beyond what the surveillance camera had previously recorded.

Deputy Pearson read April her rights shortly after Sheriff Ostermier informed her of the charges against her.

1. Selling alcohol and tobacco products to minors.
2. Selling alcohol after hours.

3. Selling meat products mixed with illegally obtained venison.
4. Selling wild game without a permit.
5. Possession, with the intent to deliver, controlled substances, namely marijuana, cocaine and heroin.
6. Harboring known criminals.
7. Failing to cooperate with authorities during a criminal investigation.
   And last but not least,
8. Prostitution.

After being presented with the overwhelming evidence against her, April declined the legal option of having an attorney present. She sensed having or not having an attorney present would make little difference. Her only sensible option would be to made a deal with the Sheriff, after answering the questions she knew were coming. Saving her own skin was April's top priority, and to hell with anyone else. She'd talk, and "let the chips fall where they may!"

Special Agent Oaks was successful in nailing down the final piece of evidence linking Cory Welchek to the murder of Tony Ramonni. After introducing himself to the manager of the convenience store, and explaining what he was searching for, the manager quickly cooperated.

The young clerk who was on duty on the evening when Tony Ramonni was killed was called in to be questioned. He too was very cooperative. The clerk related his conversation with a man who claimed to be a newspaper reporter from "downstate", and seemed to be intent on locating a man named Cory Welchek. Agent Oaks did not divulge the real occupation of the "downstate newspaper reporter". The clerk also remembered one other customer was present in the store at the time the reporter arrived.

Last but not least, the surveillance camera's tape from the evening in question was viewed several times. It clearly showed the victim enter and leave the store, as well as a scruffy looking man with what looked like a week's worth of stubble on his face. It also appeared that the faded baseball cap the bearded man was wearing was covering a head that had been recently shaven.

Agent Oaks took a picture of Cory Welchek from his briefcase, and using a black magic marker darkened the face on the photo to simulate a short growth of whiskers. The young clerk took one look at the altered photo and exclaimed, "That's the guy! That's the guy who bought all the beer and left the store just before the newspaper reporter left."

Sherman Oaks was very good at putting two and two together and coming up with "four". Cory Welchek had done an excellent job of changing his physical appearance. And now the authorities would know what the man they were searching for REALLY looked like!

The effort expended by Special Agent Terry McQuarie, alias, Zachary Novak, likewise began to pay big dividends. Through a highly coordinated effort with local conservation officers and local police departments, a series of arrests took place in Michigan's Upper Peninsula and Northern Wisconsin. Over three dozen alleged poachers, the owners of a half dozen supper clubs, and four grocery store owners were arrested and charged with various violations pertained to obtaining, storing, selling or distributing illegally obtained wild game.

Armed with search warrants, the local authorities had timed their raids to occur on the same day, at nearly the same hour. By day's end, most of the individuals who had been arrested were, as Paul Vandenburg joyously exclaimed later, "spilling their guts".

At about the same time as the authorities in the U.P. and Wisconsin were pulling in their nets, federal conservation officers and government health inspectors were descending upon Mackinaw Meats, Wholesale and Retail, inc. All the various places of business that had been receiving deliveries in trucks owned by Mackinaw Meats, Wholesale and Retail, inc. were likewise raided. Many of the "fish" netted in these raids were much larger than the smaller cogs in the poaching operation's machinery, namely the poachers themselves. The once twisting trail, that had baffled the investigators for weeks, was rapidly becoming much straighter. And the trail was leading directly towards the illegal operation's top organizers.

Similar scenarios were being played out in a dozen or more states, all timed to coincide with each other. The national poaching scandal that had accidentally been uncovered by slain Conservation Officer Brian Matson, and pushed in the right direction by a seasoned, veteran woodsman by the name of Eric Sever "Hap" Larson, was about to be exposed and severely damaged. And that was a very good thing!

A swat team and a half dozen detectives from the Detroit Metro Police Department descended upon the offices suspected to house some of "The Mob's" top leadership. The federally obtained search warrants had been somewhat difficult to obtain, but the authorities had been successful. Phone records, computer documents and testimony dragged from reluctant mob members tied William Kerletti and Tony Ramonni directly to the arm of the crime syndicate that specialized in "hits".

And lo and behold, one informant was willing to testify that a senator from Michigan's Upper Peninsula, a senator named Randolph Redman, had paid the mob ten thousand dollars as a down payment to have two brothers "liquidated".

Senator Randolph Redman was arrested and charged shortly after he emerged from a committee meeting at the State Capitol in Lansing, Michigan. Of course, he strongly professed being totally innocent of the charges against him. His outrage at the allegations was expressed with vocalized ranting, liberally laced with personal accolades.

"I'll have you know I'm the SENIOR MEMBER of the Michigan State Senate, and SPEAKER of the same intuition. I'm also a MUCH respected citizen and role model for those citizens who stand for decency and law and order. It's an insult and a miscarriage of justice that I, Senator Randolph Redman, should be so accused of such unspeakable acts!" Senator Redman used his legally allowed one phone call to notify his lawyer.

Once Attorney Benjamin Silverstein arrived, the arresting officers showed the senator and his "mouthpiece" a copy of the surveillance tape, which had been recorded upon his arrival at The Howling Beagle. The senator paled considerably upon seeing April's hand attach itself to the lump in the crotch of his pants and whisk him inside her living quarters. Attorney Silverman lowered his head, sighed and closed his briefcase.

Next, the damning testimony that had been obtained from April Ravovich was presented to the senator and his attorney. It concerned the senator's deep involvement with the Welchek brothers, the poaching operation, and the "marijuana factory" that had been housed in the old farmhouse on Highway 77, as well as arranging deliveries of cocaine and heroin.

The final charge against Randolph Redman drove the last nail into the senator's coffin. He and his lawyer were presented with the evidence obtained by the Detroit Metro Police Department. Attorney Silverstein requested to speak with his client,...alone! The officers left the room.

Fifteen minutes later the senator's attorney motioned the officer's back into the interrogation room. The senator had been reduced to a chair filled with quivering flesh. His attorney spoke.

"My client would like to make a deal."

Somehow, as usually happens during investigations of this magnitude, rumors leaked to the press. And also as usual, many of the media hounds expounded theories and rumors rather than the actual facts, which of course they still lacked. Reports from newspapers, radio and television soon alerted their readers, listeners and viewers that "a mammoth poaching and illegal drug distribution operation has been cracked. Arrests of the organization's leadership are eminent." The "news" carried on the media grapevine spread quickly.

Senator Redman's attorney settled for the best deal that could be negotiated. For the senator's complete and honest cooperation with the authorities, they promised to obtain "some degree of leniency" when the senator went to trial. The authorities had offered up a crumb, and the soon to be jailbird had gobbled it up.

The senator's testimony quickly resulted in arrest warrants for two other high-ranking officials who were MAJOR players in the massive illegal organization. Warrants to search their offices, homes, bank accounts, and phone records were also obtained.

With Senator Redman's information in hand, the investigators followed a path to the door of Corbet O'Keefe, Director of Criminal Investigations for the State of Michigan. Mr.

O'Keefe had vacated his office just an hour earlier, bound for the airport with a ticket to Argentina. His was a valiant effort, but all in vain. Upon reaching his destination in South America he was greeted by a squad of Argentine police. The director realized something he had uttered many times during his tenure as Michigan's Chief of Criminal Investigation. "You can run, but you can't hide."

A second "big fish" had been netted.

Agents from the Washington D.C. Office of the Federal Bureau of Investigation made their way to the office of Mr. Kenneth Bradford, Deputy Secretary of the Department of Interior. Here the authorities met with a totally different situation. Finding the door to his plush office locked, his secretary informed the agents that her boss had still been at his desk when she left work the previous afternoon. She had tried the door, found it locked, and had also received no response when she tried to reach him by phone and the intercom. Not having a key to unlock the massive hardwood door, the agents forced it open. A grisly scene greeted them.

Mr. Bradford was slumped on the floor behind his desk. Near his right hand rested a .38 Special Colt revolver. The back of Mr. Bradford's skull contained a gapping hole and portions of his brain were smattered on the wall and window behind his desk. It was apparent Mr. Bradford had heard the "news" or had been "tipped off". Obviously, he had opted to end his life rather than "face the music". This had been accomplished by sticking the barrel of his handgun in his mouth and pulling the trigger.

The biggest and final fish no longer posed a problem.

Now but one loose end remained. Cory Welchek!

Chapter Fourteen: "Netting The Final Fish"

Part One: "Plan B"

Although Cory Welchek had a long list of shortcomings, including lower than average intelligence, a violent temper and poor work ethics coupled with lousy personal hygiene, his inability to make positive choices and sound, sensible plans of action would ultimately be his final downfall.

His early childhood education was riddled with failing grades, playground fights, bullying younger children, sexually harassing girls, and being expelled from school numerous times. His mother tried, God bless her soul she tried. He tried as hard as she could to curb his hostile behavior and plant the seed of social decency into his thoughts and actions. His teachers also tried. And tried and tried to do likewise. But to no avail. Liberals would later label him "a victim of his environment". In reality Cory Welchek was simply a "bad seed".

Cory's violent and sudden temper, plus his inner feeling "the whole world is against me", finally resulted in being expelled from high school in the second semester of his sophomore year. This expulsion was permanent.

He knocked around the county for six or seven years working at a variety of menial jobs. Pumping gas at the small gas station in Curtis, cutting pulp for a local logger, doing yard work, bagging groceries at the IGA supermarket in Newberry and tending bar at several small taverns. In every case his inability to get along with other people always climaxed with a violent argument or a fight with a customer or fellow employee. This violent anti-social behavior doomed all his attempts at earning a living wage working at "normal jobs".

When Cory was twenty-six he found steady employment working for Senator Randolph Redman.

Todd, Cory's younger brother of two years, was somewhat different. Certainly he was not blessed with a brilliant mind, but his I.Q. tested slightly above one hundred. During his formative years Todd tended to be a person who generally took the path of least resistance and basically tried to get along with most people. However, he had a different attitude towards completing a project or assignment using the "normal route". Todd was a master at finding some way to "take a shortcut".

By earning average grades and generally abiding by the rules, he did finish high school. Upon graduation Todd completed a six-month course in auto mechanics at a trade school in Sault Ste Marie and found employment working as a mechanic for an auto dealership in Newberry. This job lasted for nearly four years until his boss began to suspect Todd was dipping his fingers in the cash register. After his firing, the community rumor mill planted the seed that neither of the Welchek brothers where hiring material and Todd's attempt to find a new job hit dead end after dead end. Rejection after rejection. His earlier demeanor of trying to get along with people changed considerably.

When Todd was twenty-four he found steady employment working for Senator Randolph Redman.

Cory always looked upon his younger brother as a friend and companion. As kids, they often hunted, fished and did a bit of trapping together. The two brothers became inseparable. Cory actually looked up to his younger brother as their "leader". Todd usually found a way to get their chores done more quickly, although the finished product generally lacked quality.

Occasionally there were disagreements between them. Disagreements that became more frequent after their father disappeared one day and was never heard from again. There is no doubt the loss of a father figure for the two teen aged brothers contributed greatly to their ever increasing negative attitude towards society and it's laws.

And both brothers gradually took up a hobby of drinking too much. By the time they were thirty they were both alcoholics.

The rapid descent of Cory's Honda down the embankment caused his head to be severely banged against the ceiling of the car. Although the blow did not cause him to loose consciousness, it did cause his head to throb and made him feel groggy for several minutes.

The vehicle settled deeply into the mucky swampland to a depth that made it impossible to open the car door. Cory made his escape by rolling down the driver's side window and crawling out, landing "kerplunk" in six inches of slimy, stagnate swamp water. He regained his feet, shook himself like a dog, and kicked the side of his car as hard as he could. Next he repeated every vile swear word that was stored in his vocabulary.

Reaching through the open window he removed his Duluth pack and the supplies he had purchased at the convenience store and carried them to solid ground. Sitting down in the grass on the rain soaked embankment, he popped the tab on a can of beer and drained the contents in several gulps. Cory was already wet from his fall into the swamp water, so he simply tried to ignore the downpour that continued to pound earthward. He thought to himself, "Now what the hell am I gonna do?" His thoughts were interrupted by the sound of an approaching vehicle on the road above him. Scrambling up the steep, slippery, embankment he crested the rise just in time to see a Dodge pickup with a topper pass his location, heading north. Inside the cab Cory vaguely made out the silhouettes of the driver and two passengers. Although it was very dark, the glow from its taillights indicated the truck was dark green in color. At the moment, Cory's mind did not recall where he had seen a pickup just like that one, nor remember who the owner was. His memory would recall those facts a few hours later.

Two days passed before Cory's Honda was located nestled in the muck and mire in a swamp along highway H-33. Two young girls, out enjoying a bike ride, happened to spot the abandoned vehicle as they were riding their bikes along the shoulder of the road. Stopping to investigate, they took off their athletic shoes, rolled up their pant legs, and cautiously examined the car to see if anyone was still inside. Upon reaching their home twenty minutes later, their mother called the sheriff's office. Deputy Nordahl reached the crash location a few minutes later. He recognized the Honda as being the one Cory Welchek was driving, but unfortunately, the fugitive was no longer present. The downpour that occurred during the early morning hours when the accident had taken place did an excellent job of removing any footprints to indicate in which direction the accused felon may have fled. Once again Cory Welchek had slipped through the fingers of the law.

After consuming two additional beers, Cory's mind had devised an alternate plan. He loaded his supplies in the Duluth pack and started walking south on the dark, wet, deserted highway. In less than an hour he reached The Howling Beagle. The light of the lone mercury vapor lamp, which illuminated the bar's parking lot, allowed him to check the time on his watch. It was a quarter past four a.m. The rain had finally ended and occasional breaks in the clouds revealed a sky full of twinkling stars. Checking the eastern horizon, Cory was able to detect a thin strip of softening darkness indicated dawn was approaching.

Behind the bar he once again found April's red Jeep Cherokee. He had taken it once, now he badly needed it again. Cory quietly opened the door and squinted slightly as the interior lights flicked on. He looked at the ignition. The key was missing! April had apparently learned to remove the key from the ignition! Resisting the urge to slam the door and swear, he gently closed it, shouldered his pack and once again headed south down highway H-33. The road to the old hunting shack was still nearly three miles away and soon daylight would be arriving. He had to hurry!

Deputy's Jim Pearson and Vincent Palino had been summoned from their respective homes shortly after three thirty a.m. Both officers knew the jangling telephone by their bedsides, which had dragged them out of well deserved sound sleep, meant something out of the ordinary was taking place. Both were not scheduled to return to duty until six a.m. The two officers, as well as many other area law enforcement personnel had been working overtime attempting to locate and arrest Cory Welchek. Sheriff Ostermeir had set six a.m. as the departure time for his team of deputies to launch the raid on the old hunting shack where it was suspected Cory Welchek might be hiding out with his two kidnap victims. But the phone call from the sheriff's dispatcher quickly informed both deputies that Hap Larson had already "raided" the shack and rescued his wife and her granddaughter. The sheriff's original plan had been cancelled.

After receiving their new orders, the two drove to the sheriff's office, armed themselves with sawed off shotguns, and departed for the location of the old deer-hunting shack. The time was four forty three a.m.

Cory finally reached the two-rut trail that led east off H-33 towards the old shack where he had left his prisoners. A check of his watch indicated the time to be a few minutes after five a.m. Dawn was rapidly replacing the night's darkness, making visibility and progress towards his destination much easier. While he been hurrying towards his objective, his mind had been whirling, trying to come up with a plan to replace the one that had been cancelled when his car, minus the front wheel, ended up in a swamp.

Besides whirling, his mind has also quickly rebuilt his anger and rage. Anger that so many things kept getting in the way of allowing him to reap final retribution on Hap Larson. Just as it seemed everything was falling into place, which would allow him the joy of killing Hap Larson little by little, the sky had fallen on him.

First was his chance encounter with the bastard who had pretended to be a newspaper reporter. But Cory had seen through that lie! And justice had prevailed. The son of a bitch had got just what he deserved! So had his partner, the one who shot Todd in the back with a load of buckshot! The time expended to execute Tony,……whatever his last name was, had put Cory's plan behind schedule.

Next had been that damned flat tire! And then the spare had also been flat! Another three or four hours had evaporated before he figured his way out of that dilemma. Then the feeling of urgency to leave Newberry had denied Cory the phone call he had planned to make to Hap Larson. That phone call was the key ingredient in his plan. The phone call was going to be the bait, which would lure that Larson asshole to the jaws of Cory's trap. At the time, not making the phone call had been but a minor interruption in his schedule.

Then the front wheel of his car had come off, which caused Cory and his car to end up in a swamp! He touched the lump on the top of his skull where his head had come into contact with the roof of his vehicle during his downhill slide into the muck. "Ouch"! It still hurt.

All this had put his entire plan in the garbage can. Without a vehicle there would be no way to easily reach a phone to make that all-important call. Without a vehicle there would no way of transporting his two captives to the location he had chosen where Hap Larson would have been directed to meet them. And as he continued to trudge down the muddy two rut trail, cold and wet and covered with muck from his plunge into the stagnate swamp water, Cory's rage continued to increase, as his mind replayed additional memories concerning his sworn enemy.

It had been Hap Larson, snooping around the old farm, who had discovered the pot plants in the basement. It was Hap Larson who had embarrassed Cory by escaping from the old chicken coop at the Welchek's farm. It was Hap Larson who had thrown a coffee can full of urine and chicken shit into Cory's face, then pulled him head first into a iron pipe, knocking him out. It had been Hap Larson who had chained Cory to the very post to which he had confined Hap Larson! It was Hap Larson who had led the cops to the Welchek property and taken him into custody. It had been Hap Larson who had discovered the body of that goddamn game warden who had found the brother's "butcher shop dumping grounds". Hap Larson, Hap Larson, Hap Larson. He hated the sound of the name and hated even more the person who owned it! Cory hated Hap Larson more than anything he had ever hated in his entire life!. And come hell or high water, the son of a bitch was going to pay,......and pay dearly!

Cory continued to manufacture a new plan of action. His mounting rage rushed the process to completion. Once he reached the old deer-hunting shack he'd take his time having some "fun" with his two captives. He wondered if the young girl was still a virgin. He smiled inwardly as he thought, "she ain't gonna be no virgin when I get finished with her. I'll show her a few tricks I learned from April. And I'm gonna make that red headed bitch watch while I do it to her pretty little granddaughter! And when I finished havin' my fun, I'm gonna cut their damned throats and watch 'um bleed to death! Then when I do corner that son of a bitch,......that Larson asshole, I'm gonna give him a play by play account of what I did while I carve the dirty bastard into little pieces." Cory had a new plan.

Just a few hundred yards short of the intersection of the two rut he was walking on, and the trail that turned north towards the old shack, Cory heard the sound of a vehicle coming down the old road behind him. He quickly leaped into the brush that lined the roadside and flattened himself to the ground. Seconds later a squad car containing two deputies drove slowly by.

Part Two: "Plan C"

Deputy's Pearson and Palino drove their squad car beyond the intersection of the two old roads. They parked the cruiser beyond a curve, so their vehicle could not be seen by anyone turning north towards the location of the deer-hunting shack. They walked back to the intersection and inspected the tire tread marks in the soft mud. The most recent tracks had certainly been made by a vehicle much larger and heavier than a Honda sedan. It appeared the person they hoped to capture had not as yet returned.

However, they carefully approached the old shack, separated and stealthily closed in from two sides. The door was wide open and all was quiet. Finally entering the building, they discovered it to be vacant. Closing the door, each officer took up a position at a window to watch for the expected return of Michigan's most wanted fugitive. Five hours later they realized their wait had been in vane. For whatever reason, Cory Welchek had decided not to return to the shack.

Life at the Larson's home returned to near normal. Edna and Gwen's faces, arms and ankles, compliments of hundreds of mosquito bites, looked like they had a severe case of measles. Other than that, the two former captives were physically o.k., but it would take a few weeks for the mental trauma they had suffered to subside.

Hap's cousin, Charles Baldwin and his wife Shirley, returned from there short trip to their home in Sept lies, Quebec amid great excitement and expectation of enjoying the remainder of "the warm months" at their new cottage on Manistique Lake. What they weren't very happy to hear was the news that Cory Welchek had returned to their cottage and spent a few more days living there. And what upset them even more, was the horrible information about Edna and Gwen being kidnapped and abused by the now notorious outlaw.

Hap and Edna continued to feel very uneasy. Edna's account of Cory's numerous threats against her husband's life caused a great deal of apprehension. The veteran woodsman put himself on an elevated state of alert, and carried his .44 in it's shoulder holster when ever he ventured out of doors or traveled anywhere in his truck.

To upgrade the nighttime security, Hap built a simple doghouse at each corner of the Larson's home. At bedtime, rather than leaving all his dogs in their kennel, he stationed one dog at each location to act as sentinels. Should anyone venture near their dwelling, a loud barking alarm would be sounded. Hap was taking no chances while Cory Welchek was still at large roaming the countryside.

As the news media increased their coverage concerning the inability of the authorities to corner, capture or kill the chief suspect in three of the four recent murders in Luce County, likewise, the intensity of the search was increased. The newly appointed Chief of Criminal Investigation for the State of Michigan, who replaced the now jailed former chief, Corbet O'Keefe, sent a dozen state troopers into Luce County. The immediate result was that nearly all local residents maintained strict adherence to the posted speed limits. Squad cars seemed to be everywhere. Everywhere that is except where Cory Welchek was!

Cory Welchek's skill as a "woodsman" had been well honed. Much of his life had been spent in pursuit of fish, fur and game. Usually the methods he used in that pursuit were illegal, or the game he killed was "out of season", and generally the amount of fish and game he took was "way over the limit".

But still, he had acquired a vast amount of skill in using the woods and waters to subsist. Besides both being males, skill in using the woods and waters to subsist was the only similarity between Cory Welchek and his sworn enemy, Hap Larson!

Upon seeing the two deputies in a squad car approaching the old deer-hunting shack where Cory had imprisoned his two victims, he used his stealth and knowledge of the landscape to ease within a few yards of the old shack. As daylight gradually increased visibility in the dense grove of balsam and spruce that encircled the hunting shack, he easily made out the forms of the officers who were inside the building sitting by the windows watching for his expected return. "Well", thought Cory, "I've returned, but not exactly how ya thought I was gonna return."

It was then, as Cory lay hidden beneath the thick, drooping branches of a bushy spruce tree, the vision of the green Dodge pickup he had seen on highway H-33 shortly after his accident came hurtling back into his mind. "That son of a bitch, Hap Larson owned a truck just like that one! Sure as hell it was him, and them other two sittin' in the cab was his red headed bitch and her granddaughter! How the hell did that asshole find where I hid 'um?" Cory had viewed a green Dodge pickup parked at Hap's home, when he had spent time "checking out the lay of the land" and organized his original plan to "get even" with his sworn enemy. And now as his mind finally comprehended the fact "the bait for his trap" had been set free, Cory's anger and rage soared to new heights!

Cory's original plan had been well thought out, at least in his mind's eye! He would wait in the forest that surrounded the Larson's home until he was sure they were fast asleep. Then he'd sneak in under the veil of darkness and circle the house while he deposited gasoline around it's entire exterior. Then he'd ignite the volatile liquid. Cory knew full well the old cedar log home would become an instant inferno. After all, this was the same method he used to burn down his own house and garage! If the Larson's were lucky, they might make it out of the building in time. Cory hoped they would. He'd be waiting for them with his 9-mm pistol. But kill them outright with a merciful bullet to a vital area? No way! A well-placed bullet in each leg,...he planned to aim for the knees,...would end any chance of a successful escape from the flesh charring flames. And if Hap, or his red headed smart mouthed bitch tried crawling away from the burning building,...well,...a little more gasoline sprinkled on their bodies would coax the flames to just the right spot to complete a slow and painful death. And as a bit of "desert" after Hap and his woman had finally screamed their last painful scream, Cory would pour gasoline on his damn dogs and burn them up also. That would get even for the fact two of Hap's damned dogs had chewed up his brother, Todd! Cory had drifted off to sleep many nights with this sweet, wonderful thought on his mind. The thought of how his plan would climax had been the source of his energy that kept him going!

But after Edna, Colleen, and the two granddaughters had blundered into Cory's hiding place at the Baldwin's cottage, he had changed his plan somewhat. The ease of which he had kidnapped his two victims made his original plan still workable,...with some slight modifications.

"Plan B" had been worked out while Cory walked from the scene of his auto "accident" towards the old shack where he had been holding his two victims prisoners. He intended to use Edna and Gwen as "bait" to force Hap to come to the shack,......alone! And once he arrived he too would become a prisoner. Cory spirits had risen considerably as he envisioned the fun he would have watching his sworn enemy die very painfully, a little bit at time. And Cory knew Hap would have to follow his orders to come to the shack after he described in detail what he would do to the red headed bitch and her granddaughter IF Hap did not come.

But now, Plan B had been trashed! Somehow the dirty bastard had located Cory's new hiding spot and had freed his captives while he had been detained in Newberry, and then detained further when the front wheel of his Honda parted company with the rest of his car. And in Cory's deranged mind,......it was ALL Hap Larson's fault!

After watching the old shack for a few minutes longer, Cory concluded any attempted confrontation with the deputies would be foolish and do nothing to help achieve his goal of inflicting final retribution on Hap Larson. Carefully easing away from his hiding place beneath the bushy spruce, Cory slipped away into the forest. His mind had already developed "Plan C".

Part Three: "Final Retribution"

The nationwide roundup of suspected poachers, processors, distributors, and sellers of illegally obtained wild game continued. The investigations and arrests, which were dubbed "Operation Roundup" by the media, had already netted several thousand individuals in various sting operations in twenty-three states! And the authorities vowed there would be many more arrests over the next few days and weeks. That was the good news.

The bad news, especially for the folks living in Michigan's Luce County, was that Cory Welchek was still at large. Despite an ever-increasing army of law enforcement personnel, the accused murderer of three men and kidnapper of a woman and a female teenager, continued to avoid capture. And with each passing hour, Hap Larson's apprehension grew.

Although Cory Welchek continued to roam freely throughout Luce County, his ability to avoid capture was not without personal suffering. His supply of food and beer had been exhausted. What remained in his backpack was a pitiful small amount of supplies and equipment. A small plastic tarp. A threadbare wool blanket. Knife, binoculars, and a small coil of hemp rope. A light jacket and several pairs of dirty socks. Also, the clip in his 9mm pistol contained but six cartridges.

The small reserve of money he had taken from the can that had been buried in his garage, just before he torched it, was nearly gone. And even if he had possessed a million, risking going into any place of business to purchase something was out of the question. As he had slipped unseen through the woods, which bordered highway H-33, it seemed that every third or fourth vehicle passing by was a squad car of some sort. It was evident the search for Cory Welchek had intensified!

During the three days and nights, which passed since Cory had silently slipped away from the old deer-hunting shack, the weather had settled into a prolonged period of cloudy skies and frequent periods of rain. Daytime temperatures struggled to reach the upper fifties. And at night, temperatures dipped into the upper thirties. The pools of standing water throughout the forest teemed with mosquito larva, which daily produced bumper hatches of biting, bloodsucking, pesky insects. Actually, it was typical U.P. early June weather.

Cory's diet consisted of morel mushrooms, tree bark, and a few green leaves from shrubs known to be non-poisonous. Water was an easier commodity to obtain, but by day two the impurities which it contained had given Cory a raging case of what the "Yoopers" referred to as "the Hershey Squirts".

At night, when Cory made a primitive camp by erecting his plastic tarp as a roof to keep off the intermittent rain showers, he avoided building a fire. He was well aware that the airplanes he heard flying overhead after dark were probably aerial search planes looking for just such a beacon. Wet and cold and hungry, Cory was forced to endure the multitude of discomforts. But worst of all was the alcoholic pain in his stomach, coupled with, as Cory put it, "The pain in my ass caused by Hap Larson!"

Despite the slow progress towards his ultimate destination, Cory felt confident "Plan C" would be successful. Cory estimated the Larson property was still a bit over twenty miles from where he had camped for the night after day three of his journey. He was making about five miles per day, so he expected to be in position to carry out his final retribution in about four or five more days. He was becoming a patient man, with his continuing strength being supplied by thoughts of completing his only remaining goal in life. Killing Hap Larson and enjoying watching his suffering and agony as his life slowly ebbed away!

It had been eight days since Hap rescued Edna and Gwen from the clutches of Cory Welchek. Eight days and nights of worry, frustration, and,……hope. Each time the phone rang he prayed the voice at the other end would be Bill Ostermeir informing Hap and Edna the ordeal had ended, and Cory Welchek was either in custody or dead. Hap hoped it would be the latter.

Refusing to take any sleep producing medication, Hap spent the night time hours tossing and turning, picking his head up from his pillow at each and every suspicious night time sound. Even with his faithful dogs standing guard, he worried.

During the day, when the grandchildren were outside playing or fishing off the dock, Hap sat on the deck with his scope mounted .30-06 loaded and ready, an added compliment to his .44 magnum revolver which rested in his shoulder holster. He did likewise when Edna and Colleen went into the garden to water the vegetables or pull up weeds and quack grass. Time passed as slowly, as Hap put it, "as a snail crawls in January".

Cory's northeasterly route crossed but one highway, up until he reached Michigan Highway 28, and that crossing took place under cover of darkness. He came upon highway 28 just a bit west of the tiny community of McLeods Corner. It was here he obtained one necessary piece of "equipment", which he would need to complete his planned attack on the Larson's home.

Several houses were scattered along the highway in the area where Cory needed to cross it, and a careful nighttime search of the beds of several pickup trucks resulted in locating the item of his quest. The third truck's cargo bed contained a chain saw and a gallon can of gasoline.

The following morning the logger discovered his can of gasoline was missing. He was sure he had put it in the back of his pickup when he finished his workday, but then again, maybe it was still sitting on the ground next to the last tree he had cut down the day before.

By then, Cory Welchek was already over two miles closer to his destination.

The period of cloudy, rainy weather finally came to an end. The skies had cleared during the afternoon, and by dusk the royal blue sky had been completely swept clean. A light breeze drifted in from the northwest off Lake Superior bearing with it a strong hint of frost by morning.

Daylight was rapidly waning when Hap fed his dogs and chained one to each of the four temporary dog houses which were situated at each corner of his home. Wolf was housed in the kennel and Sadie followed Hap into the house. The time was nine forty five p.m.

Edna, Colleen and the three grandchildren were engrossed in a rousing game of Monopoly at the dining room table. Hap smiled as he watched them for several minutes as they took turns shaking dice and jostling for position on the board of the popular game. Then he sat down in his favorite chair and turned on the evening news broadcast from channel 8 in Escanaba. As usual, not much of major interest was happening in the U.P. except for a routine announcement that Michigan's most wanted felon was still at large. The search for his whereabouts was still in progress.

After watching the weather report, which agreed with Hap's prediction that frost was likely by morning, citizens in the listening area were reminded to cover their budding flowers. However, tomorrow would warm nicely into the low seventies with a gentle northwest breeze.

Hap turned off the TV set, said "good night" to the Monopoly players, and went to bed.

The board game broke up shortly before eleven. Carla had won! Her winnings of nearly 25,000 Monopoly dollars had bankrupted the other four players. By eleven o'clock all the lights in the Larson home had been extinguished and everyone was snuggled into their respective beds.

Shortly after midnight Cory Welchek reached the edge of the clearing about two hundred feet south of the Larson's home. "Plan C" would be put into effect shortly!

Earlier that same day, April Ravovich appeared in court to be officially informed of the charges against her, and make a plea. Her defense council was one of the county's public defenders. Due to the fact that Ms Ravovich had cooperated completely with the authorities, and was the major witness against

Senator Randolph Redman, the county prosecuting attorney had dropped or reduced most of the charges against her.

Upon hearing the Circuit Judge read the list of charges against her, she spoke briefly with her attorney and entered a plea of "no contest" to the charges.

Judge Wendell Montgomery sentenced Ms Ravovich to serve five years in a yet to be determined women's prison. While there, she would be placed in a drug rehabilitation program. She would be eligible for parole after three years. Upon being released from prison, she would continue to be on probation for an additional four years. Also, she would be required to report to a parole officer once a month until the conclusion of her probation period.

Furthermore, property taxes levied against The Howling Beagle Bar and Grille had not been paid for two years. The County of Luce was authorized to foreclose on the property and auction it off at a Sheriff's Auction.

All in all, April Ravovich had gotten off with a fairly light penalty.

Hap found sleep impossible to achieve. He and Edna had quietly talked briefly after she had come to bed, and then she had quickly fallen asleep. Hap stared at the bedroom window, watching the multitude of twinkling stars that decorated the heavens of the inky black sky above. Even though the window was opened a few inches, hardly a sound could be heard. Hap quietly got out of bed and stood at the bedroom window,...looking at the beauty of the night sky,......and thinking.

He cranked the window wide open and deeply inhaled the cool night air. It smelled so wonderful, laced with the faint fragrance of spring flowers, cedar and balsam. Far to the north he could see a minor display of the Northern Lights dancing on the horizon. From the west came the distant howl of a wolf, perhaps signifying the end of a successful hunt. Somewhere down in the river valley a great horned owl softly whispered, "Who, who who, whooooo". The land was so peaceful and quiet during the darkness of night; it was difficult to imagine there could possibly be any trouble in the world. Here, at least for a short time while Mother Nature worked her soothing magic, there was no war, no hunger, no greed, no violence, no road rage, and no danger of any kind. But Hap knew it was all a beautiful illusion. Out there the real world was home to all those man made horrors, and in many places those horrors could be found in abundance. And even here, in the generally peaceful Upper Peninsula, possibly somewhere fairly near Hap's home, a mad man was stalking him. A man bent on destroying Hap Larson's life. A sick, evil, anti-social, brute of a human being who cared little or nothing for most all living things. And who could predict where he was at the moment?

After all the lights were extinguished in the Larson home, Cory lay at the edge of the forest for what he guessed to be over an hour. He wanted to be sure everyone in the house was sound asleep before he put the final phase of Plan C into effect. Rising to his feet, he removed the can of gasoline from the Duluth pack and stealthily moved towards the darkened building. The tiny sliver of what remained of the moon had long since vanished behind the screen of trees that comprised the western horizon, and the night was what one might describe as "pitch black". Cory moved his feet slowly and carefully; feeling his was across the open area towards the shadowy bulk before him that was the object of his intentions. He smiled inwardly as he envisioned the havoc he was about to unleash. Now within only a few feet of the dwelling, Cory removed the cap on the end of the gasoline can's spout. He extracted his lighter and flicked its ignition wheel to make sure the lighter was dry and in working condition. The lighter failed to ignite on the first two tries, but lit successfully on try number three. The action was about to begin!

Of the four sled dogs Hap had posted to act as alarms, Star had been assigned the southwest corner of the house. The Malamute/Husky mixed breed had fallen asleep two hours earlier, curled up in his makeshift doghouse.

A faint grinding noise pulled the dog into consciousness and it's head raised in an attempt to identify the foreign sound. At about the same moment the distinct odor of a human reached Star's nostrils. The foul odor of a human he had never smelled before, and his nose told him the unknown intruder was close. The ninety eight pound dog was instantly on his feet, snarling with rage and charged to the end of his restraining chain, which stopped it's attack but inches from Cory Welchek's legs! The action had indeed begun!

Needless to say, Cory reacted like anyone would who was suddenly and unexpectedly attacked by an enraged, snarling beast of unknown origin! The gas can flew up in the air, as Cory stumbled backward falling heavily to the ground. The open spout of the gas can allowed gasoline to fill the air, which quickly settled over everything below it, including Cory and his clothing. Still clutching the lighter, he rolled away from the snarling dog and groped blindly for the gas can, which was laying on its side spewing gasoline into the grassy lawn on which it rested. Finally locating it, he regained his feet and began running away from the snarling animal that had nearly attacked him.

Knowing the element of surprise had been taken away, as Cory reached the front of the house he stopped and poured what little gasoline was still in the can on the floor of the front deck. Then spinning the ignition wheel on his lighter, he bent down and ignited the volatile liquid. The quickly spreading fumes burst into flames with a hissing "Whoooooosh" sound. Cory was just a bit too slow in moving his arm away from the flames. The gasoline that had been deposited on his clothing likewise burst into flames and spread quickly to nearly all parts of his body. He screamed in horror as the scorching heat immediately blistered his exposed skin and began burning holes in his clothing, exposing more of his body to the flames! Knowing a river was situated just below the Larson's home, Cory screamed again and made a mad dash towards its life saving waters!

Hap was jarred from the peaceful nighttime environment he had been quietly enjoying by the sudden and savage snarling sound from one of his "alarm dogs". Mixed with the vicious snarling came a distinct sound like a metal object striking the ground. In an instant, Hap grabbed his .44 off the top of his nightstand, and dressed only in a pair of underwear and a t-shirt, he bolted from the bedroom. As he reached the front door and was groping for the light switch, which would turn on all the outside lights, a brilliant flash of flame exploded on the deck.

Hap retreated backwards several steps, his mind trying to comprehend what was happening, but then through the window of the front door he saw the outline of a man engulfed in flames. The ruckus outside the house had quickly awakened the remainder of the inhabitants who were inside the house. Edna was the first to arrive in the living room.

"EDNA", Hap yelled, "GIT THE FIRE EXTINGUISHER OUT OF THE CLOSET! SOMEBODY SET THE DAMN DECK ON FIRE!" Edna responded.

Looking back through the window, Hap saw the individual who was nearly engulfed in flames race towards the rear of the house, screaming in agonizing pain. Hap ran through the kitchen, flipped on the light switch that activated two outdoor flood lights, and opened the back door of the house. Stepping out on the deck which overlooked the river, he could easily see the arsonist, who himself was now on fire. Just as the flaming individual reached the riverbank, Hap's mind realized who the intruder must be!

Speaking out loud, his voice dripping in anger, Hap muttered, "It's that son of a bitch Cory Welchek! He's trying to burn down my house!" And with that Hap raised his .44 in a two handed grip and squeezed off a shot, just as Cory jumped off the end of Hap's dock.

The water extinguished the torturous flames that had burned nearly two thirds of Cory's body. The cool water did very little to ease the excruciating pain that radiated throughout his blistering body. He surfaced at the rear of Hap's boat, which was next to the pier, it's bow resting on the riverbank. Looking up the hill at the Larson's house, he could see his hated enemy standing on the deck and pointing a pistol in Cory's general direction. In all the confusion, and the searing pain, he had not heard the sound of Hap's revolver. Cory pulled the 9mm from his pocket and fired three quick shots towards Hap!

Hap could not see Cory in the water, as the river was too far away to be illuminated by the light provided by the outside flood lights. But Hap did see the flash from the muzzle blast of Cory's pistol. A chunk of the deck's railing splintered just to Hap's left. A second bullet zoomed just over Hap's shoulder, striking the kitchen window and showering splintered glass throughout the room. Hap was already laying flat on the deck when bullet number three punched a neat hole in the door in front of which Hap had been standing.

Meanwhile, the interior of the house was in turmoil! While Edna was spraying chemicals to extinguish the fire on the deck, Carla was crying, Scott was telling her to shut up, Gwen was telling Scott to stop yelling at her little sister, and Colleen was holding her hands over her ears and yelling, "Oh my God, Oh my God"! And Sadie was trying to find a way outside to retrieve whatever was being shot!

Outside, all five dogs were barking and snarling, trying to get loose from their restrains and attack the intruder.

Cory tossed his pistol in the boat, braced his feet on the bottom of the river and gave the boat a backward jerk. The bow slid off the bank, which allowed the relentless current of the mighty Tahquamenon River to begin carrying it eastward. Although, his body racked with pain, Cory hoisted himself into the boat and fumbled with the controls on Hap's little five horse power outboard. It started on the second pull.

Hap, who was still lying prone on the deck waiting to see if Cory would continue to direct fire at him, heard the motor spring to life. Suddenly realizing what was happening, Hap yelled in frustration, "THE SON OF A BITCH IS STEALING MY BOAT! THE SON OF A BITCH IS GETTING AWAY!"

Hap made a mad dash for the river, but upon arriving at his dock, Cory was already around the first bend in the river and out of sight. Hap stood helplessly and listened until the sound of his Johnson Sea Horse faded in the distance.

Cory Welchek had escaped once again!

Forty-five minutes later the Larson's yard was filled with various emergency vehicles. Sheriff Ostermier and Deputy Nordahl arrived in one squad car. Jim Pearson and Vincent Palino arrived in another. Special Agent Oaks followed the continued arrival in an unmarked tan colored Plymouth sedan. Next came one of the Newberry Volunteer Fire Department's fire trucks. And last but not least was a search and rescue vehicle. Edna's hysterical phone call had activated everyone except the National Guard!

Hap was fuming! "Can ya believe it Bill? That son of a bitch tried to burn our house down! Shot at me three times he did! Good thing the bastard's a piss poor shot with a pistol. An' he took my boat and motor! Roared right down the river, headin' east. He's gotta come ashore someplace. Better git organized and start lookin' for that dickhead before he does somethin' else to hurt or kill somebody". Hap finally ran out of gas.

"Not much we can do until daylight, Hap. I'll have to get our plane up to find where he came ashore. Then we can start a land search. Doug, get on the radio and call our dispatcher. Tell him to wake Sam Goecks up. Tell him to get his bloodhound over here to the Larson place by sunup. We'll use the dog to track him this time. I think this time Mr. Welchek has cooked his own goose!"

"Speakin' of gittin' cooked,......he's probably burnt pretty bad. He musta spilled gas on hisself and when he set fire to our deck, it got him too. He was blazin' pretty dang good by the time he made the river and jumped in. By the way, I got off one quick shot myself,...don't know if I hit the son of a bitch or not. Probably not. If my .44 slug woulda plunked him somewhere he' be floatin' in the river rather than stealin' my boat."

"Well", began Sheriff Ostermier, "I'm sure he won't turn your boat around and come back here. So I think you and your family are safe. Thank God, nobody got hurt......I mean none of you folks. Mr. Welchek,......well I sure can't feel sorry for him. I'd say he got a good dose of his own medicine! We're going to head back to Newberry and get organized to start what I hope will be the final search for Welchek. Hap, I really feel this time we're going to get the bastard!"

Hap and Bill shook hands. The Larson's nighttime ordeal was over. Hap, Edna and their four guests watched the line of emergency vehicles wind their way down the dark driveway and out of sight. Hap gave Edna a kiss on the cheek and an affectionate squeeze. Then looking at his watch he exclaimed, "Dang, it's almost four a.m. Edna! Time sure flies when yer havin' fun! How about some breakfast? I'm starved!"

Cory Welchek's flight through the night was one of pain, suffering and agony beyond anything he imagined a human being could endure. Using an empty metal can that once had been filled with nightcrawlers, Cory poured cold river water on his numerous burns. It helped some, but not much.

Once out of sight of the Larson's home, Cory throttled back the engine and slowed the boat so he could stay near the middle of the river and not run aground in the shallower water along the banks. He continued at a modest pace for almost two hours. Dawn was just beginning to soften the eastern horizon, with bands of yellows and reds, when the outboard motor ran out of gas. It sputtered several times and died. Cory knew what the trouble was, and a quick search of the boat informed him no additional gas was on board.

Every movement sent waves of excruciating pain shooting through his tortured body. He tried rowing the boat but the motion required in doing so resulted in pain so great he could not stand it. He slumped to the floor of the boat and fell into unconsciousness.

Dawn arrived. Brilliant rays of sunshine spewed over the landscape promising a spectacular late spring day. The folks living the U.P. were going to have a wonderful weekend to enjoy doing anything they intended to do!

The area law enforcement officers were primed and ready to complete what they intended to do,...capture Cory Welchek,......or kill him if he decided to put of a fight. After all, he WAS armed and dangerous!

But there was one resident who was not going to have a wonderful weekend. Cory Welchek drifted back to consciousness only to be greeted by the unbearable pain from his burns, which was increasing with each passing moment. Slightly dazed, he lifted his head to see where he was. His escape vehicle was drifting with the current, which seemed to have increased during the time he had been unconscious. And Cory had no idea of how long he had been unconscious. Also, now that it was getting light out, Cory noticed a large spot of blood on the floor of the boat. Where it was coming from was of little importance considering his physical condition, and Cory dipped up more water and poured it on his burns.

Once again he slumped to the bottom of the boat and began to contemplate his impossible situation. Normally Cory would have been in a state of raging anger. He always became wildly angry when things did not suit him, or turn out as he expected they would. But now, he simply hurt too much to register any anger, rage, or any emotion. Pain was his constant and unwelcome companion.

He finally began to realize his botched attempt to kill Hap Larson was without a doubt the last opportunity he would ever have. Looking at his badly burned body, he knew he'd be lucky to survive the ordeal. He knew badly burned persons became seriously infected without major medical help. And help needed to come quiickly. But how would he get help? He couldn't. Even if somehow, someone found him and took him to a hospital, he would be recognized and the cops would be summoned. He dipped the can in the river and poured more cold water on his burns.

The sun was now up over the eastern horizon, bathing the landscape in radiant, brilliant sunshine. Hugh Mancini was at the controls of the Luce County search plane, with Chief Warden Paul Vandenburg and Warden Wayne Maki acting as observers and spotters. Flying the plane along the twisting course of the Tahquamenon River at an altitude of three hundred feet, there would be no chance of not locating Hap Larson's boat. And once located, a virtual army of law enforcement officers would be directed to the area to capture or kill Michigan's Most Wanted criminal!

Cory began to slip in and out of a dream world, a world that was laced with writhing pain. His throbbing brain had no notion concerning the passage of time nor much of anything else,...but pain. Relentless and horrible pain. He raised up slightly to dip more cold water from the river. As he did so, two sounds reached his ears. One was the sound of a low flying airplane, and the other sounded like a strong wind rushing through the treetops. Looking up with bloodshot eyes he saw a plane zoom over his location, then the motor revved higher and the plane began to bank back in his direction. Cory then looked further down the river in the direction of what he thought was the sound of wind. His eyes grew large with additional horror at what he saw! Less than a hundred yards away was the brink of the Lower Falls of the Tahquamenon River! And the current was rapidly sucking him towards it! He fought his pain and once again tried to row. He pulled as hard as he could on the oars, trying to make it to the nearest shore! It was too late, and the current was too strong! He was going to be pulled over the falls!

The search plane made it's turn just in time for it's occupants to watch Hap Larson's boat and Cory Welchek topple over the crest of the falls. Later, the witnesses would tell the press, "It seemed to be happening in slow motion."

Cory was tossed from the boat and landed heavily on the rocks below. His left hip struck a large, jagged boulder, shattering his pelvis, hip socket, and femur. Hap's wooden rowboat likewise struck the rocks and splintered into hundreds of pieces! The outboard motor, jarred loose from the transom, bounced off a slippery rock and landed on Cory's back, crushing two vertebras. The current rolled him over and over, which caused all parts of his body to come into violent contact with numerous additional rocks. The damage was extensive,……and eventually fatal. His battered and burned body washed up on the shore a quarter mile downstream from the falls.

"Final Retribution" had been achieved, but not how Cory had envisioned it!

The doctor who performed the autopsy discovered nearly every bone in Cory Welchek's body had been broken or shattered! It had been, as the coroner stated, "A hell of a way to die".

The coroner told Sheriff Ostermier one additional fact about one of Cory's injuries. Bill grinned, and then laughed out loud, although the information was a little on "the sick side". Next he called Hap Larson.

"Hey Hap, I've got some news you might get a chuckle or two out of." Hap was silent, waiting for Bill to tell him what it was. "Are you there Hap?"

"Ya, I'm listening. What's so funny?"

"Your shot at Cory Welchek wasn't a clean miss. You aimed a little low and your bullet when between his legs." Bill paused for effect. "But the bullet was just high enough to clip off the end of his dick!"

"Would you believe that's what I aimed fer? Ha, Ha, Ha."

"No, I wouldn't believe that, but it was a shot that legends are made of. The staff here at my office laughed their asses off. Talk to you later, Hap."

Hap turned to Edna with a silly grin on his face. "Edna, you'll never guess where my bullet hit Welchek!"

Epilog

The final chapter was finally closed. Sheriff Ostermier breathed a collective sigh of relief. Special Agent Oaks said his good-byes and headed back to his regional office in Chicago. Paul Vandenburg and the conservation wardens who served under his command created a memorial fund honoring their slain fellow officer, Brian Matson. The monies raised would be placed in a trust account to pay for his children's educations. Hap and Edna Larson were eventually able to realize their summer dream to, as Hap put it, "Lounge around and do jist what we damn please!"

Hoards of media personnel descended upon Luce County to gather material for newspaper articles, feature magazine stories, television specials, and radio news broadcasts and talk shows. They came to interview anyone and everyone who had been involved in the biggest manhunt the Upper Peninsula of Michigan had seen in over thirty years. Many of the media hounds remembered the name "Hap Larson", "The Hero of the Wilderness", as the Canadian media had dubbed him just one year earlier. And it was Hap Larson most of them wanted to interview.

Crews representing local and major TV networks recorded Hap's long drawn out tale of his involvement in the case from start to finish. The finished product was a televised "Special Presentation, "SEARCH FOR A KILLER", which lasted ninety minutes! There were video shots of Hap's home, the Baldwin's cottage, the old deer hunting shack where Edna and Gwen had been held prisoner. They filmed The Howling Beagle, inside and out, the little cabin where Todd Welchek was ambushed and Cory Welchek shot Billy Kerletti. The hotel where Tony Ramonni was brutally stabbed to death was filmed, as well as the old farm on Highway 77, including the grove of pines where all the "left over parts" from the illegal deer had been dumped. Dewey and Betty Matson were interviewed, as well as Brian Matson's widow and children. No one escaped the media monsters! And of course there was considerable footage shot at the waterfall, which had been Cory Welchek's final downfall. And as one reporter printed after making that exact remark, "Pardon my pun".

Within another week after Cory's grisly death, life around Newberry began to return to normal. Colleen's husband, Andrew, arrived and stayed with Hap and Edna for a few days, after which Edna's daughter and her entire family left for their home in Canada. Both Hap and Edna sighed a collective sigh of relief.

There was one additional thing that Hap needed to do to put his heart at rest. He and Edna visited the site of Brian Matson's grave. After placing a wreath at the grave marker, they both kneeled and said a silent prayer. As they were about to leave, Hap took Edna's hand, and looking at the granite marker he whispered, "I promised I'd see this thing through ta the bitter end, and Brian,…I want ya ta know I kept my promise." Then looking at his wife Hap added, "Ya got a Kleenex Edna?"

As the couple drove home from the cemetery they passed the old farm on Highway 77. This time there were no crows hovering over the wooded area behind the barn.

Reaching their driveway, Hap stopped the truck to let Edna get out and check their mailbox. Besides the usual bills and junk mail, there was one letter, which had been postmarked in Quebec, Canada. It was from Professor Pierre LeBlanc.

Edna ripped open the letter and read it to her husband as he drove down the driveway towards their home.

Dear Hap and Edna,

I sincerely hope this letter finds both of you in fine health, good spirits and both of you are thoroughly enjoying a relaxing retirement.

I'm writing this letter to let you know our Historical and Cultural Theme Park you had a big hand in helping us get off the ground will be finished on schedule. Next year we are planning to set aside the entire month of June to celebrate our park's Grand Opening.

You indicated you'd love to come back to Quebec when it opens, and this letter is your formal invitation to be one of the honored guests. The Society will pick up the entire tab for your trip here and provide you with deluxe accommodations during the duration of your stay.

Let me know of your intentions, and please don't say "NO"!

With kindest personal regards,
Pierre

P.S. Don't forget to bring your dogs.

Hap looked at Edna, grinned and remarked, "Looks like another relaxin' summer on the horizon."

TO BE CONTINUED!

Printed in the United States
1300600002B/61-558